BESTSELLER COLLECTION

popular reprints by bestselling authors

Jane Porter

The Secretary's Seduction

Christos's Promise

Mills & Boon™

DID YOU PURCHASE THIS BOOK WITHOUT A COVER?
If you did, you should be aware it is **stolen property** as it was reported
'unsold and destroyed' by a retailer.
Neither the author nor the publisher has received any payment
for this book.

First Published 2002
Second Australian Paperback Edition 2012
ISBN 978 1 743 06752 9

First Published 2001
Second Australian Paperback Edition 2012
ISBN 978 1 743 06752 9

THE SECRETARY'S SEDUCTION
© 2002 by Jane Porter
Philippine Copyright 2002
Australian Copyright 2002
New Zealand Copyright 2002

CHRISTOS'S PROMISE
© 2001 by Jane Porter
Philippine Copyright 2001
Australian Copyright 2001
New Zealand Copyright 2001

Except for use in any review, the reproduction or utilisation of this work in whole or in part in any form by any electronic, mechanical or other means, now known or hereafter invented, including xerography, photocopying and recording, or in any information storage or retrieval system, is forbidden without the permission of the publisher, Harlequin Mills & Boon®, Locked Bag 7002, Chatswood D.C. N.S.W., Australia 2067.

This book is sold subject to the condition that it shall not, by way of trade or otherwise, be lent, resold, hired out or otherwise circulated without the prior consent of the publisher in any form or binding or cover other than that in which it is published and without a similar condition including this condition being imposed on the subsequent purchaser.

All rights reserved including the right of reproduction in whole or in part in any form. This edition is published in arrangement with Harlequin Books S.A..

This is a work of fiction. Names, characters, places, and incidents are either the product of the author's imagination or are used fictitiously, and any resemblance to actual persons, living or dead, business establishments, events, or locales is entirely coincidental.

Published by
Harlequin Mills & Boon®
Level 5
15 Help Street
CHATSWOOD NSW 2067
AUSTRALIA

® and ™ are trademarks owned by Harlequin Enterprises Limited or its corporate affiliates and used by others under licence. Trademarks marked with an ® are registered in Australia and in other countries. Contact admin_legal@Harlequin.ca for details.

Cover art used by arrangement with Harlequin Books S.A.. All rights reserved.

Printed and bound in Australia by
McPherson's Printing Group

The Secretary's Seduction
Jane Porter

Jane Porter grew up on a diet of Harlequin Presents® romance novels, reading late at night under the covers so her mother wouldn't see! She wrote her first book at age eight and spent many of her high school and college years living abroad, immersing herself in other cultures and continuing to read voraciously. Now, Jane has settled down in rugged Seattle, Washington, with her gorgeous husband and two sons.

Jane loves to hear from her readers. You can write to her at P.O. Box 524, Bellevue, WA 98009, U.S.A. Or visit her Web site at www.janeporter.com.

DEDICATION

For my great friend, Barb. It is a fairy tale, isn't it?

CHAPTER ONE

IT WAS sweltering. No one, but no one, married in Manhattan in the middle of July. No one but Winnie Graham that is.

The organist paused and the packed congregation in St. Paul's Cathedral seemed to rise in unison and all four hundred and fifty heads turned to stare at Winnie where she stood at the back of the church in her twenty-thousand-dollar silk bridal gown.

White silk gown.

Just like her white garter, white silk hose, white flowers, white carpet, white, white, white for a virgin bride.

For a twenty-five-year-old virgin bride who knew so little about life and men, that she was about to walk down the aisle without ever being kissed.

Well, she had been kissed once, *badly* kissed, back in seventh grade when Rufus Jones practically stuck his tongue down her throat at a junior high birthday party. She'd been so disgusted by the kiss that she'd nearly thrown up afterward, so that kiss didn't count.

And now she was about to marry the love of her life except he didn't love her and he'd never kissed her and she'd actually signed a contract agreeing to this horrible public society wedding which meant nothing to him.

What in God's name was she thinking? What in God's name was she doing?

How could she be a wife before she'd ever had a date?

Winnie closed her eyes, drew a deep breath and tried to calm herself but she was losing it, knew she was losing it. She was shaking so hard now she could barely keep her teeth from chattering. Funny how your teeth could chatter when you're burning up. Perspiration covered her skin. Her heart raced. She couldn't get enough air.

What a fool she was. What a perfect idiot.

Yes, she loved Morgan Grady. Yes, she was madly in love with Morgan Grady, but how could she sell herself like this? How could she sign away her life?

A contract.

She'd signed a contract to become his wife.

How could she love herself so little and him so much?

The organist struck the keys with fervor. Bars of music filled the cathedral, four hundred and fifty people seemed to inhale all at once, waiting for her to take the first step forward.

Winnie's head swam. The people became a blur of white noise and heat. It was so hot in here. There were too many people and not enough air. She felt as though she were suffocating. She couldn't breathe. Couldn't think. And they were all waiting for her to move. To take that first step. Morgan was waiting for her to take that first step.

So she did. She took a step, she turned around, she ran.

Winnie dropped her bouquet of white lilies, roses and orchids in the cool foyer, dashed through the cathedral's paneled doors, down the wide marble steps and jumped into a passing taxicab.

CHAPTER TWO

"Where to?" the cabdriver asked, sweating profusely and craning his head to get a look at her in the back seat, the stiff petticoats in her wedding gown making the white silk billow like huge sails on an eighteenth-century schooner.

The cabbie needed a shower. The inside of the car stank of old sweat. Winnie cranked her window down, dangerously close to throwing up.

"Anywhere," she choked, needing air, but the hot muggy air outside only made her more nauseous.

The driver shot her another glance. "I got to go somewhere, lady."

Where to go, where to go after leaving her family, Morgan and four hundred and fifty people behind in the church?

She had to go someplace that no one would

find her. Someplace where no one would be. "The Tower, on Wall Street," she said, sinking against the seat, naming her office building.

It was Saturday, the office would be deserted, and not even Morgan would think to look for her there.

Closing her eyes, Winnie sagged against the sticky vinyl seat and tried to forget that she'd just run away from her own wedding, that she, Winnie Graham had left Morgan Grady, New York's Sexiest Bachelor, standing at the altar.

But eyes closed, she saw it all, saw how it happened.

She even knew the day—the hour—the moment—that everything in her life had changed.

June sixteenth. His office. Her insecurity.

"Willa, I need copies of these immediately," Morgan Grady said, thrusting a sheath of papers across the desk without looking up, "and the top two sets faxed to the client noted on the cover page."

Winnie's heart fell. Five and a half months she'd been working for him. Five and a half months and he still didn't know her name.

"It's Winnie," she corrected faintly, growing warm as color crept into her cheeks.

"What's that?"

She balled one hand and pressed her thumb across her knuckles. She'd never liked her name, never understood how her parents could look into her face as a newborn and think, *Winnie, yes, you with the little puffy eyes and tiny mouth, you're our Winnie*. But if Winnie was bad, Willa was far worse.

She'd corrected him before, several times actually, but he'd always been on his way in or out, or in the middle of something important, so she forgave the slips, and made up excuses for him.

But after five and a half months, the excuses had worn thin. Her patience had worn down. And her outer skin had worn *off*. She couldn't do this anymore, nor could she handle being invisible. It was definitely time to move on.

Winnie's lungs ached and she exhaled, feeling the elastic of her panty hose pinch her waist. She'd gained some weight over the winter, her usual extra five or ten pounds and she'd been slow to lose the weight this year. "You called me Willa."

He didn't look up. His attention never wavered from his Palm Pilot where he was making copious notes. "Yes."

Her panty hose was killing her. She couldn't remember when she felt so frumpy or dull. And worst of all, it wounded her pride that Mr. Grady was completely oblivious to her existence, while she knew—and was expected to know—*everything* about him.

Morgan Louis Grady. Born August first, Boston, Massachusetts.

A Leo, he took four newspapers daily, but didn't start reading until he'd hit his treadmill and weights for his morning workout.

He read all the important business sections of the paper between six and seven in the morning, during which he drank exactly two and a half cups of very strong, very black coffee. He had nothing until lunch—light salad and chicken from a caterer that delivered every day—and worked without interruption until three when she brought him a shot of espresso from the coffee cart downstairs.

Shirt size: sixteen and a half. Shoe size: eleven.

Height: six foot three. Weight: two hundred and five muscular pounds—*he* never varied in weight.

Impeccable dresser.

His hair was another matter. That couldn't,

wouldn't be tamed. Thick, glossy and nearly black, he had a cowlick at his temple and he wore the back longer than the rest. He could cut it all short but he never did.

She knew all this, and more, and yet he didn't even know her name. Drawing a deep breath she blurted, "Mr. Grady, my name is Winnie, not Willa. I'm Winnie Graham and I've worked here since January second."

His dark head lifted. "Oh."

She stood a bit straighter, pulled back her shoulder blades, trying to project that she was taller, more impressive than her five feet, five inch height. "I replaced Miss Dirkle. And Miss Dirkle replaced Miss Hunts. And Miss Hunts, I believe, took over for Mrs. Amadio."

"Yes. Miss Dirkle, Miss Hunts, I remember."

They were making progress. Eye contact had been established. He recognized some names. He appeared to be listening. Good.

Now was the time to mention Friday.

Friday, four days from now, she had a final interview with a company in Charleston for a position much like the one she held now, executive assistant to the CEO of a major Fortune 500 firm. The job responsibilities and salary were equitable with what she had now, except that the cost of living in Charleston was much more affordable than Manhattan, and she'd be working for a kind, grandfather-like gentleman in his sixties rather than Morgan Grady, Wall Street's Most Eligible Bachelor. "About Friday, Mr. Grady—"

"What about Friday?"

"I sent you a memo."

"I don't recall."

There were moments she wondered how he could possibly be New York's youngest, shrewdest, most aggressive money manager. Everyone said he was brilliant. His firm received more press than any other investment firm on Wall Street, citing his leadership, insight and intuition, but he didn't display a bit of that insight and intuition with his assistant.

Flushing, Winnie pressed the stack of paperwork to her chest. "I left you a memo two weeks ago about needing Friday off, and then a follow up e-mail last week—"

"Sorry." He shook his head once, a short cryptic shake even as his gaze dropped to his desk and he reached for his phone. "Anyway, Friday's bad. Can't do. Wait until later in the summer, right?"

Wrong. Wrong, wrong, wrong. Not only had he said no, but she'd lost his attention.

Twenty seconds of conversation and he'd mentally checked out.

She glared at him, fighting tears, wondering just what went on inside that head.

He was heart-stoppingly beautiful. Women fell at his feet in droves.

Last year he'd even been voted Wall Street's Most Eligible Bachelor, six months ago he'd been selected New York's Sexiest Bachelor, and the florist deliveries continued to stream in. Long-stemmed red roses, potted palms, elegant orchids. Socialites, models, actresses, *other* men's wives…they all wanted him.

Including her.

She tried to study him dispassionately but there was nothing dispassionate about her feelings for him.

He had a great nose, a strong nose, with the smallest hump at the bridge and serious dark blue eyes, matched by the best mouth and most perfect chin in all of New York. Correction, the most perfect face in all of New York.

Manhattan was the place of beautiful people and he was the most beautiful of all. But she couldn't handle it anymore, couldn't handle being a nothing, a nobody and so soon she'd be gone, off to another job, a slower pace of life, and an elderly white-haired, bespectacled boss.

"I can print off another memo, Mr. Grady. The original's still saved on my hard drive."

He shook his head, hung up the phone and began to place another call all without a glance in her direction. "Doesn't matter. Friday's not good."

"But I asked you two weeks ago." She heard her voice falter, and immediately strengthened it. "You didn't say no then."

"I didn't say anything at all."

"Exactly!"

"You can't take a non-answer as a yes."

"But, Mr. Grady—"

His dark head lifted abruptly. "Is this a family emergency?"

"No."

"Death in the family?"

"No."

"Death of a friend or former colleague?"

"No deaths. Personal leave."

He was staring at her and he had beautiful eyes, not exactly sapphire, more indigo, and when he looked at her like that, she could swear he saw straight through her. Literally. Straight through her to the wall behind her with the big clock and the fancy framed Chagall. She'd lost him. He wasn't even thinking about her request. He was thinking numbers, odds, research, stocks, options, you name it, anything and everything but what she needed.

"Personal leave," he repeated softly, a crease between his brows.

"Yes, sir."

He was still staring at her, eyes narrowed slightly. "On Friday."

"Yes, sir."

"During the shareholder's meeting?"

She had his full attention now and she felt oddly warm, and very uncomfortable, feeling the weight of his scrutiny. "I've found a replacement," she said, her voice cracking, her composure cracking. "She's highly qualified, shorthand, word processing, data processing—"

"No. Sorry," he cut her mercilessly off. "Reimburse yourself for the ticket from petty cash and leave me a copy of the ticket voucher."

Mr. Grady picked up the phone again and rapidly dialed a new number. Clearly he was done talking. "And those faxes, *Winnie,* you'll see to those immediately?"

Morgan Grady watched the rigid lines of

Winnie Graham's back as she marched from his office, her sensible one-inch black heels clicking across his floor, her dark glasses sliding low on her nose.

"Shut the door, if you would," he added pleasantly, picking up the phone again.

She reached for the doorknob and her brown tweedy blazer gaped, exposing her severe cream blouse with the wing collar. The tweedy blazer wasn't appropriate for the heavy heat of June, and the cream blouse didn't flatter her complexion, but then, nothing she wore was fashionable and that suited him just fine. Work was work. Pleasure was pleasure. The lines never crossed.

Yet he couldn't help noting a faint tremor in her hand and he'd have to be a moron to not recognize that she was upset.

Well, that made two of them.

He knew exactly why she wanted the day off Friday and it made him madder than hell.

Miss Graham, his quiet unassuming Miss Graham had an interview scheduled on Friday in South Carolina.

His assistant was looking for another job when she was needed here. When *he* needed her here.

The press were digging into his past, looking for tidbits as if it were King Tut's tomb. They were making calls, investigating leads, trying to find out if Morgan Grady was really the fairy-tale story he appeared to be.

Morgan smiled grimly. Fairy-tale life? Hardly. But the details of his past belonged to him and even now, twenty-five years after being adopted, he still knew the stigma that came with being from Roxbury instead of Beacon Hill.

The Gradys were saints, he thought, swallowing hard. They'd known from the beginning who he was, where he came from, and they'd taken him in anyway. They'd made him one of them. Gave him their name, their love, their security, and it had been wonderful, but now the spotlight was intensifying and the heat was becoming unbearable. It wasn't that he was ashamed of his past, but he didn't want Big Mike to take any credit, or get the attention, or savor his son's success.

The only way to juggle the pressure of personal and professional was to keep a tight rein on his emotions, to remain focused, to stay on schedule.

And no one but no one was better than Winnie Graham at keeping him on task.

She knew her job. She was the best damn secretary he'd had in years, and after going through a half dozen in less than a year, he'd like to keep her, thank you very much.

Morgan stared at the closed door for a moment, remembering the pinched expression at Miss Graham's mouth and briefly considered calling her back in.

But what would he say then? *I know you're job hunting and I don't want you to leave?* Absolutely not.

He was the boss. She was the executive assistant. He made the decisions. She implemented them.

Impatiently he reached for the phone, placed another call, feeling the intense pressure he'd been under for months. In the last year his business had skyrocketed. Work was nothing short of insane. The sheer volume, and value of the deals, staggered him.

Winnie Graham couldn't leave. He needed her. Depended on her. Give Miss Graham Friday off? Not a chance.

Back at her desk, face still burning, Winnie numbly copied and faxed the documents Mr. Grady gave her before swiftly sorting through the afternoon's e-mails accumulating in her in-box.

She worked on automatic pilot, answering the most urgent e-mails, forwarding what was necessary and printing out the spreadsheets required even as her mind raced.

She couldn't, wouldn't, miss the job interview.

She could go back in and argue about leave time again, or she could just not show up Friday morning. It wasn't as if Mr. Grady didn't have other secretaries on the staff able to cover for her. Grady Investments was made up of a team of seventeen, which included the two assistants for the research analysts and the two assistants for the traders.

She was not essential on Friday. Any one of the other assistants could take notes, pour coffee, and smile grimly. Although the other secretaries would probably be delighted to assist Mr. Grady, she reflected, gritting her teeth in disgust. Everybody loved Mr. Grady.

Including her.

There, the truth. She'd admitted it at last. The reason she couldn't stay: Winnie couldn't bear having her heart stepped on anymore. It was time to get smart. Time to think about self-preservation.

Winnie's head began to pound and her stomach chose that moment to rumble. She'd just started a new diet—her third attempt this summer—and she still hadn't gotten used to working from lunch to dinner without the midafternoon cookie or candy bar. What she needed was some fresh air and something cold to drink.

Winnie reached into her top right desk drawer and scooped out her wallet before taking the elevator to the forty-second floor, and changed to the express elevator that whisked her to lobby level in less than ten seconds. It was a drastic free-for-all in her tummy and she swallowed hard when the elevators slid open a second time.

Life with Morgan Grady was a bit like riding the Tower elevators: a giddy ride up and down but nothing solid in between.

Yet after six months of wild rides, she was ready to get off.

She wanted a job with decent hours, solid benefits, and an elderly boring boss so she could sleep again at night.

Outside, Winnie drew a short breath, momentarily blindsided by the heat and noise. As she walked to the hot dog vendor on the corner, a truck roared past, followed by a dozen streaking yellow cabs, half leaning on their horns.

Winnie bought a can of icy soda and popped the top on her way back to the Tower's entrance. It was midafternoon and Manhattan's skyscrapers had already reduced the light into little grids of sun and shadow on the sidewalk.

When she announced she was moving to New York to work, her family had predicted she wouldn't survive a month. Instead she'd lasted over four years.

She didn't particularly want to leave Manhattan now, but she needed distance from Morgan and all her impossible, outrageous fantasies. At night she dreamed of him over and over and it only made reality worse.

Morgan Grady would never go for her. He dated socialites, models and actresses. Not pudgy secretaries who stuttered when nervous.

The Tower's revolving glass door turned and a woman Winnie only knew as Tiffany, joined her on the sidewalk in front of the building.

"It's that time of day," Tiffany said, tapping out a cigarette and lighting up. She was tall, slender, with lots of blond highlights in her hair. She looked like the type that had tried to model in high school. "Just three more hours."

Winnie felt a stab of envy. "You go home at five?"

"Most of the time. If I'm lucky." Tiffany dragged on the cigarette and exhaled. She cast Winnie a bored glance. "Where do you work?"

"On the seventy-eighth floor."

"The seventy-eighth?" Tiffany's eyebrows arched, her interest piqued. "Then you must work for Grady Investments."

Suddenly Winnie didn't feel like talking anymore. Women always wanted to be friends with her if they thought it'd get them closer to Morgan Grady. "Yes," she answered, voice clipped.

"So what's he like?" Tiffany persisted.

Winnie pushed her glasses higher on the bridge of her nose. "Who?"

Tiffany let out a little laugh, her pink-painted lips parted. "Very funny. Morgan Grady, silly. You work in his office. You must have met him. What's he like…I mean, really, what's he *like?*"

"Busy."

"Of course. He's huge. He completely dominates the investment world. Everyone pays attention to his market forecasts."

Winnie forced a small, tight smile. "Isn't that nice?"

"But the part I find most amazing, is that he's not just this brilliant brain in a glass jar—he's gorgeous, too." Tiffany sounded positively giddy. "No wonder he's been named New York's Sexiest Bachelor twice in a row. He's sexier than sin. I'd kill for a moment alone with him."

"And I should just kill myself," Winnie muttered beneath her breath, feeling painfully inadequate. Living on the periphery of Morgan Grady's world was about as excruciating a thing as Winnie had ever experienced.

Thank God she'd soon be working somewhere else. Maybe then she'd get some self-esteem back.

Tiffany had a one-track mind. "What's he like as a boss?"

"Let me loan you my book, *Never Work for a Jerk,* and then you tell me what you think."

Tiffany giggled. "Is there really such a book?"

"Yes."

Tiffany laughed even harder. "And you have a copy?"

"No, not yet. But I plan on buying it soon."

Tiffany was laughing so hard she had to wipe her eyes. "I had no idea you were so funny," she cried, tapping her cigarette. "Who would have thought?"

"Yes, who would have thought?" A voice coolly cut in. It was a deep voice, husky and distinctly male, a voice Winnie knew far too well. "She's a woman of many hidden talents."

Winnie felt ice water flood her limbs. *Mr. Grady!*

"And her next job," he continued dryly, "will be working as a standup comedian."

CHAPTER THREE

IT COULDN'T be. He couldn't be here. He didn't hear her say that...did he?

Paling, Winnie turned to discover Morgan Grady behind her, a black trench coat thrown over his arm, his long dark hair almost tidy.

"Mr. Grady," she whispered, her mouth drying. "Heading out?"

He gazed down at her, his expression curiously hard. "I've been trying to reach you."

Heat surged to her cheeks. "I came down for a soda."

"I see."

There was a moment of strained silence between them, something that had never happened before. He'd always talked; she'd always listened. He'd never been silent with her before. "Did you want something?"

"You had a phone call from a Mrs. Fielding. She said it was urgent. I left the number on your desk."

Winnie couldn't remember Mrs. Fielding and wondered what could possibly be urgent. "Thank you."

His dense black lashes lowered, his mouth compressed. "Next time you might want to remember to take this," he added, extending his arm to reveal her small pager.

Winnie moved to take the pager from him but tensed as her fingers brushed his palm and a sharp current of sensation sizzled through her.

He was angry.

In her five and a half months with him he'd never displayed any emotion and yet now he was angry.

Quickly, to hide her confusion, Winnie clipped the pager to the waistband of her skirt even as Tiffany dropped her cigarette, stubbing it out with the spike of her high heel.

"Mr. Grady," Tiffany murmured, her voice dropping an octave as she held out her hand.

He hesitated, turned ever so slightly, and smiled a cool quizzical smile. It was a smile he must have practiced for moments like this, when he needed to put distance between himself and others without appearing aloof. The smile was a little slow, a little crooked, and made his rugged jaw wider, his cheekbones stronger. "We've met?"

"Once," Tiffany answered archly. Her smile stretched as his hand closed around hers, her cheeks glowing with the faintest touch of pink. "Well, we sort of met. You had business with one of the firm's partners and I notarized the paperwork."

"Ah." Morgan's teeth had never looked so straight or white and he continued to hold her hand in his. "You work with Jeff."

"Yes. He thinks the world of you. We all do."

A black limousine slid next to the curb, and the driver shifted into neutral but the car remained on, engine idling. Morgan Grady released Tiffany's hand, glanced at the limo, and then back at Tiffany. "I must run, but it was a pleasure meeting you, Miss—"

"Saunders. Tiffany Saunders. And I work with Jeff."

"On the sixty-third floor, right." He smiled again, and Winnie could see why women melted at his feet. There was something in his eyes, something in his energy and intensity that made you feel—however brief—that you were special. That you were the only one alive.

Winnie sucked in a painful, self-conscious breath.

He'd never looked at her once that way.

He'd never even gotten her name right.

A lump filled her throat and Winnie wished with all her heart she'd never worked for Morgan Grady.

Mr. Grady started for the waiting car, conversation forgotten, no goodbyes necessary. Move On, seemed to be his unwritten motto, no time to linger, no patience for niceties. Just move on to the next thing on the agenda.

But suddenly he stopped and turned back. It was muggy hot, the muggy hot of New York in late June when the air felt thick and yellow, yet he looked coolly elegant in his black suit and shirt.

She wondered how he did it, how he handled the heat and pressure without sweating or wilting or fading.

How did he predict the market before the market knew what it was going to do?

How did he juggle dozens of complicated, million and billion dollar deals without worrying, panicking, overeating?

She didn't know. She couldn't know. He was nothing like her.

Mr. Grady was staring at her now, his high tanned brow slightly furrowed. "Are you job hunting, Miss Graham?"

It was the last question she expected from him, the absolutely last thing she expected him to say, and Winnie wobbled in her sensible heels.

She reached for a handkerchief from her pocket and came up with nothing. Instead she gripped the pager in her perspiring hand. Good Lord. Did he know about her job interview, too? Or was it just a joke, a follow-up to his comedian remark moments ago?

Winnie blinked, swallowed, and blinked again, her glasses fogging slightly, her thoughts spinning in no logical direction.

What was she supposed to say? How was she supposed to answer that?

"No," she blurted at last, cheeks darkening. "Of course not."

His eyebrows lifted. He stared at her hard, his lips twisting ever so slightly.

Her blush deepened. She felt like a willful child with a hand caught in the cookie jar.

"Of course not," he echoed softly, mockery in his voice. "I'll see you later," he said.

"Right."

Then he turned away and climbed into the back of the waiting limousine.

Tiffany silently disappeared into the lobby of the Tower's building leaving Winnie alone on the sidewalk.

For a long moment Winnie didn't move, her heart thumping hard and fast. What had just happened out here? What did Mr. Grady mean?

Finally she shook off her fear, threw away her lukewarm soda and returned upstairs.

Winnie worked until dinner and then when she'd done all she could for the day, turned off her computer and took the subway home.

She was back at the office the next morning at six-thirty. As usual she was the first of the administrative assistants to arrive and Winnie made it her job every morning to turn on the office lights, check the thermostat and get the coffee brewing.

Coffee percolating, Winnie left the employee break room and headed toward the back office suite, flicking on lights as she went.

She arrived at Mr. Grady's office and froze.

Mr. Grady was already in, he was sitting at

his desk, and his door was ajar. He never left his door ajar. He was a man that preferred privacy always.

She stood there, transfixed, listening to him type, his fingers tapping away at his computer keyboard.

Something was wrong. The door shouldn't be open. He shouldn't be at his computer yet. He should still be reading his papers.

What had happened? Was it something to do with the press? She'd had three calls yesterday from various media sources, or was this more personal? Did this have anything to do with…her?

The tapping on the keyboard briefly stopped and Winnie felt the strangest, most physical sensation shoot through her. She could *feel* him.

Her brain told her that he hadn't left his desk but her body was reacting totally different. The fine hair on her nape rose. Her skin prickled. Her body felt incredibly sensitive all over.

She'd never been so keenly aware of him before. It was almost as if he was standing right here next to her, touching her.

Heat banded across her cheekbones. She drew a slow breath. She was being overly dramatic, she lectured herself, forcing herself to action.

Winnie headed for her desk, took off her lightweight trench coat and hung it on the hook next to the filing cabinet before moving to her desk.

As she rolled out her chair she spotted a book with a lime green cover lying in the middle of her desk.

She didn't remember leaving a book on her desk last night. She always left her desk clean, virtually spotless.

She moved closer, lifted the book. *Never Work for a Jerk*.

She dropped the book as if she'd been burned. Good God. The book. It was *the book*. The book she'd mentioned to Tiffany. He'd gone out and bought her a copy.

Winnie sagged into her chair, sitting down in a heavy heap, her purse falling to her feet.

He was going to fire her. That's why his door was ajar. He was waiting for her to get here so he could give her the ax.

It wasn't supposed to go like this. She'd been the one looking for a new job. She'd been the one hurt. It was her feelings that had been trampled.

And yet had he ever badmouthed her? Had

he ever publicly insulted her? Had he ever insulted her even in private?

Why had she said what she'd said to Tiffany? Why had she let her emotions get the better of her? What was the saying? Open mouth, insert foot?

Well, it was more like, open mouth, insert body.

She felt really, deeply embarrassed.

The small intercom on her desk made a faint clicking sound. "Miss Graham, when you've a minute, I'd like to see you."

Her heart jumped. She couldn't make herself move, unable to find enough strength in her legs.

But she couldn't ignore him. She was already in trouble. She might as well get this over with, go face the firing squad.

Winnie rolled away from her desk and stood up, pressing her blue pleated skirt smooth, making sure every pleat fell straight. It was her smartest skirt, the one she wore when she needed to feel extra crisp, extra professional. If ever there was a day she needed it, it was now.

The intercom clicked again. "Oh, and Miss Graham, you don't need to bring the book with you."

Morgan watched Winnie enter his office, her eyes wide behind her dark glasses, the black frames resting halfway down her straight nose. She sat down gingerly on the edge of the chair that faced his desk and folded her hands across the notebook and pen she'd brought with her.

He struggled to be civil. "Good morning."

"Good morning, Mr. Grady."

He leaned back in his swivel chair. "How are you?"

Her lashes fluttered behind the lenses of her glasses. Her lashes were long and they brushed the glass. "I'm fine, thank you."

Her voice sounded firm, decisive, every inch the competent secretary he'd been relying upon these past six months.

She swallowed hard. "About the book—"

"I don't want to discuss the book."

A pulse had begun to beat rapidly at the base of her throat. "You don't?"

"No. I knew you wanted it, so I bought a copy for you. Happy Secretaries Day."

"That was back in April, Mr. Grady."

"Better late than never." He sat forward, touched a button on his keyboard and checked the European market before it closed. His gaze skimmed the various stock prices before sitting back again.

"I have to be able to trust my staff," he said after a moment, grateful his voice could sound so calm when he didn't feel the least bit calm, and hadn't since overhearing her flippant remark yesterday in front of the office building.

His perfect secretary was a fraud.

Until now he'd thought of her as a future Miss Robinson, Miss Robinson being his first executive assistant and hands down, the best. Miss Robinson was tidy, precise, efficient, intelligent, controlled. She was always one step ahead of him and practically anticipated his every need before he even knew the need himself.

Miss Robinson had been with him for seven years, and retired eighteen months ago, just before he bought out Bradley Finance in a friendly acquisition. Trying to fill Miss Robinson's shoes had been impossible and he'd gone through assistant after assistant until he inherited Winnie Graham through the Bradley acquisition.

He hadn't thought he'd like Miss Graham, hadn't expected anyone who hid behind large dark glasses and a mass of pinned-up braids to be as effective as his esteemed Miss Robinson but Winnie Graham wasn't just good. She was great. She was the future Miss Robinson, the superlative secretary who knew what he wanted before he even wanted it.

"I need to trust you," he said. "You have complete access to me. You know details about my personal life, my family, my finances. If you're going to talk to Tiffany from the sixty-third floor, what's to say you won't talk to a friendly reporter?"

Her head lifted and her unblinking gaze met his. He watched as she adjusted her glasses. "Because I won't," she answered crisply.

"But you did yesterday—"

"And it was a mistake!" She rose from her chair. She'd never interrupted him before, never contradicted him and her passionate response surprised both of them. "I'm sorry, Mr. Grady, I feel terrible about what happened yesterday. It was careless of me, but I honestly didn't mean anything by it—"

"Are you looking for a new job?"

Her lips parted and color seared her cheeks but no sound came from her mouth.

She didn't answer because she couldn't answer, he thought, rocking forward in his chair, reaching for his phone, needing something, anything to do to keep his temper in check.

How had this happened? Where had he misjudged her?

"Never mind," he uttered shortly, unable to remember the last time he felt so cheated, or deceived. "I know you want Friday off. Take it off."

Winnie sank back into her seat. "Please forgive me," she whispered, cheeks stained red, fingers kneading in her lap. "I admire you so much. I think the world of you."

"It didn't sound like that yesterday."

"I know, but it's not why you think." Her fingers tightened together. "Tiffany was gushing. Everyone gushes and…" She took a deep breath. "I don't want to sound like one of them. I wanted to be…cool."

"Cool?"

"Cool," she repeated shakily. "I've never been cool in my life and women are always asking about you, beautiful glamorous women, and I get insecure. I can't believe I'm even telling you this but it's true. I'm a geek. I just wanted Tiffany to think I was like her."

"Like her?"

"You know, sophisticated."

He hadn't heard anything so pitiful in years. His incredibly intelligent and capable assistant wanted to impress a ditzy airhead like Tiffany? *Why?*

He stared at Winnie hard, trying to see past the glasses and firm press of her lips and what he saw was a young oval face with a high, pale forehead and small rounded chin.

"You have my approval," he said after a moment. "Why do you need hers?"

She didn't move a muscle. Her fixed expression didn't change. Her stillness coupled with the heightened color in her cheeks reminded him of a painting, an oil portrait from the turn of the century.

"That's a good question, sir."

"Think about it," he said, frustrated, angry and not at all sure what to do. Should he fire her? Could he trust her? What was supposed to happen next? "Are you going to a job interview on Friday?"

She hesitated for the briefest moment. "Yes."

He was out of patience. Sitting forward, Morgan punched another button on his market monitor. The market was open. Trading had begun. "If you take the job, I'll expect two weeks' notice."

Winnie looked away, stared past his shoulder to the wall of windows behind him. There was no emotion in her face. She looked like the serene, capable assistant he'd always known. "How did you find out about my job interview?"

His stomach felt hard, tight. He hated conflict. Hated feeling mistrustful. Charlotte had done a number on him, and while it'd been fifteen years since she betrayed him, some things were impossible to forget.

But Morgan didn't let any of his emotion show. He'd learned years ago to keep his personal life private. "Mr. Osborne's office called on Monday doing a reference check. I spoke with Mr. Osborne personally."

Winnie's head lifted, and her gaze met his, eyes large and worried behind the heavy glasses. "What did you say?"

He felt his lips twist into a ghost of a smile. "That you were the best damn secretary I'd ever had."

"Morgan, we're worried about you. Reed's worried about you." Rose Grady's precise diction was even more vigorous than usual. "Every time we turn on the television, you're there. We can't pick up a magazine without a story about you."

Morgan finished pulling his T-shirt over his head, having stripped off his suit and changed into jeans and a T-shirt now that he was home.

"You're sick of my press?" he teased, shifting the phone from one ear to the other as he headed for the kitchen.

"That's not what I mean," Rose retorted indignantly and Morgan could picture the elegant arch of her eyebrows rising higher. "We know how hard you've worked at putting the past behind you, but now these reporters are digging into everything. And I do mean, *everything*."

Morgan popped open the mineral water and took a long cool drink. "It's going to be all right," he said, wanting to believe his own optimism as he leaned against a stainless-steel counter, his kitchen huge and modern, big enough to accommodate a fleet of chefs. "The reporters will hound someone else soon. People get bored and move on."

"That's not all, Morgan. There's something else, and I'm not sure how to tell you, or even if I should tell you, but I don't want you to hear this from anyone else."

"Then tell me."

Silence stretched across the line. "I saw Charlotte."

Morgan froze. *"What?"*

"Charlotte came to the house."

It felt as if he'd been slammed on the chest with a shovel. He couldn't catch his breath. "Alone?"

"Yes."

He set the water down so forcefully the bottle rattled on the counter. "What did she want?"

"To hear about you. To know what you've been doing all these years."

Charlotte. *Charlotte.* "What did you tell her?"

Rose sighed impatiently. "I said, read the papers. Turn on the evening news. Morgan's life is everywhere."

He nearly smiled. Trust Rose to give an answer like that.

"She says, she made a mistake," Rose continued more faintly, as if delivering this information caused her great pain. "She indicated she wanted to make amends."

"It's been fifteen years."

"You once wanted this."

"Fifteen years ago."

"Five years ago," Rose rebutted.

Morgan shook his head slowly, angrily, not understanding why this had to happen now when he had so much pressure on him, when he had so many people depending on him. "How did she look?"

"Even more beautiful. She's certainly matured well. She's a classic beauty. What do you expect?"

His chest tightened. He closed his eyes. He didn't want to hear this, didn't want to know this. "I don't want to talk to her."

"Fine."

"And I don't want to see her."

"Then don't."

But even as he said the words, he was laughing at himself. Who was he kidding? Even fifteen years after she disappeared from his life he still wasn't over her.

"Rose…Mom.." Morgan pressed a clenched fist to his forehead, battling fears that very few knew about. "What do I do? How do I get out of this?"

"First of all, forget Charlotte, she's inconsequential," Rose said crisply, comfortable taking charge again. "And second, get rid of the press!"

"How?"

"Morgan, you're smart. Throw them a bone. Give the media a story…and I don't mean Charlotte!"

CHAPTER FOUR

RIDING the subway to work the next morning, Winnie heard Mr. Grady's words ring in her head. *The best damn secretary he'd ever had*. It was the highest compliment she could be paid. It was the highest compliment she'd ever been paid, and as pitiful as it sounded, those words from Mr. Grady meant everything to her.

She shifted on the subway seat, already sticky and warm despite the air-conditioning. Winnie told herself it was the summer heat wave making her feel a little hot, and more than a little bit crazy, but really, it had less to do with the thermometer than it did with her own feelings.

Two days from now and she'd be on a plane for the final interview in Charleston and she dreaded the interview now in Charleston, she dreaded her last day at Grady Investments, she dreaded everything to do with leaving.

Don't think about it, she told herself, as the

subway arrived at her stop and she lurched to her feet. *You have two weeks before you have to say goodbye. No reason to cross that bridge today.*

The advice had been sound, but the moment Mr. Grady walked into the office, Winnie's heart did the same wild lurch it always did, making her feel as if she were on the subway or elevator again.

What was it about him that she loved so much? She stared at his eyes, his mouth, his chin and while the features were all perfectly shaped, her interest had less to do with the physical perfection than the intensity beneath.

There was something about him, she thought, putting the top of her pen to her mouth, something deeper, more complex than he wanted to reveal. But what?

"Good morning, Winnie."

"Good morning, Mr. Grady." She managed a firm, professional smile. It was the competent smile she knew executives preferred. "The president of Shipley's Bank just called. Would you like me to get him back on the line?"

"Not just yet. I have a couple of things to take care of first. I'll let you know when I'm ready."

"Of course, Mr. Grady. Is there anything else I can do for you right now?"

"No. Just hold all calls."

"Yes, Mr. Grady. I'll do that, Mr. Grady."

His door closed and she sank back into her chair and covered her face with her hands. Could she possibly sound more pathetic? *Mr. Grady. No, Mr. Grady. Isn't the sky perfectly blue, Mr. Grady?*

She sounded like a simpering idiot. *Winnie, you need a life.*

You need to be good at something besides typing. You need to have interests other than Morgan Grady. You need to stop waiting for something good to happen.

And suddenly tears filled her eyes, ridiculous tears that had nothing to do with work and everything to do with wanting so much and not knowing how to accomplish any of it.

Once the tears started, she couldn't seem to make them stop. Suddenly she was crying because she was the middle daughter and the uninspiring daughter and the only one of her sisters who wasn't spectacular. Alexis and Megan were stunning, and talented, and incredibly popular. Unlike Winnie who'd never even been invited to the prom, Alexis and Megan had never missed a high school dance.

She'd never been beautiful or special, and as horrible as the tears were, as embarrassing as they were, they were real. It's hard to be plain and unexciting when the world embraces style and beauty.

The tears continued to stream and Winnie, who firmly believed that tears didn't belong at the office, grabbed a tissue from the box of Kleenex and blew her nose before being forced to pull off her glasses and wipe her eyes dry.

"Are you all right?" It was Mr. Grady, and his voice was coming from above her desk. She hadn't heard his door open or his footsteps approach.

Winnie struggled to hide the tears and quickly tossed the damp tissue away. "Yes, Mr. Grady. I'm just great."

His skeptical gaze swept her face. She knew she was a wreck when she cried. Some women were delicate weepers. She was not. Her nose went shiny. Her eyes turned pink. Her complexion took on a mottled hue. But she squeezed her lips into a smile and prayed it'd work.

It didn't. His brow creased deeper. "You look

like you're in agony. Do you want to go home? Take an early lunch?"

"Heavens, no. It's not even nine-thirty, sir, and it's nothing…it's just…it's just…"

"Just what?"

"I've made a mistake."

"I'm sure it can be fixed."

"No, it's too late."

"Is it a stock order? A market transaction?" he asked, clearly dumbfounded.

"No, it's about my job. This job, and the job in Charleston. I don't know what I'm supposed to do anymore. I don't know what's right anymore—" She broke off, eyes welling up again, and Winnie struggled to get her glasses back on, but in her haste she bypassed one ear and the black frames ended up dangling off her face.

"I think you've missed something," Morgan said surprisingly gently.

"An ear, sir." She hiccuped, took the glasses off, and slid them on correctly, hooking the glasses around each ear with as much composure as she could muster considering the fact that her nose had gone stuffy and her voice sounded thick and she'd just been sobbing her heart out. She wasn't making sense. She knew she wasn't making sense and it only made her feel worse.

"I'm sorry," she said, drawing a deep breath, trying to calm herself. "I'm fine now. I just had something in my eye—"

"I think those are called tears, Winnie."

She smiled faintly at his joke. It was a feeble joke but she appreciated it. "Yes, you're right. And I'm fine now. Please, go back to work and put this out of mind."

"Easier said than done."

"It's an achievable goal, sir." She turned to face her computer, her fingers hovering above her keyboard and fixing her gaze on her computer screen she waited for him to disappear.

He did not. He remained where he stood, just across her desk, his tall, solid body a delight in Italian wool and Egyptian cotton. She could smell his fragrance, smell the tantalizing hint of musk, and her gaze slowly lifted, traveling up his white shirt, past the elegant gray and black tie to the square cut of his chin and his impressive lips. She thought sometimes she'd do just about anything to have a kiss from those lips…

And there she went again, fantasizing, like she'd spent half the night last night.

Last night she'd imagined driving around

Manhattan in the back of Morgan's black stretch limo and she was wearing something silky and clingy and they were kissing madly. His hand was cupping her breast and she was making desperate little whimpering sounds and she couldn't get enough of his mouth, of his hands. In her dream she wasn't stodgy old Winnie, but someone exciting, someone smart and funny and beautiful. But of course morning came and she woke and dragged herself into the bathroom for a reality-check shower.

And still he stood there, before her desk. She didn't know what he wanted, what he was waiting for. Winnie dropped her hands back into her lap. "Do you need something, Mr. Grady?"

He was looking at her most strangely. Looking at her as if she wasn't Winnie but someone else. The slash of his black eyebrows drew closer together and a lock of dark hair fell forward on his brow. "Yes. I want to know more about the job in Charleston. Why were you interested in it?"

Heat filled her, a warm slow heat that made her tingle from head to toe. She knew what she was, and saw herself all too clearly—slightly pudgy, rather frumpy, and prone to panic attacks—but oh, how she loved him and oh, how she wanted him. But living in fantasyland was just about to do her in.

"Change," she answered huskily, wishing yet again she were someone else, someone with style, someone with grace, someone that men would fight to ask out. Although, really, she didn't want *men,* she wanted just one man. Morgan.

What a stupid, futile wish. What a stupid, futile path she was traveling.

Sniffling, she jerked open her desk drawer and dug around for a paper clip to stop her eyes from welling yet again. She had to get a grip. She had to get on with things. Because even if she wore a red dress and put hot rollers in her hair, she wasn't the supermodel of Morgan Grady's world. Wake up, Winnie. Grow up, Winnie. You're never going to be his type.

"But you like New York?" he persisted.

She swallowed the lump in her throat. Of course she liked New York. *He* lived in New York. She'd love Timbuktu if that's where he was. "Yes, Mr. Grady."

"So the problem is here, at the office."

Her chest felt raw, her lungs ached with bottled air. "Yes."

His black eyebrows drew even more tightly together. "You don't like working for me?"

Like didn't exactly factor into it. It was more of a love-hate thing. She loved working for him but hated being a nobody. She didn't want to be his secretary. She was dying to be his lover.

Winnie bent her head, rolled her eyes. How perfectly Ninny Winnie.

"So it is me," Morgan repeated.

"No!" She looked up at him, emotion so strong she was sure he could see what she was feeling in her eyes. But she did need to tell him something because obviously, she was having a problem right now. Her job search. The book on her desk. Her emotional breakdown just now. This wasn't the dependable, rational Winnie Graham he knew. She wasn't exactly a rock this week.

"It's not you," she said hoarsely, ashamed that she was practically disintegrating again. "It's me."

He shook his head, lines fanning from his eyes, deep grooves etched beside his mouth. "I don't understand."

Her eyes burned and she fought the urge to sniffle. She knew her nose must be bright red and her glasses were fogging up. "I've fallen in love."

There was a moment of dead silence and then a small muscle in his jaw popped. "With someone here? At Grady Investments?"

He couldn't have sounded more incredulous. "Yes."

It wasn't a lie. She had fallen in love and she was in a muddle and she'd never been so emotional in all her life.

He leaned on her desk, leaned so close to her she caught another hint of spice. "He doesn't love you?"

Her eyes burned and she swallowed hard. "Oh, no, sir. He's not interested in me."

"Is he married?"

She shook her had swiftly. "No."

"Has he taken advantage of you?"

She couldn't help blushing. "No. No, it's not like that. The problem is, he doesn't know I exist while I…I—"

"You what?"

"I'm crazy about him." She averted her head, wishing she could just crawl into some city manhole and hide. "Hopelessly crazy."

"That does sound bad."

"It is," she answered huskily, her voice

breaking. She could feel his gaze rest on her, felt what seemed to be sympathy, and she didn't want it from him. "Which is why I started looking for a new job. I knew this wasn't working out and I thought change was necessary. I thought it'd be wise to put some distance between us."

Mr. Grady looked troubled. "But if he doesn't know…?"

"It doesn't matter if he knows or not, *I know*. I know when he's here. I listen for his footsteps, for his voice, for everything." She bit her lip, fought for control. "But it's too painful. I can't do this anymore."

He studied her for a long silent moment and then shook his head. "Fine. Tell me his name and I'll fire him."

Winnie nearly fell off her chair. "Mr. Grady!"

"I'm not going to let one of my most valuable staff members ruin her career."

"You can't blame him!"

"I don't. But I'm also not going to stand by and watch you walk out because some guy here is knocking around your heart. If you can't stand coming to work because Mr. Heartbreak works here, then give me his name and let's get this over with."

She couldn't believe he was serious. He'd fire someone because she wasn't happy here anymore? "You can't be serious."

"He'll get an excellent severance package."

"Mr. Grady!"

"And the best references."

"No."

"I want his name."

"No." Her phone rang and she looked at the handset where the number and name of the caller flashed. "It's Shipley's Bank again," she said, heart hammering, hands shaking and yet incredibly grateful for the interruption.

"His name, Winnie."

Her phone rang again. She tensed, muscles tightening everywhere. When the phone rang a third time she couldn't keep silent. "I'm going to answer. Do you want to take the call or should I take a message?"

He didn't say a word, his dark blue gaze locked with hers. He didn't look angry as much as determined, jaw jutted, expression intense.

Winnie reached for the phone, "Mr. Grady's office, may I help you?"

He gave his head a slow shake and mouthed the words, "This isn't over, Winnie," before returning to his office.

★ ★ ★

He remained sequestered in his office on the call with Shipley's Bank for nearly two hours before leaving directly for a meeting across town.

After he left, Winnie let out a long sigh of relief. She'd been sitting on pins and needles the past two hours and wanted nothing more than to get a break herself. She opted for a rare luxury—lunch out, heading down the street to her favorite deli two blocks away.

But not even a lunch out could erase her worry. Business and pleasure didn't mix. Careers were destroyed over office romances. It'd be disastrous for her to remain at Grady Investments much longer. She felt it in every bone of her body.

Winnie walked slowly back to the Tower's building, trying to ignore her reflection in the mirror-glass building fronts but it was impossible to deny the black glasses, beige blouse, hair scraped back from her face which screamed, uptight. Make that uptight, unsatisfied *virgin*.

Yes, an uptight, unsatisfied virgin. That's exactly what she'd become.

Winnie stopped and stared at her reflection and hated what she saw. This wasn't her. This isn't how she felt on the inside. On the inside she was madly passionate, daring beyond measure. On the inside she wanted everything and was willing to risk all—

On the inside.

There lay the problem. No one knew about Winnie on the inside. No one saw the fun side, or adventurous side of her. No, she kept that side buttoned down and pressed back because once upon a time she decided if she wasn't going to be popular and sexy and fashionable then she damn well better get respect.

Respect. Augh! Respect was fine for seventy-year-old matriarchs, but she was twenty-five. She had no social life. No dates. No romance.

No wonder.

Impatiently Winnie reached up and undid the top button of her stiff blouse. She didn't want to be uptight. She didn't want to be unsatisfied. She didn't want to go through life without ever experiencing anything.

Winnie unbuttoned the next button. Checked her reflection again. Still boring, still a virgin, still really really not sexy.

And let's face it, two buttons unfastened on a beige blouse were not exactly a makeover.

What she needed was a miracle. What she wanted was a life-changing experience.

She'd give up everything, she thought, if for one week—no, make that a month—she could look like Tiffany from the sixty-third floor. Sexy, curvy, sensual. A woman that made men hot. A woman that made men melt.

Crossing the lobby Winnie's sensible heels clicked loudly on the floor. She pressed the elevator up button and waited. A moment later the elevator doors opened. People streamed out. Winnie stepped back to let the others pass. As she moved out of the way, Tiffany Saunders grabbed Winnie's arm.

"Hey," Tiffany cried, latching onto Winnie's sleeve as if they were life-long friends. "I just heard the news. It must be nuts upstairs!"

"What news?"

"About Morgan Grady. *News Weekly*'s Man of the Year. Isn't it incredible?"

Winnie blinked blankly. "But Mr. Morgan isn't Man of the Year, he was Sexiest Man—"

"No, no. This just happened. The magazine doesn't hit the stands until tomorrow but it was announced on the noon news broadcast today. The media are everywhere. They're swarming upstairs—" Tiffany broke off, eyes widening. "You didn't know? Where've you been?"

Winnie's throat dried. "Out to lunch."

"Well, honey, you better check in because your Morgan Grady is Man of the Year."

The express elevator to the seventy-eighth floor always left Winnie's stomach at her feet, and today was worse than ever.

Stepping off the elevator, she walked into a frenzied sea of reporters and carefully picked her way through the crowd to the reception desk. The young receptionist at the front desk, flagged Winnie down. "Thank God you're here," the receptionist choked. "They won't go away and they just keep arriving and I don't know what to do."

"They're here for Mr. Grady?"

"Yes. It's about the Man of the Year award. The phones keep ringing—" She was interrupted by the telephone and her face crumpled as she sat down again to take the call.

Winnie sized up the crowd. Tiffany was right. It was bedlam in here. Every reporter from every paper and TV station must have a representative in the reception area.

Poor Mr. Grady.

The receptionist hung up the phone. "So what do I do, Winnie? How do I get rid of them?"

"Tell them he's not here."

"I did, but they don't care. They won't leave. They want Mr. Grady and they're going to stay until he arrives."

Winnie recognized the stricken look on the poor girl's face and her conscience pricked her. She couldn't leave this eighteen-year-old from Nebraska to deal with this snapping, yapping throng. The journalists had been kept waiting for over an hour and they were impatient, hungry, and doing a very good imitation of a pack of wild dogs.

She also knew how Mr. Grady would hate returning to face this crowd. He'd never sought out the media, had never wanted to be a poster boy for the gorgeous and eligible. He routinely declined interviews, shunned society events, donated anonymously instead of funding charities publicly.

In the last six months she'd witnessed first-hand how the media hounded him. Board meetings, morning runs in Central Park, and dinner dates were nothing more than photo ops for the determined press.

Just last week a reporter with a microphone

jumped out from a stall in the men's washroom in hopes of getting a good sound bite for the evening's news.

Morgan Grady was a hunted man.

Winnie felt a wave of loyalty, laced with pity. Facing the noisy throng she put two fingers in her mouth and whistled. The piercing sound silenced the crowd. "Thank you," Winnie said briskly. "Now is there something I can do for you all or are you here applying for a job?"

Winnie's question drew some reluctant laughs and the crowd jostled closer. "Is Morgan Grady here?" one reporter shouted above the rest.

"No, he is not," she answered.

"Where is he now?"

Winnie crossed her arms over her chest. "In a conference across town."

"Does he know he's been selected *News Weekly*'s Man of the Year?"

Winnie's eyebrows arched. "What do you think?"

The crowd laughed again. Another reporter stepped forward. "When do you expect him back?"

"Not until you're gone."

And they laughed harder, real chuckles

mixed with mock groans. Winnie couldn't help smiling back, realizing that some of the tension in the reception area had finally dissipated. For the first time in days she felt as though she'd finally done something right.

Just then, from the corner of her eye, she saw the elevator doors slide open and inside the gleaming paneled elevator stood Morgan Grady.

Her heart lurched.

His gaze met hers and held. Her smile faded and she felt the most intense longing for all the things she'd never had, for all the passion she'd never known.

What impossible desires, she thought, *what painful impossible dreams.*

She shook her head slightly, a nearly imperceptible shake that only Morgan noticed. *You don't want to get off here,* she tried to tell him. *You don't want to go through this now.*

Morgan remained inside the elevator and the doors slid soundlessly closed.

He'd escaped.

CHAPTER FIVE

HE'D escaped.

Morgan let himself into his Fifth Avenue apartment and shut the door behind him. A row of extravagant floral arrangements crowded the marble-topped eighteenth-century mahogany sideboard with dolphin feet. Those were new.

He scanned the florist envelopes, reluctant to open any of them. He could guess who'd sent the arrangements and he could imagine the sentiment expressed. It wasn't that he didn't appreciate the support—it was wonderful to have such a loving family—but he didn't feel celebratory.

How ironic that a big day like this should leave him cold. He hated the fuss. Didn't know how to internalize success like this.

The phone began to ring and Morgan started to move, but stopped as he heard Mr. Foley, butler and chef, answer it. Mr. Foley was taking a message, murmuring thanks and saying goodbye.

The phone rang almost immediately again, and then the doorbell chimed.

Morgan closed his eyes, pressed a fist to the middle of his forehead, and wished he were anywhere but here. Most people would have loved the honor *News Weekly* bestowed on him today, but it was the last thing Morgan needed. He couldn't bear to be the focus of so much attention. The hype reminded him too much of where he'd been.

The doorbell chimed a second time.

He had to get out of the limelight, had to do something soon. But first, the door.

Morgan opened the door, accepted an even more lavish bouquet, a huge crystal vase filled with lilies and orchids. There was no room left on the crowded table and Morgan set the vase down on the limestone floor.

Mr. Foley appeared in the doorway. He wore a dark suit, white shirt, dark tie, all very crisp and formal. "Congratulations, sir."

Morgan struggled to smile as he nodded his thanks but the smile never came. He hadn't felt this lonely in years. "Thank you, Mr. Foley."

The butler bowed. "Can I get you a drink, sir? A celebratory champagne, perhaps?"

"Gin and tonic is fine."

"Of course, sir. And congratulations again, sir."

No, lonely wasn't the right word, Morgan thought, correcting himself as he glanced around his expansive entry hall, teeming with flowers and the overpowering sweetness of lilies. He wasn't lonely. He felt alone. It was a subtle, but significant, difference.

It was a difference that continued to haunt him hours later as he lay in bed. How had he become this larger-than-life figure?

He wasn't a cool, sophisticated playboy, nor was he Wall Street's Boy Genius and he hated the cult of personality. The Morgan Grady the media glorified had never existed. He saw what they saw—Ivy League schools, gorgeous girlfriends, tremendous wealth. On paper, he looked good. In an Italian suit, he looked even better. But scratch a little at the surface polish, peek beneath the diplomas, the social life, the tailored suit, and he was Morgan O'Connell, Big Mike's terrified kid, a kid so desperate to escape his neighborhood that he took all kinds of jobs to get him off the street and away from the fighting.

He'd folded newspapers at four in the morning, delivered them on his bike at five, collected payments from the high-class neighborhoods in the afternoon.

When he'd finished delivering papers, he collected beer bottles and Coke cans, and then started mowing lawns. He'd made up flyers and pasted them on bulletin boards, stuck them in mailboxes, pushed them under people's doors.

Morgan O'Connell. Yardwork, Painting, Cleaning, Odd Jobs. Excellent work at cheap prices. References available. Will work after school and every weekend.

Anything for a buck.

Anything to escape the decrepit building called home.

Anything to avoid Big Mike's mean temper and quick fist.

Eyes burning, Morgan grabbed his pillow, and turned over on his stomach. The sheet slipped low on his hip, leaving his torso bare.

The Gradys helped him leave his old neighborhood behind, and he'd made enough bucks now to ensure financial security. But he still didn't feel as if he'd made it. And work, which had been his safest haven, had become a nightmare. How to do this? How to continue like this? How to be someone he wasn't?

Closing his eyes, he rested his cheek on the cool cotton pillowcase. But with his eyes closed he saw a dark shape, and the shape became a squiggly black-green tattoo on Big Mike's arm. Wouldn't the press love to know that Morgan Grady was really Morgan O'Connell from Roxbury, not Beacon Hill?

Charlotte had found out and look what had happened. She'd hadn't just left him. She'd run away.

Morgan couldn't do this anymore. Rose had said to throw the media a bone, to give them a story. A story...

Morgan Grady gets married.

Morgan Grady no longer a bachelor.

No longer sexy, now just a boring old married man...a very boring Morgan Grady.

Morgan took a deep breath and the pressure in his chest began to ease.

He'd get married, get away from the hype, get back to being just a regular guy.

And it came to him as the tension melted, that he knew the perfect woman, knew the most sensible, practical woman who handled the press with ease, could manage his schedule, and already knew his many foibles—Winnie.

She'd been the best damn secretary. She'd be the best damn wife.

In the end, Winnie went to the interview at Osborne Manufacturing. It didn't seem right to cancel at the last minute and she thought she'd be smart to keep some avenues open. But while Mr. Osborne was just as nice in person as he'd been on the phone, Winnie knew the life she wanted wasn't in Charleston. The life she wanted was on Wall Street in downtown Manhattan, and just thinking of Morgan made her heart jump, more pain than pleasure in the swift rush of emotion.

On the late flight from Charleston to New York, Winnie plucked the pins from her chignon, freeing her hair. It fell past her shoulders in a heavy tumble.

The plane touched down in one big bump. Drooping a little in her taupe suit, she filed out with the other passengers, hair still loose, her travel bag dangling from her shoulder.

She'd kill for a long soak in the tub, followed by a pint of Rocky Road ice cream. No, make that a half gallon. To hell with her diet. Diets didn't work anyway. All the experts said so.

Wearily, she moved with the crowd through the terminal until she reached the curb, searching past the whizzing cars and buses for an available taxi.

"Need a lift?"

Him, it was him. Winnie half closed her eyes, thinking she'd never grow tired of that voice, never grow tired of the rich husky inflection. Air catching in her throat she turned around.

"Hello, Morg—Mr. Grady." It was the first time she'd slipped like that. Must have been the glass of wine she'd had on the plane on the way back.

He smiled faintly, creases fanning from his eyes, making him even sexier than ever. "Hello, Willa."

"Winnie."

"I know." His smile stretched and moving forward he took her travel bag from her and slung it on his own shoulder. "How did the interview go?"

"Fine." She frowned a little, realizing that he was here at the airport when he was supposed to be out to dinner with members of his board. "What are you doing here?"

"I came for you."

"Your shareholder's meeting—"

"Canceled." His mouth quirked but he wasn't exactly smiling anymore. In fact, he looked fierce, hard. "I was waiting at the gate but somehow missed you," he added, gesturing toward the terminal, black blazer falling open over his fine knit black shirt. He almost always wore black.

"Ah, there's my car now," he said. "We'll talk on the way."

She fell into step beside him. "Talk on the way where?"

"Dinner."

Nothing was making sense, she thought, reaching up to rub her temple, her thick hair falling forward against her cheek. She felt so tired and unkempt. Her hair down, her suit creased, her feet aching. And he wanted to take her to dinner now, like this?

She'd fantasized about having dinner with him but it hadn't been like this in her fantasy. In her fantasy she felt fresh, elegantly dressed, relaxed. In her fantasy she'd been in control.

That certainly wasn't the case now.

The limousine pulled next to the curb, black and sleek. Morgan opened the limo's back door. "Come," he encouraged. "I don't want to miss our dinner reservation. I've already pushed it back twice."

Winnie flashed him a worried glance before sliding into the back of the luxurious limousine. As the car pulled from the curb he pushed a dozen long-stemmed red roses into her arms, the stems perfectly straight, tied with a wide purple silk ribbon, and the roses still in identically shaped buds.

He'd never given her flowers before. Not even on Secretaries Day.

Winnie's heart twisted, a jagged little pain going through her middle. She was surprised how much all this hurt. She'd always wanted this from him but now that it was happening, it was wrong. It felt wrong.

Flowers were supposed to mean something, she thought wildly. Dinner was part of romance. But this wasn't romance. This was business.

He wanted her back. He was determined to get her back. She clutched the flowers so tightly they shook in her hands.

"He offered you the job?" Morgan's voice sliced through the dim interior, an edge to his voice, anger, too.

She jerked her head up. Her gaze met his. "Yes."

"Did you accept it?"

"Not yet," she answered, drawing a swift breath, drinking in the fragrance he wore. It was relatively light but on him it made her head swim.

She loved the way he smelled. He didn't always wear cologne, but when he did, it knocked her off balance, affected her coordination. Other men wore the same cologne but it didn't make her dizzy and hungry to bury her face against the neck and just breathe him in…

"Good. Because I have something to propose to you."

"What?"

"Let's wait until we get to the restaurant. I just ask you to keep an open mind."

An open mind? What did he mean by that?

Nervous, Winnie drew the flowers up and sniffed the blossoms. Compared to him, they had no fragrance, no spicy or musky scent, nothing like the roses in her mother's garden.

She glanced at him and his blue gaze locked with hers. The intensity in his expression took her breath away.

"An open mind," he repeated softly as the limousine pulled off the interstate and made a series of turns before drawing up in front of a small rustic restaurant with a nearly deserted parking lot. "That's all I ask."

The driver parked in front of the restaurant, put the car in neutral, and hurried around the side to open the door.

"Where are we?" she asked, sliding across the leather seat and stepping out into the warm night.

"We're just outside the city. This is Franco's. It's a favorite place of mine."

As Morgan stepped aside to let her pass, a car pulled out of the shadows, headlights blinding, and drew next to them. Morgan muttered an oath and Winnie glanced at him in alarm. The driver of the car leaned out and a camera flash exploded in their eyes. Morgan's driver charged the photographer.

"Come on, let's get inside," Morgan urged her, shielding her eyes from the blinding strobe of light.

She wanted to move, but fear and too much adrenaline held her in place.

It wasn't until the photographer peeled out of the parking lot, tires screaming as the car rounded the corner that she let go of Morgan.

She drew a shuddering breath, trying to calm herself. She'd been so afraid. When the photographer had first pulled up, she'd thought it was a gun he held, not a camera, and she'd felt absolute terror when the flash exploded.

All her fears about big city life and crime had come to life. She felt violated. Her safety stripped.

Trembling, she turned on Morgan. "What was that about?"

He shook his head, shadows in his eyes. "Just more of the same."

She drew another shuddering breath. "That was awful."

"I'm sorry."

"He had no right."

"They do it all the time, Winnie."

Morgan's voice was quietly apologetic, but she heard his frustration. He endured this on a daily basis lately.

She was beginning to calm down but she still felt chilled, and her nerves were jittery. "It's just such a shock. Where did he come from? How did he know you were here?"

"He probably followed the limo from the airport."

"You mean he's been tailing you this whole time?"

He sighed wearily. "Most likely."

Winnie was horrified. She glanced out, to the street and beyond. "They need to leave you alone."

"They will. Eventually." He reached toward her, placed a light hand on her back. "You're all right now?"

Her anger had dissipated, and the shock was wearing off, but she wasn't all right. She felt hot and tingly, and just the light pressure of his hand made her feel too sensitive.

He'd never touched her in six months of working for him and his hand sent rippling shock waves through her middle. "I'm fine," she answered, her voice huskier than normal.

The restaurant door opened and a gentleman in a red smoking jacket and black trousers stood in the doorway. "Mr. Grady, we've been expecting you. Welcome."

"Hello, Franco. Thanks for accommodating us."

Morgan steered her up the three front steps. She felt his warmth and it was a tangible thing.

Franco led them to a table at the back. The restaurant was dark and dimly lit, with deep crimson cloths and lots of little votive candles on what would otherwise be empty tables.

Winnie slid out of her blazer and Franco took it with him. Winnie felt a little naked in the cream silk blouse but tried to focus on other things. "Is Franco's Italian or French?" What a dumb question. "I guess it doesn't matter," she added quickly. "It could be either. Italian or French."

She was babbling. She was barely coherent. This evening was going to be bad.

"Don't be so nervous. This is just me. Morgan Grady. That jerk of a boss you work for—"

"Don't," she wailed, slinking lower in her seat. "Please don't bring that up now."

He smiled. "I'm playing."

He played? That was a revelation. "Okay."

Morgan had been studying her. "Now I know why I missed you at the gate," he said, almost relieved. "You don't look like you. I was looking for the—" he pointed to his head, finger circling "—braids."

"Oh."

He was still staring at her. "I've never seen you wear your hair down."

"Not by choice, no. But I had a headache earlier, on the plane, so I took the bobby pins out." He didn't say anything and she shifted uncomfortably. "You don't like my hair down, do you? It is on the messy side—"

"It's nice. I'm just not used to seeing you like this, but it—you—look very nice."

His voice had deepened and she felt absolutely terrified again. This wasn't normal. She didn't know what to do, or what to say. It didn't help when Franco arrived with a bottle of champagne.

Champagne. Her heart did a painful flip. Morgan was really going all out.

Franco held the bottle before Morgan, waiting for his approval, and once getting it, pushed the cork off with a soft pop.

Her first bottle of real champagne, French champagne, in a restaurant named Franco's with *News Weekly*'s Man of the Year. This wasn't her life. She was living Morgan's ex-girlfriend Annika's life. Only problem was, she didn't know how to be Annika.

Winnie smiled nervously as Morgan filled her glass before filling his. The champagne was a pale gold and very fizzy. Hundreds of tiny bubbles rose swiftly to the surface and she realized she'd better say something intelligent soon, do something semi-sophisticated.

Winnie seized her flute. "To *News Weekly*'s Man of the Year," she proposed, voice quavering. "Congratulations, Morgan. You deserve it."

She sounded so sincere, so artless, Morgan thought, lifting his glass and clinking his flute against hers. The candlelight flattered her, her pale skin luminous in the candle's flickering yellow-white light.

She wasn't like the women he dated. She was far more grounded, more real. He liked her lack of sophistication; it suited him better than glamour and glitz. Everyone assumed because he'd made enormous sums of money that he liked the trappings, preferred the trappings. The opposite was true.

"It's been quite a year," she added. "You're everyone's favorite person."

"Not yours," he answered mockingly.

Her cheeks turned pink. Her gaze dropped to the tablecloth. "You're talking about the book, but I really do hate it when you bring this up because the last six months have been amazing. I mean, let's face it. You're amazing."

Something in her voice wrapped around his heart. She had a softness in her that constantly surprised him. He didn't know many women anymore that were still so tender, still so…innocent.

Morgan frowned, momentarily confused. He wasn't entirely comfortable with this slight shift in feeling. He wasn't comfortable with feeling, period, but he hadn't selected her as a wife candidate based on emotion. It was reason. She was the most logical choice.

"And to think a week ago I felt underappreciated," she said with a wry smile. "I guess I can't feel that way now, can I?"

"You felt underappreciated?"

"You didn't even know my name!"

He felt a stab of guilt. That was bad. She had a right to be upset, but she also had to learn to accept responsibility for herself. Stand on her own two feet. "I wish you'd corrected me the first time I said it wrong. Tapped me on the shoulder, buzzed me on the intercom—"

"Would never happen," she interrupted with another husky laugh, and in the candlelight he realized her eyes were a hazel green, mostly green, with just a touch of yellow. "You... you're...you."

"Brilliant deduction, Miss Graham."

She smiled at him, pink suffusing her cheeks and something shifted inside him yet again. This emotion was new, and rather protective, and more than a little bit jealous.

Mr. Osborne couldn't have her. Morgan wasn't going to lose her.

Dinner over, Franco cleared their plates and the empty champagne bottle was replaced with coffee. Winnie leaned back against the booth, relaxed, sated.

"Lovely," she sighed and then was forced to cover her mouth to smother a yawn. She hadn't looked at her watch but it had to be way past midnight. "This was like a dream."

"It doesn't have to end." Morgan leaned forward, black knit shirt pushed up on his muscular forearms. "I have an idea, and it's going to sound a little crazy, but I think it'd work, and I think we'd both be happy."

"You're going to give me a raise?"

His eyes met hers and held. They were such a dark blue, gleaming like water beneath a full moon. "You could say that."

He reached down, drew a small black-velvet

jeweler's box from his trouser pocket and set it on the table.

Winnie's heart stopped for a moment. She felt odd, a prickly sensation shooting from her middle to her limbs.

He slid the jeweler's box across the table. "Marry me."

She'd begun to shake. She felt so cold. She couldn't believe he'd do this. She couldn't believe he'd treat her this way. "That's not funny." Her hands felt stiff as she groped about on the seat for her purse before remembering she'd left it in the limo.

"I'm not making a joke."

"Put it away," she choked.

"Winnie—"

"Don't Winnie me." She felt naked in her silk blouse, bereft with her hair down. It was as if he'd caught her skinny-dipping. She felt so bare, so exposed.

Winnie slipped out of the booth and onto her feet. "Don't get up," she said quickly, cheeks feverish, her skin burning with shame. And she did feel shame. She felt completely humiliated. "I'll just grab a cab."

Morgan dropped cash on the table and followed quickly. "Wait, Winnie." He barred her exit with an arm strategically placed across the doorway. "Don't leave. Not like this."

"I think we've both had enough drama for one evening," she choked, unable to look at him, her arms bundled across her chest.

He'd always thought of her as comfortable and solid, but without her blazer he realized she wasn't very big at all and definitely not comfortable and solid. He could see the outline of a delicate collarbone through her thin silk blouse and the slender bra strap across her straight back. With her head averted he glimpsed her neck and the pale creamy skin beneath her ear. She looked so small. And terribly defenseless.

"Winnie, don't be angry. I'm not trying to hurt you. I'm trying to tell you that I need you."

Need her? Winnie thought, trying hard to keep the tears from falling. He didn't need her. He was Morgan Grady, New York's Sexiest Bachelor. How could he need anything? "This is like a prank high school boys play. This is something they'd do—set you up, make you feel special, and then humiliate you afterward.

But I never, ever would have expected this from *you*."

He caught her by the shoulders. "But this isn't a joke. The proposal is real, and I'm very sincere, but obviously I approached it wrong."

She closed her eyes. "Have some pity, please."

But he wouldn't stop talking and his fingers dug into her shoulders. "I should have told you at the outset that this is business. I should have prefaced the proposal by telling you it's a job. I do want to marry you but it wouldn't be all fun and games. There's the media to contend with, and tremendous social pressure, but I'd take care of you financially. I'd make sure you had everything your heart desires."

His fingers tightened yet again. "Everything," he repeated more forcefully.

The Wedding Of The Year! New York papers proclaimed. Wall Street's Most Eligible Bachelor No Longer Available.

Winnie tried to avoid reading the papers, not wanting to get caught up in the hype but every now and then she'd sit back at her desk and stare off into space and just smile. She, Winnie Graham, was marrying Morgan Grady in just four weeks.

There was paperwork to sign, a contract and a rather tersely worded prenuptial agreement, but the business aspect didn't bother her. He needed her, and that was enough.

Planning the wedding was even more exciting. For the first time in years she and her mother had something in common and they spent hours on the phone discussing wedding traditions and making decisions about the ceremony and reception.

Winnie confided to her mother one evening that she felt like Cinderella getting ready for the ball. Everything was just so perfect, Winnie enthused, life couldn't be better.

"You really love him, don't you?" her mother had said gently, maternal pride in her voice. It was almost as if she couldn't believe that Winnie, her most awkward daughter, would soon be a radiant bride.

"Of course!" Winnie didn't even have to think about it. There were no questions in her mind. She was doing the right thing. Morgan needed her and she needed him. "I'm crazy about him. I couldn't love anyone more."

Her mother hesitated. "And you're sure he's right for you?"

"Mother, I *love* Morgan."

Her mother hesitated even longer this time. "Yes, darling, but are you sure he loves you?"

CHAPTER SIX

Morgan glanced at his watch. That must be a record. It'd taken five frantic weeks to put the wedding together and only twenty-three minutes to empty the congested church, call the St. Regis, and cancel the reception.

Thank God everyone had gone, and having given the priest a generous contribution to the church, Morgan headed to his waiting limousine, unfastening his snug bow tie as he walked.

Who said lightning didn't strike twice? Twice he'd been engaged, twice he'd planned a wedding and both times the bride bolted.

What the hell was wrong with him?

He'd proposed to Charlotte out of love, and proposed to Winnie out of need, but both brides had turned around and run.

So much for Sexiest Man in New York.

Swearing, Morgan slid off his coat. All he wanted now was a cold drink, a change of clothes, and his plane. He was getting out of this miserable city for the rest of the summer and figure out just what had gone wrong with his life from the very private, very pristine island he owned in the Bahamas.

But on reaching his limousine he discovered Winnie's parents waiting for him. Mrs. Graham was crying. Mr. Graham looked stoic. And Morgan really didn't want to talk to either of them.

"Do you have a minute, Morgan?" Mr. Graham asked, still dressed in his black tux, sweat beading his brow. It was damn hot, unbearably hot with not a hint of breeze anywhere.

Morgan paused. He didn't feel like talking. He had no desire to make any conversation but he couldn't very well brush off Winnie's parents. He might be furious with Winnie but he didn't hate her.

"Of course," Morgan answered, wondering for the first time if perhaps the prenuptial agreement he'd presented to her had been too terse. It'd been business to him but really, had he been fair with her? Could he have been more generous financially?

Mr. Graham cleared his throat. "We're not

happy at all about what happened today. Winnie's mother and I want you to know—"

"She was wrong," Winnie's mother interrupted tearfully. "There's no excuse. I don't know what came over her. She's always been a little high-strung, but really to run off like that…" Mrs. Graham shook her head, peach-lipstick lips quivering. "It makes no sense at all, especially as she's so crazy about you."

At least Winnie had done something right, he thought grimly, trying to keep his expression pleasant as he ground his teeth together. She'd convinced her parents she was marrying for love, something that all parents wanted to believe. Including his.

"I guess she had second thoughts," he said, jaw aching with the effort it took to maintain a smile.

"For whatever it's worth, she does love you. She's absolutely head over heels in love with you. And if you don't believe me, ask her yourself—"

"Margie," Mr. Graham remonstrated, placing a hand on his wife's arm. "Don't do that to Winnie."

"But it's true," Mrs. Graham vigorously defended. "Winnie can't lie. Her face gives her away. She gets a tic, on the left side. We use to catch her all the time when she was small."

A tic? On the left side? Morgan rolled his eyes as he stepped from the elevator in his building to his third-floor apartment. Give me a break, he thought, opening his door and stepping in. He didn't need that kind of nonsense today.

Mr. Foley appeared from the cool air-conditioned recesses of Morgan's apartment. "Would you care for a drink, sir?" he asked, taking Morgan's tuxedo jacket and cast-off tie.

"A cola on ice would be great."

"I'm sorry about today, sir—"

"I don't want to talk about it."

"Of course." Mr. Foley inclined his head but he didn't budge.

Morgan suppressed a sigh. "Yes, Mr. Foley?"

"Is she all right, sir?"

Morgan wished he could pretend he didn't know what Mr. Foley was talking about. He wished he were already in his plane on his way to St. Jermaine's, his tiny island with the most beautiful white sand anywhere in the world. But he wasn't on his plane, and he'd just come from the cathedral and he couldn't forget that Winnie had a tic when she lied and that somehow her mother earnestly believed that Winnie loved him.

Winnie, his dutiful talented assistant, loved him. What were the words Marge Graham had used? *Head over heels.*

"I'm sure she's all right," Morgan answered wearily, feeling the first pang of guilt. But he didn't want to feel guilty, there was no reason to feel guilty, it wasn't as if he was taking advantage of her. She was being compensated. Cash, savings account, new penthouse, credit cards in her name...

And she'd left it all, and him. She'd run off, jumping into a yellow taxicab, her white skirts filling up the car's back seat.

Morgan had chased after her to the steps of the cathedral, had watched the taxi pull away from the curb into the stream of traffic. He'd gotten a glimpse of Winnie from the back window, saw a sheen of white, and pale skin. Saw her hand reach up and press tiara and veil to the top of her head.

Did she love him?

He told himself it didn't matter, that a contract was a contract, and business was business, but it did nothing to assuage his growing guilt.

If she loved him, it changed everything. He hadn't been strategic at all. Instead he'd taken advantage of a naive young woman's affection.

Winnie dragged her crescent-shaped tiara and starchy white veil from the top of her head, plucked the pins that twisted curls back from her face and slumped at her desk, chin in hand.

Well, the fairy tale was finally over.

The prince had kissed the frog who claimed to be a princess and it turned out the frog was really just a frog and very green and very lumpy.

Winnie had never felt like such a lumpy green frog in all her life. There was no more pretending, no more fantasies of true love. She'd taken those three little words, *I need you,* and turned them into something huge and elaborate—a castle in the air.

Yes, he needed her, but not the way she wanted him to need her. He just needed a smokescreen. A shield. A semiwarm body to deter the press.

She'd been fine with that, too, had told herself that being needed was practically the same thing as being loved, but standing in the church, dressed up like a princess bride, she realized she might be able to delude the press, but she couldn't delude herself. She was too much of a romantic to settle for marriage without love.

Sighing at her folly, and wondering if she'd just messed up her one chance to do something really different with her life, Winnie rolled back in her chair, away from her desk, to look around the office.

This was Morgan's world. She'd loved his world.

She'd really miss his world.

For a moment she couldn't move, could hardly breathe, remembering how she'd come here four years ago on a job interview.

She was fresh out of college and Grady Investments was looking to hire an entry-level position for their research department. Grady Investments was Wall Street's hottest investment firm and they only took on the best and the brightest for their research team and Winnie had been thrilled when they read her résumé and requested an interview.

She spent two weeks preparing for the interview. She read every Fortune 500 press release available, tracked the hot stocks and graphed companies she believed were overvalued.

Winnie couldn't have been more prepared. Yet when she arrived for the interview she bombed. It was just like at the church today. She started thinking and criticizing herself and before she knew it she lost all her confidence.

She stood in Grady Investments's entry, hugging her briefcase that still had the new leather smell and she watched the people come and go through the reception area, all deep in conversation or engrossed in reading, and she felt like a fish out of water.

She wasn't smart like these people. She wasn't sophisticated like these people. She wasn't successful like these people.

The longer she stood there the more nervous she became. By the time she was led to the conference room for her appointment, she was a mess. Every intelligent thought had left her brain. Less than five minutes into the interview, Winnie apologized, picked up her portfolio, and ran.

It wasn't until she reached the busy street that the terror gave way to grief. Despite her degree, her university honors, and the expensive wool suit, she still couldn't do anything right.

That botched interview changed her career path. Instead of pursuing entry-level positions in finance she accepted a clerical position with another finance company. Her future had been decided.

Just like it'd been decided today.

Morgan had given her the opportunity of a lifetime—so what if he didn't love her? She could still have been part of his world and traveled and tried new things—but no, she had to overanalyze and overthink and ruin everything.

She'd blown it again.

"Going somewhere, Winnie?"

That voice was the voice she'd heard on the intercom for the last seven months and she responded to it even now, heart accelerating. *Morgan.* Slowly, Winnie turned in her chair, hands resting on her white silk skirt. "What are you doing here?"

"Looking for you."

Her stomach did a somersault, her pulse leaped, and she felt like a teenager all over again. "I'm here."

"So I see," he said, advancing toward her and moving the box from her desk to the ground. He sat on the edge of the desk, facing her. "How are you?"

Her stomach flip-flopped again. He'd

changed from his tuxedo, but even dressed down, casual in a black knit shirt and khaki slacks, he looked gorgeous. The black shirt made his eyes look bluer, his hair glossier, his jaw more pronounced.

"Fine." She swallowed convulsively, nerves and tears battling for each other. "How are you?"

"Fine."

The strained civility made her want to laugh. Or cry. This had been one of the worst days of her life. She had no idea what would happen now.

Morgan hesitated, appeared to pick his words with care. "It was rather awkward with you leaving so suddenly."

She had a mental picture of him standing up front at the altar with the priest and the ring boy and the flower girl watching Winnie turn around, white skirts billowing, as she ran.

It was an awful mental picture and she pressed her nails to her skirt to erase it. "Was it that terrible?"

One of his black eyebrows lifted. "What do you think?"

So it was really terrible. No use kidding herself. He'd been humiliated. Winnie swallowed hard around the lump filling her throat. "I'm sorry."

He shrugged. "Fortunately I've been through this before so I'm getting adept at handling high-strung brides."

Her eyebrows puckered. "Be serious."

"I am." He smiled faintly, but hard glints shone in his dark blue eyes. "Don't believe me? Ask my mother. Rose will tell you all about it. It was fifteen years ago. Her name was Charlotte and I thought we were deeply in love."

Winnie didn't know what to say. The office seemed too huge and empty, too silent. She flexed her fingers, knuckles aching. "Did she really leave you at the altar, too?"

A small muscle pulled in his jaw. "Not exactly. She gave me a little more notice—she was kind enough to cancel a week before. But that didn't make it less difficult. People want to know what happened. They don't want to ask, and most don't, but every now and then you get the daring few who do."

"What was her reason for canceling?"

His shoulders shifted and he walked to the window to gaze out at the enormous Federal Reserve Bank of New York. "It's complicated, but the bottom line was that she had concerns about my..." He hesitated, searching for the correct words. "Family tree."

The Gradys were one of the oldest most-respected families in Boston. How could anyone have a problem with his family? "That doesn't make sense."

He looked at her over his shoulder, his expression almost mocking. "It does if you know my family tree. In terms of lineage, I'm an O'Connell, not a Grady. Charlotte didn't discover this until a couple weeks before our wedding and she panicked—" he broke off, wincing at the word "—changed her mind. She didn't want an O'Connell. She wanted a Grady. A *real* Grady."

Winnie struggled to assimilate his words, and the meaning. "You're not Rose and Reed Grady's son?"

"I'm their *adopted* son." His lips twisted tighter, his smile harder.

"Same thing."

"Not to Charlotte."

Indignant, Winnie rose from her chair. "Then she didn't deserve you! She doesn't have a heart and she never loved you—"

"Who are you to talk about love?" He interrupted, facing her. "You weren't marrying me for love, were you?"

Winnie turned away, she couldn't look at him, couldn't answer. She hated lying. Was terrible at lying. Her parents used to say she couldn't keep any wrong a secret.

"Do you love me?" he repeated, walking toward her, tension in every muscle of his body.

Winnie sat down again, still averting her head. But Morgan turned her chair toward him so she couldn't avoid his gaze.

She touched her tongue to her upper lip. "I—"

"You what?"

"I care about you. Yes, definitely, I care about you. I've worked with you for seven months now. We've worked closely together in the last month, too."

"But you don't love me. This was business, right?"

She slowly looked up at him, her eyes wide, her expression anxious. "Mmm-hmm."

"Say it. Tell me with words."

Winnie took a quick breath. "I don't love you," she blurted, but even as she said the words, her cheek tightened and her left eye twitched.

Morgan stood, backed away, forehead deeply

furrowed. Winnie watched him cross the floor, rub his nape, ruffling his hair.

"Was it hard to get over her?" she asked softly, thinking of this beautiful but callous Charlotte.

He shrugged carelessly, broad shoulders twisting beneath the snug black knit fabric. "She was beautiful, elegant, graceful." His hard expression eased, turning rueful. "Yes. It was."

"I'm sorry she hurt you."

His smile faded. "It was a long time ago. I was just a kid." He took a step back, sat down again on the desk. "Fifteen years," he said softly. "Fifteen years and I'm facing the same problem. How ironic."

Yes, she thought, ironic was the word for it because seeing Morgan now, being alone with Morgan now, made her realize she'd made a huge mistake today, running away from the church.

"So what do we do?" he asked.

"I don't know."

"We can't stay here forever."

"No."

"We're going to need food, rest, a change of clothes."

That's right. Clothes. Winnie glanced down

at her lavish wedding gown with the snug off-the-shoulder sleeves and the tiny crystals stitched across the fitted bodice. She could see the headlines in the morning paper: Bride-to-be Jilts Grady At The Altar. Man of the Year Claims Runaway Fiancée At The Office. "Photographers outside?"

He grimaced. "In droves."

Of course. When weren't there? Morgan Grady was still everyone's favorite bachelor. "I didn't bring anything with me."

"I've got some clean dress shirts in the closet in my office. You could wear one of my button-down shirts out with a pair of gym shorts. It's not high fashion but it's better than petticoats and silk."

Winnie changed in his office but needed his help to undo the endless little hooks hidden on the back of the dress.

It was strange having him help undress her. They'd never been so personal before, never dealt with much beyond contracts and copies, flight plans and schedules. His hands against her back, his fingers against her bare skin made her feel so much, made her want new things.

His hands, his mouth, his body, him…

She was glad he couldn't see her face, glad

he couldn't see her blushing. Winnie Graham, she silently lectured herself, you're not his type, you'll never be his type, and just because you've made a deal with him doesn't mean it'll ever be love.

Hooks unfastened, Morgan left her alone to finish undressing and Winnie slipped out of the white boned corset, unclasped the white garter belt and rolled down the white silk stockings.

She stepped into the gray cotton gym shorts he'd left on his desk and then slid her arms into his starched blue pin-striped shirt. The shirttail hung down to the middle of her thighs leaving just two inches of shorts peeking beneath.

Winnie buttoned the pin-striped shirt to her breastbone and rolled up the long sleeves so they no longer extended past her hands.

There. No longer a bride. Just plain old Winnie in Morgan's blue-striped shirt.

They rode the elevator down together, and Winnie spotted the cluster of photographers outside.

"I can't do this," she whispered, panicked all over again. "I know what the papers are going to say and it'll be horrible."

"Pretend then everything's fine."

"I can't, Morgan. That's the problem, I can't fake anything important—"

"Relax," he said as he wrapped an arm around her and brought her close against him so that her cheek nestled against his chest. She could feel his warmth and smell his skin and she felt comforted. "Take a deep breath."

She did. She stood there, close against him, and just breathed him in. Oh, heaven. This was heaven.

His hand gently rubbed up and down her back. His voice was firm, soothing. "We'll go out, we'll smile, we'll act like everything's fine. You can do that."

Immediately she stiffened. "I don't know—"

"Sure you can. You're with me, and you trust me, right?"

She looked up into his eyes, those amazing dark blue eyes, and his gaze was steady, his expression warm. He made her believe she could do anything. "Right."

They exited the lobby through a side door, but the photographers rushed toward them as the limousine pulled up at the curb.

It was still hot outside, the air heavy and sticky, and the flash of camera strobes blinded Winnie. The chauffeur had opened the back door but Morgan paused for the cameras, slid his hand low on Winnie's back and smiled.

And then the panic struck. "This isn't going to work," she choked, turning her face away from the cameras, her mouth pressed close to his chest.

"You just have to stop thinking. Let it go. Have fun," he answered, his lips against the curve of her ear.

"How?"

"Like this," he said, his voice dropping lower, deeper as he tilted her face up to his.

He was going to kiss her.

He was going kiss her *here?* Panic flooded her, drowning all rational thought. She jerked as his head dropped, but he held her firmly, his palms flat against her middle, one at her back, one at her belly.

"Relax," he repeated, just before his mouth brushed hers. "It's just a kiss."

Just a kiss, she silently repeated and then gave in to the incredible sensation of his lips slowly, very slowly covering hers.

His mouth felt cool against her hot skin, his lips were firm and he drew her closer, bringing her snugly against the hard plane of his chest and the roughness of his jaw and chin. He was built so much bigger, and harder and it crossed her mind that he knew everything about making love and she knew absolutely nothing.

But expertise seemed inconsequential as his mouth moved leisurely across hers. He was doing something to her, making a deep dormant part of her come to life. The touch of his mouth against hers was about as wonderful sensation as she could imagine, and as his breath fanned her skin, she shuddered, her body rippling in a series of explosions, nerve endings bursting into flames.

Winnie forgot everything but touch, and the newness of his touch, sighing with pleasure as the pressure of his lips increased. She welcomed the heat and the flick of his tongue against the inside of her lower lip.

Her mouth felt warm, she felt warm, she felt wildly alive. Heat coiled in her middle, heat and urgency and something so physical she craved more of him but didn't know what. Tentatively she touched his chest, fingers splaying against the thick band of muscle.

"See?" he said, his head lifting just enough to gaze into her eyes. "Kissing's easy."

The photographers got their shot, she thought numbly, as the limousine sailed through Manhattan traffic. He might hate the media attention, might dread the photographers, but he always managed a smile and a civil word.

He was amazing that way, she thought, glancing at him in the deepening twilight. Back there, at the Tower's building, one of the reporters had asked Morgan how it'd felt, being left at the altar, and Morgan had grinned, flashing white teeth.

"Felt a little awkward," he answered with the easy confidence that charmed even tabloid journalists. "But I have her now, and that's all that matters."

She turned to look out the tinted window at the flicker of light and shadow, the moon beginning to peek between skyscrapers and glimpses of water. No wonder people loved Morgan. He was everything the public admired—intelligent, articulate, insightful—and he broke hearts.

"You do that so well," Winnie said. "You're a PR dream."

"I don't feel like it."

"Then you fake it well."

"Learned early."

She felt cold on the inside, empty on the inside. She'd loved the kiss but it'd just been good

PR for him. Everything about them was just appearances. "How did you learn to fake it?"

He shrugged. "Rather Darwinian. Survival of the fittest, I suppose. People don't want to know about problems and troubles. They want success stories. I try to give them a success story."

"So you do what you have to do?"

"That's right."

Her emotions felt dangerously unhinged. "Including kissing me."

He turned, stared at her, his gaze unflinching. "It wasn't exactly a chore."

She took a moment to answer, wondering why her heart was beating so fiercely and why she had this odd weak sensation in her tummy. "I know you're not attracted to me. You prefer models. Tall blond supermodels, preferably from Sweden."

"I liked kissing you."

"No, you didn't."

"And I'd like to kiss you again but I think we have a few things to straighten out first. Our relationship, for example."

Winnie was growing increasingly uncomfortable. "We don't have a relationship—"

"We do. We had one at the office and we

came awfully close to getting married today so obviously there's something here, even if it's just friendship, and that alone deserves discussion."

"It's going to be hard to discuss anything right now. Emotions are running awfully high."

"Which is why we need some time. I think it'd be wise if we both went away for a few weeks, put some distance between us and the gossip columnists and figure out what we're going to do next."

Truthfully, she'd love to get away for a few weeks. She felt trapped right now, trapped and claustrophobic.

Winnie chewed on her lower lip. "Where are you thinking of going?"

"St. Jermaine's."

His island off the Berry Islands in the Bahamas. She thought longingly of turquoise water and sandy coves and the shade provided by coconut trees.

"I guess I could go home," she said slowly, trying to figure out her best escape plan. "Mom and Dad will be upset but I can't imagine them kicking me out."

Morgan muttered an exasperated oath. "I'm

not leaving you here to face the media alone. The pressure will be intense. If I head to St. Jermaine's, I'm taking you with me."

CHAPTER SEVEN

THEY weren't flying out until the morning and Morgan spent much of the night sitting in a leather chair in his living room staring out at Manhattan's sparkling skyline.

She did love him.

Damn. This wasn't supposed to happen. He didn't want her emotionally involved. He knew what it felt like to love someone and not be loved in return. It hurt. It was miserable. He wouldn't wish that kind of feeling on his worst enemy and Winnie was definitely not his enemy.

Hell, he liked her. A lot. And she'd looked pretty today, almost glamorous, although part of him preferred her without the eye makeup and hair goop. Winnie didn't need cosmetics to cover her up or try to improve her. She was great just the way she was.

Everything was great until today.

What had happened at the church? What scared her?

Sighing, Morgan rubbed his jaw, the bristles of his beard scraping his palm. She loved him. Fine. He liked her.

In fact, he'd really liked kissing her. She had a great mouth, incredibly lush lips, and sex would be just as pleasurable once they got past the early, awkward stage.

The early, awkward stage.

That's it, he thought, sitting up. That's where he went wrong.

He'd been rushing her too much, pressuring her without meaning to. She needed time to grow comfortable with him, with them.

He knew without asking that she wasn't sexually experienced. There was an innocent air about her. Even the way she looked at him was youthful, hopeful, lacking pretension. He knew she rarely dated. In fact, he didn't know when she'd last gone out.

No wonder she was scared. She probably stood there at the back of the church listening to the heavy-handed organist, overpowered by the lilies, and imagined all the things she'd never done, wondering if sex with him would even be enjoyable or if it'd be something she'd have to endure like the Victorian wife who stared at the ceiling, gritting her teeth and bearing it for God and country.

He reluctantly smiled. Poor Winnie.

She had no idea that he'd never, ever rush her into bed. She hadn't a clue that he loved foreplay, loved the feel of a woman, and the unique way a woman was made. He relished curves, adored the female shape, and had a particular weakness for a soft, bare mouth.

Like Winnie's soft, bare mouth.

His body hardened just thinking about the kiss earlier. She'd shivered in his arms. He'd felt her helpless response and he knew then that if she responded to his kiss like that, she'd be just as sensitive in bed.

What he needed to do was woo her. Wine her, dine her, make impossibly slow love to her. She'd eventually discover that love wasn't the only thing that helped cement a relationship. He might not love her in the romantic poetry sense, but he could offer Winnie trust, respect, companionship, and best of all, sexual compatibility.

Morgan stood up, stretched, and gratefully headed for bed. Now that he'd identified the problem, he'd come up with a solution. Now, if he were lucky, he might even get a little sleep.

Morgan's bungalow on St. Jermaine's, if five thousand elegant square feet could be called a bungalow, looked like something out of *Architectural Digest*.

It was an absolutely stunning space, all creams and taupe, floor-to-ceiling windows that opened completely to let in the cool sea breeze, with gleaming hardwood floors.

Hands on her hips, Winnie inspected his collection of folk and Caribbean art. The bright canvases and sculpture were a contrast to the cool neutral walls and furniture.

"This is not a beach house," she said, transfixed by the canvases depicting trees and oceans, exploding volcanoes and dancing people.

"Sure it is. It's just got style, that's all," Morgan retorted as Mr. Foley moved past them, heading toward the kitchen where he intended to take control of the menu, the grocery list, and the cook.

During the three-hour flight from New York, Winnie had learned that Mr. Foley accompanied Morgan on most trips, ensuring

Morgan's comfort and saving him from having to attend to irritating domestic details.

Rather like her job.

Although in her job she rarely left the office, and when she did, it was to sit across from Morgan in the limousine, take dictation, prep him for meetings, and make last-minute travel arrangements.

But she'd never been on his plane, or taken a trip anywhere with him until now.

When the Learjet landed an hour ago on St. Jermaine's narrow airstrip, Winnie felt a wave of excitement. For the next week she'd be virtually alone on a private tropical island with Morgan Grady, New York's Sexiest Bachelor. If that wasn't an adventure, she didn't know what was.

A young man in a bright print shirt driving a white Jeep had met them at the airstrip and ferried them the half mile to the house.

They'd driven through a dense grove of coconut trees on the way to the house and Winnie had peeled off her linen blazer to relish the island breeze. The blazer matched her beige linen skirt and without the blazer she was quite comfortable in her camisole top.

In the shade of the coconut grove Winnie

drew a deep breath, feeling for the first time a moment of peace. With the emerald hills, turquoise cove, and white powdery sand, it almost felt like paradise.

Morgan took her on a brief tour of the house, showing her the central living areas before leading her down a wide, highly polished hallway to a very private wing of guestrooms.

"Your room's here," he said, opening a door, revealing a spacious suite decorated in apricot and cream. "I'm on the other side. There is a house phone, though, in case you need me."

She turned her back on the massive four-poster bed not wanting that kind of visual just now. "I won't need you."

One black eyebrow rose. "You sound so sure."

Winnie shrugged, feeling a little cavalier. She rather liked being with Morgan one on one, away from the office. She felt more equal, less dependent. It wasn't as if she needed his approval anymore. What was the worst that could happen now? He'd fire her?

"I won't need you," she said sweetly, crossing her arms over her chest. "If I think about the history of our *relationship,* it's *you* that needs *me.*"

His eyebrow arched higher. "How is it that I need you?"

She felt rather feisty just then, and more than a bit wicked. He'd always been so in control and she'd followed him around like a puppy dog.

Winnie smiled.

"You're the one always desperate to find me. At work you lean on the intercom, shoot constant e-mails to me, hound me by cell phone. In fact the last time I left my pager on my desk, you practically had a nervous breakdown."

"That's a gross exaggeration!"

Winnie took a step back as he stepped forward. "Maybe, but it's still true. When have I needed you for anything?"

Her arch question was met by complete silence. His dark blue eyes met hers, held, and she saw a flicker there, in the dark blue depths, a hot blue fire she'd never seen before.

Winnie felt a tiny thrill, followed by a surge of adrenaline. Morgan was looking at her, really looking at her, and he liked what he saw. It wasn't an external thing, it was something else, something deeper, more basic, and there was heat in his eyes, heat in the way he leaned a little closer and then a little closer.

Very slowly, very deliberately Morgan placed his right hand on the wall next to her shoulders, and then his left hand, trapping her there between him and the wall.

He leaned even closer, until their bodies were nearly touching.

"I think you have needs, Winnie."

His voice was so husky. His warmth was tangible. She felt her tummy tighten. "Of course I do. I need eight hours' sleep each night, three nutritious meals every day, twenty minutes' exercise—"

"Naked, in my bed."

Winnie's mouth dropped open, then blushing furiously, she snapped it closed. She scrambled to think of something to say but nothing smart or succinct came to mind.

Morgan leaned closer still, and whispered in her ear. "Actually, twenty minutes is nothing. I recommend a minimum of forty." Glints shone in his eyes. "Sixty whenever possible."

Still blushing, she lifted her chin, her heart beating faster in a one-two dance that made her feel very aware and very alive. "Thank you for the offer, *Mr.* Grady, but I believe there'll be plenty of exercise opportunities on St. Jermaine's without having to put yourself out."

"Really?"

She fought the urge to smile. Her imagination was running wild just now. She could picture his style of warm-up, the vigorous aerobic activity and the recommended cool-down. "Better yet, the things I have in mind require *no* nudity."

"Nudity's nice."

"I prefer my clothes."

Morgan's mouth practically grazed her sensitive earlobe. "Then you haven't found the right…activity… yet."

She loved the feel of his lips on the curve of her ear and the tender skin below. A delicious shiver raced through her as he caught her ear between his teeth and held it there.

He was teasing her, tormenting her and she loved it. How bad was that? She actually liked that he was making her ache inside, making her feel a fierce and driving need.

"Come on, Winnie, admit that you'd enjoy nude activity with me."

She grinned. He made sex sound lighthearted, even fun. She was amused and intrigued. "I don't know. Maybe…after I'm tired of everything else there is to do on the island."

His lips touched her neck very briefly, very lightly. "Like what?"

"Everything," she sighed, voice dropping, heat growing.

"Name a few."

He kissed her just above her collarbone. It was a fleeting kiss but he seemed to know every nerve ending already. Winnie gasped softly as his tongue flicked the curve of collarbone.

"I'm waiting," he added, just before his mouth slid up her neck, back to her ear and she felt as if he'd set her skin on fire.

Winnie grabbed his shirt, practically clinging to his chest, and dragged herself closer, needing contact, much more contact.

"Swimming," she whispered, mouth drying, belly knotting. Oh, she wanted him to touch her, wanted his hands against her ribs, under her breasts, sliding down the length of her.

But he was too intent on keeping score. "That's one."

"Is that enough?"

"No," he answered, hands moving to cup her face and tilt her head, exposing her neck. His fingers caressed her nape. His lips kissed an invisible spot on her neck, a spot that seemed wired just for him because every time he touched her there she gripped his shirt tighter, pressed herself closer.

"You said endless," he reminded, tipping her head back so that his lips could travel up her neck to the width of her jaw.

He was touching her skin and tasting her skin and she'd never felt so much sensation in all her life. "Jogging," she choked.

"That's two."

"Jogging—"

"You already said that."

She felt his smile against her skin, felt the heat building between them. It was wild, it was something so new and yet so strong that she wriggled helplessly, seeking more contact, more pressure, more fulfillment. "Snorkeling, sailing, snorkeling, sailing...."

"Yes. But you can only count each one once."

"How about kissing?" she sighed, turning her head toward his, wanting his mouth, needing his lips.

He wouldn't kiss her though. He lifted his head and appeared to consider her question.

Winnie groaned. "Kiss me, Morgan, please."

He bent his elbows, leaned all the way in so that his chest crushed her breasts and his hips ground against hers and she felt the hard ridge of his erection against her thighs. But still he didn't kiss her, and suddenly she couldn't stand it a moment longer.

Groaning, Winnie reached up, clasped his neck and dragged his head down to hers. His mouth felt cool, he felt hard and strong and her lips parted beneath the pressure of his.

She wanted to open that way for him. Wanted to part her knees and let him in and feel him tight and hard against her skin.

Just wanting to know him, wanting to experience him, made her blood race, her body warming from the inside out. As his kiss deepened and his tongue thrust inside her mouth she felt herself soften, growing pliant against him. It was the most wonderful sensual awakening, a hint of what could be, a glimpse of what surrender would feel like.

The door banged open and the young man in the bright yellow print shirt burst in carrying Winnie's suitcase.

"Oh! Sorry," he apologized, quickly backing up once he'd realized he'd intruded.

But by then Winnie had jumped out from under Morgan's arm and Morgan was smiling faintly as he watched her smooth her linen skirt and top.

Her lips felt tender. Her body throbbed. She felt self-conscious once again.

"Thanks for the tour," she said briskly, trying to cover her embarrassment. "I think I now know where everything is."

His eyes met hers and his smile slowly stretched, laughter just beneath the surface, warmth in the blue depths. "Yes, I think I do, too."

He led her back to the center of the house, which had a distinct pavilion feel with the floor-to-ceiling windows and the oversize ceiling fans strategically positioned over dining and sitting areas.

Mr. Foley appeared as they returned to the living room. "A cold drink?" he asked, extending a sleek pewter tray.

"Thank you," Winnie said, accepting one of the tall glasses festively garnished with pineapple, banana and orange slices.

This was the life. She knew she was being spoiled, knew she'd never experience anything like this again. A small voice inside her urged her to savor every decadent cocktail, every breathtaking vista, every mind-blowing kiss, because before she knew it she'd be back in steamy New York, sweating on the subway's vinyl seat and wishing to high heaven that women's nylons had never been invented.

Morgan took his drink and Mr. Foley slid the tray beneath his arm. "There are hot and cold appetizers waiting," he said, gesturing toward the sunken living room.

"He's very formal," Winnie said as Mr. Foley marched down the hall back toward the kitchen.

"He's great, isn't he?" Morgan answered, carrying his drink down the steps into the living room eclectically furnished with antiques and low comfortable pieces.

Winnie had yet to take a sip from her glass but she loved just looking at the luscious fresh fruit garnish. She hadn't had really ripe pineapple in ages.

She followed Morgan slowly, reminding herself to remember this moment, making note of the gentle breeze created by the ceiling fan and the blue sky outside now lit with horizontal streaks of pink and orange. Even the sky here looked ripe, edible, sensual.

Morgan watched her come down the steps and approach the rattan coffee table. She was beautiful, and her beauty was natural, the kind that glows from the inside, the kind that has nothing to do with hair and makeup and elegant clothes.

It was her lovely green-flecked eyes. Her soft sensitive mouth. Her light brown hair pulled back in a simple ponytail. He loved the lines of her neck. The shape of her lips. Her curves. Oh, those curves.

He'd felt her warmth earlier, felt the promise of her softness and he'd wanted her so bad that it was all he could do to keep it slow, take it easy, stay relaxed.

She was smiling now, smiling at some secret thought and he loved the way she bit her lower lip trying to keep her smile to herself.

"Do you like the drink?" Morgan asked, indicating the glass with the frothy white mixture.

"I haven't tried it yet. Let me find out." She lifted her glass, took a little sip. "It's a banana milkshake!" She laughed in surprise.

That smile just about did him in. His gut knotted, his body hardened. He wanted to drop her on the couch, slide his hands beneath her narrow linen skirt and— He shook his head, he wouldn't last the night if he didn't get some control.

"An adult banana milkshake," he corrected,

"it's potent. Mr. Foley makes one very dangerous banana daiquiri."

She took another drink, this time a bigger swallow. "I don't taste any alcohol."

"Annika said the same thing—" Morgan broke off, mentally kicking himself. That was stupid.

Winnie had heard him. It was amazing the impact his words had on her. A moment ago she'd been so happy she literally glowed, and yet suddenly she crumpled. Folded in like a paper airplane

"Annika's been here?"

Of course she had. Annika had been his girlfriend for months but none of that mattered now. Annika was the past. Winnie was the present. Women should know these things but they never focused on the important facts.

Morgan stifled a sigh. "She came with me last spring, when we were dating."

"Did she like it here?"

"Winnie, don't do this."

But Winnie's chin was set, her expression fixed. "Did she come here often?"

"That's irrelevant. The important thing is you're here with me now."

Her eyes watered. "Yes, but that's just this week. It'll be someone else next week."

Morgan set his glass on the rattan coffee table. "I'm not going to even dignify that with a response."

She moved toward him, blocking his path. "Why not?"

"Because you're being ridiculous. You're acting...jealous, and you have no right to be jealous."

"Why not?"

"Because I proposed to you. I was at the church yesterday. I was standing with the priest at the altar in front of a huge crowd of people waiting for you. And guess what? You walked out on *me*."

Winnie didn't speak and he drew in a deep breath, surprised at the depth of his emotion. He was angry, yes, but it wasn't just anger. It was...it was...

Concern. Worry. Pain.

It'd hurt him when she left. It *hurt* that she'd walk away from him.

It crossed his mind that everything had changed. Something had happened in the past few weeks. Something had happened just yesterday. And something had happened today when he pressed her against the bedroom wall and felt her shudder beneath him, felt her body arch against him. He wasn't indifferent to her. Not in the least.

"Why did you run away yesterday?" he asked abruptly, recognizing how heavily the question had been weighing on him the past twenty-four hours.

"Why did you ask me to marry you?"

"You already know that answer."

Her head lifted, her light brown ponytail swishing as she looked up at him. "I wouldn't have asked if I knew."

This was a new Winnie. A stronger Winnie, a more confident Winnie.

Certainly a more direct Winnie.

"Because you were the best candidate for the job," he answered lightly, trying for humor, but she didn't smile. Her grim expression didn't change.

"What about Annika?"

"What about Annika?" he retorted.

"Well, she's blond and beautiful and famous. She's your Swedish supermodel and she'd have looked perfect in the paper's page six photos."

"But I don't want to be the center of the society page. I don't want to spend the rest of my life photographed. I just want to live a normal life. A quiet life. A life away from the limelight."

It took Winnie a moment for the implications to hit her. She grit her teeth thinking he had incredible nerve. He didn't want a beautiful supermodel for a wife because the press would eat it up, but he'd marry her, a chunky little secretary who'd bore the media to death.

Her stomach physically hurt. "What about love?"

"I don't love Annika."

"You don't love me."

He didn't answer. The rawness inside her chest was nearly intolerable. "You don't love me," she repeated, her tone turning savage. "Do you?"

Morgan regarded her steadily. "No."

"So why me? Why did you ask me?"

"You're different." His shoulders shifted. "You know me. You wouldn't be operating under some false romantic illusion about married life."

Because a woman like Winnie wouldn't have any romantic illusions. A woman like Winnie was practical, dependable, sensible. A woman like Winnie didn't get many offers and she ought to know that Morgan Grady wasn't just a good catch, but a dream catch.

God help her, but she was supposed to be flattered. He expected her to be *pleased*.

For the first time since working for him she thought she could actually hate him. He really had no idea who she was.

She'd waited her whole life for the magic of falling in love, for the chance to be deeply loved. Her sisters had been loved, adored, spoiled. Winnie wanted the same thing, too, but didn't think she'd ever have it…didn't think she deserved it until yesterday when she looked in the mirror at the expensive Park Avenue salon and saw what the bevy of makeup artists and hair stylists had done, saw how they'd turned her from stodgy Winnie Graham into someone utterly magical, truly beautiful.

Winnie had looked in the mirror, contact lenses in, hair glossed and pinned, makeup expertly applied and she'd seen a woman who deserved real happiness, a woman still longing for the fairy-tale ending. And a marriage of convenience wasn't even close to her idea of a happy-ever-after dream.

Yes, she'd have money, Morgan had ensured

she'd be handsomely compensated, but what was money without love?

What was anything without love?

Winnie turned away and looked out toward the ocean. The late-afternoon sun shone hot and bright, glazing the beach.

"You know they're wrong," she said quietly, "those gossip columnists who called me a gold digger. I'm not interested in your money. I've never been interested in money—least of all yours."

She shook her head once, remembering the harsh things written about her in the past couple weeks and then looked back at him over her shoulder. Her lips twisted in a brief, rueful smile. "The only one thing I want from you is love."

CHAPTER EIGHT

Morgan laughed. It wasn't a loud laugh, or harsh, but it was definitely laughter and it was the last thing Winnie expected to hear from him. "Why are you laughing?"

"Because you…you're…a dreamer."

"What's wrong with that?"

"Nothing, except you're bound to be disappointed, and you think you agreed to marry me for love—which is very virtuous—but it's not exactly the truth."

She stiffened, blood draining from her face. "You can't say that. You don't know that. You don't know me."

Morgan smiled grimly. "Actually, I'm beginning to know you. I'm starting to understand you. You're not quite the altruistic person you think you are. You might tell yourself that all you want from me is love, but that's not true. You want a lot more than that."

"Really?" She glared at him, temper rising.

"Really." He walked toward her. "You want passion, sex, glamour, adventure. You want to try something different, be someone different. You think with me it could happen, and you're right, it could. With me you can be anyone and anything you want to be—including yourself."

He stood just a foot away and Winnie had to tilt her head back to see his face. His eyes were narrowed, his expression closed, but the heat he was generating more than made up for his lack of expression.

Winnie was powerfully reminded of how it'd felt in his arms, pressed against his hard body. She felt the warmth increase now, and the slow, seductive rise in energy.

From the dark blue of his eyes, and the angle of his jaw, she realized he was feeling the change in tension, too.

"Neither of us are altruistic people, Winnie." He lifted a hand, touched the curve of her ear, rubbed his fingers lightly across the skin. His eyes met hers and held. "We both have needs—and some of these needs have nothing to do with love."

Winnie's pulse raced. His touch was amazing. He made her feel so many incredible things but her attraction to him was based on love, not lust. "Maybe you can reduce it to the physical, but I can't. I feel this way around you because I love you, not because you turn me on."

He smiled. "You're such a romantic. You want it all—love with a capital L, romance with a capital R, passion with a capital P—"

"Yes, I do, and I think it exists."

His smile reached his eyes. He had the most beautiful eyes, the most lovely shade of blue. They were the kind of blue one would never get tired of. Not a shiny plastic blue, but rich and dark, like sapphires and midnight and silk from the Far East.

His fingertips trailed down her neck. "We could be happy together, Winnie. I know I could make you happy."

His touch did one thing to her. His words did another. She felt her heart squeeze, protesting against his logic, and his cool pragmatic reasoning. "I couldn't ever be happy with you if I knew you didn't love me."

"There's all kinds of love. You're talking romantic love. I'm talking reality love. I'm talking respect, admiration, friendship—"

"Not that again!" she interrupted, drawing swiftly away.

She wanted passion, romance, love and he wanted respect, admiration, and friendship. How perfect was that?

Snorting to herself, Winnie reached for her frosty glass and took a swallow. He'd spent the last fifteen years dating models, actresses, socialites, but he wanted to marry her based on the incredibly dull virtues of respect and admiration.

He wanted to marry someone safe. Someone dependable. Someone dumpy, dowdy, dull.

"Boring!" she snapped, setting her drink down again. "I can't spend the rest of my life with a man who feels nothing for me—"

"But I do like you."

"*Like?* Morgan, I want *love.*" She was getting angrier. She needed to take a step back, calm down, but she was too irritated. "I want someone who really wants me, someone who can't keep his hands off me, someone who'd walk to the ends of the earth for me. I want the real thing, and that includes fireworks, amazing sex, and eternal love."

She felt his gaze but he didn't speak. Her shoulders slumped, anger fading. She drew a shaky breath. "I just don't want to settle for less. It'd be wrong to settle for less."

"And what if your idea of love doesn't exist?"

Her eyes burned and she blinked hard. "You're so cynical."

"Maybe. Or maybe I'm just a realist."

Maybe.

She blinked again, thinking that maybe it was possible to see life from two different perspectives, and have both be equally right. And if that was the case, while they'd never see eye to eye, it didn't mean they couldn't enjoy the moment and, let's face it, they were in the middle of paradise.

St. Jermaine's was the most beautiful place she'd ever been and from the looks of it, there'd be a gorgeous sunset later tonight. She was drinking her first banana daiquiri and soon she'd be sitting down to dinner with the love of her life.

Dinner was served on the veranda, white gardenias in a bowl, the glass table glowing with the flicker of a dozen white candles. It was the most romantic table she'd ever seen.

The service was discreet. Mr. Foley uncorked a bottle of red wine and disappeared. Morgan was being his charming best. Winnie leaned back in her chair and listened to the soft lap of waves against the sand.

I could get used to this, she thought, picking up her goblet, admiring the wine's ruby sheen. This is definitely the good life. Wouldn't it be something to really live like this? What would it be like to be Morgan's girlfriend…or his mistress?

"You're smiling," Morgan said, topping off her glass with more wine before refilling his own.

"I am," she agreed, stretching a little, very relaxed. She lifted her glass in front of one candle and let the flame glow through the goblet, marveling at the warm garnet glow, red symbolizing love…passion.

Sex.

Maybe it was the Merlot in her veins, or the balmy evening, but she felt really lazy and really happy, and swirling her glass, Winnie thought she'd like to feel this way more often.

To feel like this not just now, but always.

"What are you thinking?" Morgan asked, his dark hair gleaming in the candlelight, his teeth flashing.

She looked at him from beneath her lashes.

"That you're not bad company when you're not worrying about the stock market."

He grimaced. "I don't worry about the stock market."

"No, you obsess about it."

Lines deepened near his mouth. He was trying not to laugh. "I'd never obsess about anything."

Her eyebrows arched.

He laughed out loud. "I must say, you're not bad company when you let your hair down." His dark blue gaze met hers, held. "I like your hair down."

"Literally or figuratively?"

His eyes were doing something crazy to her insides. Her heart raced and her arms felt weak, as if the bones had turned to butter. She slipped her hands to her lap and balled her fingers together.

"Both," he answered. "Don't pin it up anymore. I like it down. I like you like this. You're an interesting woman, Winnie. You're constantly surprising me."

His compliment touched her. She felt a lump grow in her throat. "You like interesting women?" she asked, voice suddenly husky.

"Of course. Why, do you prefer boring men?"

She was feeling so much intense emotion she didn't think she had a laugh in her just then, but he'd found it and she chuckled. "Boring men, please."

"Good. I'm just your type. I'm very boring. Incredibly dull. You'll yawn yourself silly with me."

Her eyes locked with his, and his eyes were saying he wanted her. His eyes were making her feel hot and hungry again.

Blood rushed through her, from her middle up her neck, into her cheeks.

"We could have fun boring each other, Winnie." His voice was pitched so low it felt like velvet sliding across her skin.

"Yes."

"There's a lot of ways I could bore you."

Heat flooded her limbs yet again, and Winnie grabbed her water glass, took a big gulp. She'd like to be bored, if that's what he wanted to call it. She'd love to be bored as a matter of fact. "But I'm really not your type."

"What's my type?"

Winnie slowly looked up into his face. His eyes, so blue, so intense, were looking straight into hers. "Annika, Birget, Hannah—"

"Oh, yes, my blond Scandinavian supermodel type."

"It's true. It's your preference. You're attracted to tall, slender, sexy and that's certainly not me."

"No, you're not tall, and blond, but I'm still very attracted to you."

"Morgan, I don't think you understand me. I'm talking attracted as in sex."

Creases fanned from his eyes. "Winnie, I understand you perfectly. I'm talking about sex, too, and I think we'd have great sex together."

The warmth in her tummy did a sinuous dance through her middle, along her tense spine, flooding her quivery limbs with heat. Part of her brain told her she should drop the subject, back away from it now, but another part wouldn't let her. She was fascinated, intrigued by all that she didn't know and had never done. "You do? And how do you know?"

He shrugged. "I can tell from the way you kiss."

She felt hot all the way through, her skin scorching, pulse racing. She drew a breath but she wasn't getting much air. She was thinking about sex. Thinking about his mouth on her skin. "You liked the way I kiss?"

"And taste."

Winnie sagged against the back of her teak dining chair, heart thumping, belly clenching, aching in places she didn't think could ache.

His words made her want and his voice made her need and she thought she'd do just about anything if he'd teach her a few things about sex and passion and love. Or just sex and passion because she already had the love part figured out.

If he didn't insist on marriage, she could almost imagine a life with him. There'd be dates, dinners, evenings out and evenings in.

Winnie could see herself riding down Park Avenue in his stretch limo, stepping out at one of the hot clubs, treated to a private box at the opera.

He'd have seats behind home plate at Yankee Stadium. There'd be ice skating at Rockefeller Square. She'd receive invitations to all the fashion premieres.

Stylish haircuts, waxed eyebrows, year-round tan—

The fantasy came to an abrupt end. Because even tan and waxed and wearing a stylish new do, she'd never feel complete, it'd never be enough if he didn't love her.

"It wouldn't work," she said after a moment, the lovely vision bursting like a bubble inside her head. "We wouldn't survive a week."

"Why not?"

"Look at us. You're…you…and I'm…me."

He laughed softly. "Very insightful."

"I'm serious."

"So am I. There's a lot of chemistry here, Winnie, more chemistry than I ever felt with Birget, or Hannah, or Annika."

Her head jerked up. She stared at him wide-eyed. "Really?"

"Really." He pushed aside his wineglass and stood up. "Let's head down to the beach to catch the sunset."

The sun was just setting when they reached the cove and the colors at dusk were incredibly intense—blood-red, bright orange, purple and turquoise water.

Winnie slipped off her sandals to walk barefoot through the surf and when Morgan threw himself down on the beach, she sat down next to him, burying her feet beneath the still-warm sand.

It was so quiet on his island. The birds she'd heard earlier were silent and unlike New York, which was never still, here there was nothing of civilization to disturb the peace. No voices, no cars, no traffic, nothing but the gentle lap of waves against the creamy edge of sand.

"It's lovely," she whispered, pressing her hands against the sand, feeling the warm soft grains against her skin.

Morgan nodded. "I feel good here. I feel calm here. And I like having you here with me."

She leaned forward and propped her chin on her forearm, not knowing what to say. She was still rather intimidated by him, still felt some awe that she was here, in the Bahamas, on Morgan's island. It was surreal. Intimate. Exclusive. It was almost as if she'd gone on the honeymoon even though she'd missed the wedding.

Morgan stretched out an arm, pointed to the water. "Look, the sun's going quickly now."

He was right. Once the round red sun hit the horizon, it sank fast, disappearing into ocean as if it were a heavy fireball, and for one exquisite moment the ocean lit up and the surface shone ruby and gold.

Winnie held her breath the last few seconds, feeling almost bereft when the sun disappeared altogether, leaving the horizon a quiet, sullen, blue.

"That was beautiful," she said, wrapping her

arms more tightly around her knees. It was still warm out but the contrast between the intense red sky and the now gray night made her shiver.

Morgan must have noted her shiver because he reached over, touched the middle of her back. "Cold?"

"No." But she shivered yet again, not from cold as much as desire. When he touched her she felt so much, it was almost too much. She'd never known such pleasure.

For seven months now she'd battled her feelings. For seven months she'd tried to dismantle the desire, deny the need, ignore the want. She'd told herself her feelings would fade. She'd forced herself to go elsewhere, look for another job just to put distance between her and heartbreak but here she was at the end of July and she was still hoping, wanting, needing, dreaming.

Would it be so awful to stop fighting herself, to stop fighting for the higher, moral ground and to just let herself enjoy him? To just enjoy this?

Would it be so bad to be with him just for the moment and to take what she could…even if it was only sex?

"Winnie, we don't have to make any big decisions today."

She turned her head, looked at him, wondered how he could know exactly what she was thinking. "I used to believe I was really old-fashioned," she said, her throat so dry it felt as if she'd swallowed a bucket of sand. "But I'm beginning to think I'm not so very conservative."

"Winnie—"

"I don't want to marry you. If a marriage is to last it must be built on love, but there are things I'm curious about, and there are things I don't know."

He waited and she clenched her hands together, praying for courage. "I'd like if it you…" She drew a deep breath, finding these words almost impossible to say. "If you could teach me these things…show me how it works…what to do."

"You make it sound like rocket science."

"It is if you don't know how."

"Well, I don't think you need to worry. You're a natural." His lips slowly curved but the smile didn't reach his eyes. "It'll be easier than you think."

She loved it when he looked at her like that. When his eyes were serious, but she could feel the heat. He tried to check the emotion yet she felt it anyway. "That's what you said about kissing," she said a bit breathlessly.

Grooves formed next to his mouth. "And was I wrong about that?"

He was doing it again. Making her hot, making her want. Winnie exhaled slowly in the semidarkness, her skin so warm that she wanted to peel her camisole top off, push her skirt down and throw herself into the ocean.

And Winnie realized that's exactly what she wanted to do. Strip down. Get naked. Skinny-dip. She'd never done anything half so daring but this was the time, this was the night. If she didn't do something risky now, she never would.

"Want to swim?" she asked, blushing a little.

"You mean get our suits and head to the pool?"

"No." Her blush deepened, her face felt sensitive, and she thought that she'd do just about anything to make him kiss her soon. "Let's swim here." Winnie swallowed hard. "Naked."

Morgan scooped up a handful of sand and held it in his closed fist. He wasn't sure that stripping to skin and swimming was the thing he needed right now.

Winnie was having a really potent effect on him. He could feel her, smell her, still taste her. He'd been battling his desire all evening. Dinner had been a lesson in discipline. During the meal when she'd leaned forward and placed a hand on his forearm, he'd hardened instantly. Ardently.

It was one thing to hide an erection seated at the dinner table. It was another naked on the beach.

"Come on, Morgan," she entreated, leaning forward, her breasts brushing his bicep. Waves crashed not far from their feet, the salty spray coating their skin. "Swim with me."

He searched her face. She looked so eager, her face very alive, eyes wide, lips parted, her expression completely unguarded. He loved that about her—her openness, her freshness.

Beautiful women were always interested in protecting power, jostling for position. Annika had always kept her guard up. Hannah wouldn't ever compromise. Birget played coy. But not Winnie, and he thought she was just as beautiful, if not more beautiful, than the others.

He glanced behind him at his low house with the steeply pitched roof. It glowed like a mysterious Japanese lantern on a hill. The tiki torches lining the dirt path from the beach to the bungalow shimmered, yellow flames dancing and licking at the night. It was a warm night, warm enough to sleep outside, and definitely warm enough for a swim.

He opened his fingers and let the powdery sand slide through. "You really want to do this?"

"Yes," she answered, voice quavering.

"All right, but you go first."

CHAPTER NINE

"Go first?" She'd risen and now stood above him, feet slightly apart and planted in the sand.

Her hands were on her hips and her shoulders were bare. She looked very sexy and he couldn't forget the softness of her mouth, the delicate shape of her lips, or the smoothness of her skin. Just thinking about the kiss, remembering the way she'd felt in his arms, made Morgan hard again.

He craved the feel of her. He longed to put his mouth against her collarbone, feel her gasp as his tongue traced the delicate skin at her throat and the hollow beneath her ear.

"Skinny-dipping was your idea," he reminded, wondering now how he could have ever thought her big or solid. She was barely five five, maybe five four.

Without a word Winnie reached behind her, unzipped her skirt and peeled the beige linen fabric over her hips, down her legs to fall at her feet. Morgan inhaled sharply as Winnie stepped out of the skirt, leaving her in just the beige camisole and the nude-colored panties.

Winnie had legs. Amazing legs that were smooth and silky and very bare.

She looked over her shoulder, at the water, giving him a glimpse of firm thighs and a rounded bottom. Morgan was turned on all over again. "I've never done this before," she said in a small, breathy voice.

Winnie, his Winnie, the Winnie he'd worked with for the past seven months was driving him absolutely crazy. "You're doing just fine."

Her lips curved briefly and grasping the edge of her linen camisole she pulled up, lifting it over her head.

As Winnie tugged the camisole up, Morgan caught the sway of full, firm breasts. The top came off and the rising moon flooded her with light, illuminating her pale soft skin. She wasn't wearing a bra. Her breasts swayed as she dropped the camisole onto the sand.

Blood surged through him. Blood pounded in his ears, in his limbs, in his groin and Morgan felt as if he'd been taken over, hit by a wave of hunger so strong he was a sixteen-year-old kid again, looking at a centerfold.

She was lushly made—full breasts, hips, thighs—the body of a woman as a woman was meant to be.

His desire stunned him. His body actually hurt.

This was Winnie. This was the woman he'd worked so closely with for seven and a half months and he'd never known how sexy, how seductive, how sensual she was.

"You're going to join me?" she asked, hesitating slightly, as if starting to doubt the wisdom of an evening swim.

"Yes." Morgan remained where he was but slowly began unbuttoning his white Egyptian cotton shirt. His fingers weren't quite steady. In fact, he could hardly concentrate on the task at hand, still too enthralled by the vision of Winnie.

If he hadn't promised to take things slow...

"You're having trouble with that last button," Winnie said, head tilted, watching him.

He looked down at his shirt. It was true. It was all unbuttoned but the last and his fingers couldn't seem to get it undone.

Winnie crouched in front of him. "Let me help," she said, crisply, impossibly matter-of-fact.

He stared at her breasts. They swayed just inches from his face. If he bent his head he could capture one of her pale pink nipples in his mouth.

Her nipple in his mouth. His tongue against the tiny round peak. His body surged. He ached. He ground his teeth together to keep from touching her now.

But oh, he wanted to taste her skin, wanted to feel her firm nipple in his mouth and he'd suck it, warm it, make her cry his name.

"This is a tricky button," she said, her voice breathless, her fingers brushing his bare stomach. His abdomen contracted, muscles tensing at her light touch.

He could imagine her fingers on him, could imagine her soft hands against his erection and he felt nothing like controlled logical Morgan Grady but another man altogether.

God, he wanted her. He wanted to touch her, taste her, discover her.

He hadn't felt this kind of hunger in years. He wanted his palms on her breasts, her nipple in his mouth. He wanted to slide his hands beneath the snug fleshtone panties and cup her bottom. He wanted to touch the satin span of thigh, the warmth between her legs, to make her as hot for him as he was for her.

"There, got it," she exclaimed, victorious. "Now maybe we can swim."

She stood up and took a step back, her breasts perfectly round. The moon bathed her in the most delicious white light and Winnie glowed from head to toe. Her hair shone, her skin looked luminous, her shape so wonderfully distinct that he felt like a primitive man wanting a cave, a fire, and his very own woman.

He could see her stretched out on a bearskin rug; picture her in a soft leather wrap that barely covered those amazing breasts. He'd peel the loincloth from her pale hips and kiss his way from her ankle bone to the moist silk above.

Morgan shook his shirt off and, standing, he unzipped his khakis, stepping out of them. Now it was Winnie's turn to covertly watch him and his erection grew harder, bigger; his whole body ached.

He saw her gaze drop to his white briefs. There was no way he could hide his attraction now.

She bit her lower lip, worried it a little and

then her gaze lifted, back to his face. She looked thrilled and afraid all at the same time. "That just leaves the underwear."

Her husky voice just about did him in. Did she know the effect she had on him? Did she do this to everyone?

"My turn to go first," he said hoarsely, wondering when and how everything had changed on him. He'd wanted Winnie because he'd thought they'd have a simple relationship, an uncomplicated relationship, but what he was feeling now was far from simple or uncomplicated.

He wanted her, desired her, cared for her.

He *cared* for her.

Morgan swallowed. Everything was different. Every-thing was changing.

As he took off his briefs she slid her own panties off, bending over to step out of one leg and then the other.

Morgan groaned. She had the most shapely bottom, the fullest most gorgeous curve of breast he'd ever seen on a woman. In the twenty years he'd been sexually active, he'd never been turned on like this.

He felt so hard and tight and hungry that his muscles bunched, his heart raced, his groin felt hot and painful. He needed to get in the water fast.

Morgan dashed across the sand, waded thigh-deep into the water before diving under the surf. He swam a distance under the surface, arms pulling hard, feet kicking, trying to burn off some energy. The water wasn't cold but it felt significantly cooler than the fire raging inside his skin.

He was in trouble. St. Jermaine's was far removed from the world outside. St. Jermaine's made anything feel possible. Including keeping Winnie.

After a moment he swam an easy breaststroke back toward the beach. He met up with Winnie halfway. She was treading water, hair wet and slicked back, shoulders bare, globes of breast barely visible.

"Feels great out here," she said, arms drawing circles beneath the surface. "It's warmer than I expected, almost like bathwater."

And he could see himself taking a bath with her, bathing her. He could see himself spending a long, long time with her.

He floated next to her. "I've owned St. Jermaine's three and a half years and I've never done this before."

Winnie sank a little lower in the water, her chin disappearing. "Why not?"

"I don't know." He swam closer, lashes lowered as he studied her pale face in the moonlight. "It never felt right before."

Her lips curved. "And it's right now?"

It was right, he thought. At that moment, everything felt right. For much of his life he'd felt alone, distinctly cut off, but somehow with Winnie he never felt alone…or lonely. Something about her made sense to him. Winnie made sense. Even that wasn't rational or logical, simply a gut response. A heart response. *Instinct*.

And his instincts were never wrong.

The moon's reflection glinted off the water, back onto Winnie's oval face, gleaming shoulders, and pale skin.

He reached out, water running down his arm, and very gently touched her cheek. "Is it possible I've been waiting for you?"

She was staring straight at him. Her eyes were enormous. Her cheeks darkened, pink slowly staining her skin. "Morgan," she said his name softly, breathing shallowly.

Her eyes had turned very green, a sage green, and were growing darker by the moment. From the pink of her cheeks to her parted lips, he knew what she was feeling. He was feeling it, too. And he was having a damn hard time keeping his hunger in check.

"Morgan," she repeated.

Her sexy pitch turned him inside out. His body strained. His head felt light. He'd never wanted anyone like this.

"Talk to me," she whispered, as she slowly, tentatively, reached out to touch him beneath the water and her hand brushed his thigh.

Heat shot through him as her fingers glided over his leg. Hot, sharp heat, and his body tightened all over again, fresh blood surging. He was close to exploding with pleasure and pain. Stifling a groan, Morgan wrapped a hand around her upper arm and pulled her toward him, water swirling between them.

He hooked a leg around her leg, braced her against his chest, his hands encircling her waist. The water was cool but she was warm. She drew a deep shuddering breath and he could feel her tummy convulse, ribs expanding.

She'd be lovely beneath him. Lovely on top of him. Lovely every which way known to man.

He drew her even closer, her wet soft breasts crushed against his chest, her nipples pebbled and grazing his own. He wanted to be inside her. He needed her mouth, needed her wet, needed her open.

She made a soft whimpering sound as his palm cupped her breast, his fingertips massaging the nipple. "Oh, Morgan—"

"You're beautiful, Winnie. You're the most beautiful woman I've ever known."

Tears filled her eyes and she pressed her hands against his shoulders. "Don't say that. You don't have to say that."

"It's true."

"Annika—"

"Nothing compared to you," he murmured, sliding his palm up, over the peak of her breast to her collarbone and down again.

Then he couldn't stand it a minute longer. He had to have her, had to taste her and his head descended, mouth capturing hers.

She tasted cool and hot, salty and sweet, and beneath the pressure of his lips she whimpered, her hands moving, caressing his shoulders, his chest, his back, his triceps. It was as if she couldn't get enough and he couldn't get close enough and water splashed and swirled around them as their legs twined below the surface, hip pressed frantically to hip.

"Do you want to go in?" she mouthed against his ear, her hands at his nape, fingers in his hair.

He loved the way she touched him, loved everything about being with her. "A little way in," he said, and turning onto his side, he swam closer to shore, carrying her along with him.

Once he could feel the sandy floor, and stand with ease, he lifted Winnie up, parted her legs and brought her close against him. He wrapped her legs around his waist and he cupped her below the water, her smooth round cheeks fitting perfectly in his hands.

She gasped as he caressed the curve of her backside, fingers stroking out and then in until he found the very hot soft part of her.

"Morgan," she choked, wriggling against him, "I don't know about this."

He felt the delicate shape of her, the petal-like lips, the tiny hooded nerve. "You don't like this?"

Like? Winnie thought, burying her face against Morgan's damp warm shoulder, desperate to get even closer. What was there not to like? She felt wild, her senses taut, her nerves screaming. He was making her feel desperate desires. She wanted him to touch her. She wanted him to do everything to her. "I think I like it too much," she answered, her lips pressed to his neck, his skin warm and fragrant.

"I don't know if that's possible, not if you care about the person you're with."

He was touching her in such a way she couldn't think, touching her in a way that made her breath fast and shallow. His fingers played against her, played her and she felt almost helpless in his hands. "Oh, I care about the person I'm with," she murmured, feeling so much love just then.

"Good, then you can relax."

His touch was even more intimate now, his fingers slipping inside her. Winnie's thighs tensed and she wrapped her arms around his shoulders, her lips parting against the base of his throat. She'd imagined having sex but never imagined anything as seductive as this.

His fingers inside her made her ache for more of this, more of him. She writhed and he stroked her slowly, deeply and the pleasure was so intense she felt close to tears.

"Beach," she choked, practically grinding her hips against him. "Let's…go…to beach."

He carried her up in his arms and she was totally without inhibitions now. It seemed right to be naked and hot and craving each other.

On the beach they discovered a blanket, a stack of towels and two terry-cloth robes. Their scattered clothes had been discreetly removed.

"Mr. Foley," Morgan muttered, shaking his head.

"He's very attentive," Winnie said, smiling a little, fighting the nervous urge to giggle.

"Another sign that Mr. Foley likes you." Morgan lowered her down to the quilted blanket. "He's good with details, but this is a first."

The blanket felt warm, the sand was soft and inviting. Winnie felt comfortable and deliciously languid. "I think like is too strong of a word."

He knelt next to her. "He was certainly concerned when I returned from the wedding without you."

She was about to answer when he ran a hand up the inside of her thigh, his hand returning to her inner heat. She closed her eyes, sucked in air, and thought she must be a hedonist because she'd never felt anything half so good and couldn't imagine anything ever feeling better.

Morgan shifted, parted her knees wider, lowered his body between. Before she fully understood what he intended to do, his mouth replaced his hand, his tongue substituting for his fingers.

Winnie gripped the blanket, squeezed the quilted cotton in her fists to keep from crying out loud. The intense sensation overwhelmed her. Okay, she thought, trying to catch her breath, this felt even better than the other.

He was doing something with his hand and his mouth, creating a pattern of feeling, a rhythm within her. She tried to make sense of the tightness coiling in her middle, her belly clenching, her legs beginning to tremble.

Without changing position, without shifting focus or losing tempo, Morgan placed a palm on her tummy just above her pubic bone. The pressure of his hand coupled with the rhythm of his tongue was quickly building tension, layering sensation on top of sensation like children's blocks stacking all the way up, past the coconut trees to the starlit sky itself.

"But wait," she said, her voice raspy in the night, "I want you with me."

He kissed the inside of her thigh. "I'm with you."

"But I want it different for my first time, I want you in me."

"You might not be able to come. It can be hard for women—"

"I don't care. It doesn't matter." She reached down, ran her hand across his upper back, his muscles so beautifully hard, his skin silky smooth. "I'd rather feel you inside me...if that's okay with you."

He didn't say anything. He didn't have to say anything. Morgan shifted, braced himself on his elbows, stretching out over her.

With his knees he pressed her legs up and wide. His body touched hers. She could feel the tip of him and she sighed. Morgan caught her hands in his, and even as he lifted her arms up, over her head, he thrust smoothly into her.

Winnie sighed, tightening around him. His hands pressed against hers. He thrust harder, now a little deeper, then briefly stopped. "Are you okay?" he asked, buried all the way in her.

She couldn't help smiling. Okay? She felt perfect, fantastic. "Yes, oh, yes."

But he was still concerned. "I don't want to hurt you."

"You're not, you couldn't, you feel wonderful. Besides, I was ready for you."

She felt him smile against her neck, then he

kissed her most tenderly on the sensitive place near her ear. "I have to agree with you on that."

What followed was without time, without definition, without words. He was with her, so completely with her that she no longer knew him from her. He touched her and moved with her so that it felt as if they were part of the air, the earth, the sky. Beautiful, Winnie thought, I feel really truly beautiful.

She gave in to him and the rightness of being together. She gave in to the warmth, the touch, the exquisite pleasure. It was thrilling being so close, healing, too. The energy was intense, the heat formidable. To be held like this, touched like this, loved like this.

Loved.

Morgan rolled over, drawing Winnie on top of him. She felt naked for a moment, and stiffened. But Morgan caressed her breast and drew her head down and kissed her. "Don't stop moving," he whispered, lips brushing hers. "You'll like this, I promise."

She wasn't sure, and she felt a little awkward but Morgan clasped her hips and shifted her a little and suddenly it all made sense. The heat was back, the tension building. The self-consciousness receded, the strangeness disappeared. She was his again. He was hers. They were together, neither was distinct, and as she moved against him light flashed against her closed eyes. Hot liquid sun, hot summer sun, red hot, so hot, and Morgan held her tighter, moved her faster. Winnie didn't think she could stand it, the tension growing, her muscles clenching, but he wouldn't let her escape.

"Morgan—" she choked, the heat so great, her skin so hot, beads of moisture forming everywhere.

He rose up to meet her, driving hard, fierce, and she couldn't contain it any longer, couldn't control it and with a cry she felt launched into the sun. Waves of light and heat rolled through her, waves of light and heat and pleasure until she shuddered from head to toe.

"I can't hold on much longer," he said, voice hoarse, muscles knotted hard.

"Then don't."

He lifted her off him, drew her down to his side. Groaning, he held her as he came.

Winnie waited a moment before gently touching his face. "You didn't have to pull out."

He leaned on his elbow and looked down at her, his expression gentle, rueful. He pushed back a damp lock of hair from her forehead and kissed her warm brow. "Yes I did. I really wanted to be in you, but it wouldn't be fair. I'm not about to trap you into marriage."

She stared up at him, into his eyes. His black lashes were so thick they cast shadows on his face. "You've changed your mind about marrying me?"

He pulled her back on top of him, slid a hand up the length of her back. "Not at all, sweetheart, but I think you need to live a little first."

His lips were creating havoc on her skin. His hands were tracing the shape of her spine. Her body was stirring to life again. How could he still make her feel so much? Want so much?

"Live a little?" she gasped as he drew her nipple in his mouth. The warm wet feel of his mouth, the pointed flick of his tongue was driving her crazy, making her need and want and ache. Her breast ached. Between her legs ached. She was dying to feel him inside her again.

"Live," he said, his breath fanning her wet breast. "Experiment. Do all the things you've always dreamed of doing."

"I think…I think…" she said, voice breathy, faint, as he flipped her over onto her back and parted her knees with his own.

He smoothed the hair back from her face and trailed his hand from her breast to her belly and back to her breast again, his touch light, tantalizing, maddening. "Yes?"

"I think I'm…" She exhaled as he entered her again, his body so hard, his tension barely leashed. "…doing them."

And it was, she thought, as he filled her body, and filled her heart, the most beautiful experience she'd ever known. The reality of making love to Morgan was far better than anything in her wildest imagination.

CHAPTER TEN

Later they put the robes to good use, wrapped themselves in the plush terry-cloth, and walked back to the house.

It was well past midnight, and Winnie stumbled a bit on the dirt path, the tiki torches burning so low that several had burned themselves out.

Morgan touched her elbow, steadying her as they reached the stone steps leading from the lower terrace to the house.

She smiled her thanks, so calm she didn't need words. Talking seemed redundant after all that had taken place. It had been the most amazing, perfect night. She knew she might not ever experience a night like this again, knew that the intensity, the chemistry and the passion she'd felt were unique to being with him.

Winnie didn't need to be told that not everyone clicked like this. She didn't need a dozen partners to recognize that what she'd found, what she'd felt, was something few people ever knew. Somehow she had been blessed. Somehow she'd been one of the lucky ones.

The house was quiet, most of the interior lights dimmed. Here and there a small light illuminated a work of art, and some of the large bronze sculptures. But lights were unnecessary with the windows unshuttered and the moonlight pooling in. The house felt like an extension of the warm sultry night and Winnie held her breath a moment, telling herself to remember, telling herself to forget nothing.

This is a taste of heaven, she thought, holding her breath a moment, keeping the joy within. To be loved like this. To be touched like this. To feel so good, so amazing with someone else.

Morgan brushed her elbow, prompting her forward, directing her past the dining room to the kitchen. In the kitchen a light glowed above the large French stove, the stove painted a cheery color red. "Hungry?" he asked.

She nodded. "And thirsty."

"Grab one of the bar stools."

Winnie sat at the counter, discovering that sitting she was more tender than standing. Definitely no longer a virgin. Thanks to Morgan she knew a great deal more than she had this time yesterday.

Morgan foraged in the huge stainless-steel refrigerator, gathering fruit and cheese and bottles of chilled mineral water.

He carried everything to the counter, before locating a loaf of bread, butter and a sharp knife.

It was like a picnic, sitting at the counter in the virtual dark. They ate bread and cheese, and while Morgan cut juicy slices of mango and papaya, he didn't talk.

She was glad; words would spoil it. Winnie liked the silence, the stillness, and the sense of mystery.

Until tonight she'd never really lived. Until tonight she'd never fit her skin. She'd always felt so plain before, so heavy and awkward, but in Morgan's arms and against Morgan's chest she felt lovely. Lovely on the inside as well as the out.

No longer a girl, but now a woman.

There are certain rites of adulthood and tonight she'd been initiated into the most meaningful of all.

It wasn't about sex, she thought, sucking the juice from a papaya slice, but about living. It was one thing to love a man with your heart, but something entirely different to love him with your soul.

She loved Morgan through and through, and making love had only deepened her trust, cemented her loyalty. No matter what happened in the future, she would always be part of him, and he'd be part of her.

Satiated in more ways than one, Winnie yawned. She tried to cover her mouth with her hand but Morgan still caught the yawn and laughed softly.

"You're beat," he said, handing her a damp paper towel to wipe her sticky fingers clean.

"I am beat," she admitted, scrubbing the juice from her fingers and the palm of her hand.

He watched her for a moment before leaning forward and kissing her on the forehead, then on her mouth. "Thank you."

Winnie set the crumpled paper towel down. "Why are you thanking me?"

"Because." His dark blue eyes looked almost black in the dim kitchen light.

Winnie waited, forcing him to articulate.

His smile was small, his eyes shadowed with things he still hadn't shared, stories and history he kept buried inside. "It was good tonight. It was really good between us. It just felt right."

It did.

It felt really right.

Warmth filled her. Her eyes burned, and the emotion she felt was so different from other happiness. This happiness was something permanent, something she'd always have because she'd had one perfect evening, one most perfect setting, and one most perfect lover. "I love you."

She hadn't meant to say it, had thought the words, had felt the words, but hadn't meant to say anything at all. But now that the words had been spoken, she didn't regret it. How could she? It was the truth, and if she couldn't be honest with him now, when could she?

Morgan held her face in his hands, his thumbs against the curve of her cheekbones. "Winnie, I believe in you." He kissed her mouth gently, in a long lingering kiss. And when he lifted his head he added, "Now it's time for you to believe in you."

He kissed her briefly and they said good night. Winnie closed the bathroom door behind her, turned on the shower, dropped her robe and stepped inside the wide white-marble enclosure. She let the hot water pulse down, rinsing all the salt and sand and perspiration away.

Hair clean, skin clean, Winnie toweled off, brushed her teeth, slathered lotion all over and climbed into bed.

But sleep was fitful. Hours later her body was still so sensitive that she'd wake, certain that Morgan was with her, that his hands were on her and they were making love again.

By the time morning came Winnie felt exhausted. She woke up at five, went to her window, folded the shutters back and pushed open the sliding French door.

For nearly a half hour she sat on her balcony and listened to the waves roll and crash and felt the cool night air slowly warm.

She'd always believed that love was the most important thing between a man and a woman, and she'd promised herself years ago that she'd wait to make love until she was truly in love. Well, she'd done that. She'd waited to make love, she'd waited for Morgan, and last night proved that the wait had been worth it.

But what happens now?

She curled up in the chair and watched the

sun begin to rise, the purple sky lightening to weak yellow and pale blue.

From her balcony she could see a strip of white sand and she thought of them last night, out there, in the water and on the beach. She could picture Morgan naked in the moonlight, his broad shoulders and chest a gorgeous sun-kissed shade of gold. She could still see him, the way he'd looked reclining on the blanket on the sand. He'd been passionate and yet gentle, confident and loving.

It'd been such an amazing experience. The dinner, the sunset, the late-night swim. These things didn't usually happen in her life. These were the kinds of storybook events that happened to other people—people like her sisters, people like Annika, people who were poised and sophisticated and physically beautiful.

Morgan had said last night he found her beautiful but that was last night in the heat of the moment. Would he find her beautiful later, when back in New York? Would he find her as sexy and compelling when life returned to normal?

Winnie stirred restlessly, uncomfortable with the questions she posed to herself. She didn't want to answer those questions, didn't want to think about the future.

She got out of her chair, left the balcony to return to her bed. She drew the sheet up, covered herself all the way to her chin as if she could somehow block the little voice of doubt already whispering in the back of her head.

Things here might feel idyllic but this is paradise. What happens when you leave heaven for Manhattan? What happens when you're back in the Tower's building and working for him?

It was after ten when she woke up again and this time she was more rested. Dressed in a light green sundress, Winnie wandered through the house, outside to the veranda and, hearing Morgan talk, she followed the sound of his voice.

As she descended the stairs to the pool terrace she caught snatches of his conversation.

"How can she be having trouble already?" Morgan said shortly. "I'm not even there. There shouldn't be anything stressful for her to *do.*"

Winnie opened the wrought-iron gate and closed it behind her. As she rounded one large pot teaming with hibiscus flowers she spotted Morgan on the phone, pacing by the pool.

He wore nothing but navy cotton shorts, and his skin, burnished bronze, glistened. Winnie spotted a pair of shoes next to one of the chaise longues and realized he'd only just returned from a run.

"No!" he thundered, voice rising. "I shouldn't have to be dealing with this now. I'm on vacation."

He didn't know she was there, she realized, recognizing he was on a business call, probably with someone from the office. It was Monday morning and most people were back at work.

Morgan swore softly and raked a hand through his dark damp hair. "You're not listening," he interrupted sharply. "The whole point of hiring her was to ensure I didn't have to be doing this while I was gone. If she can't handle the job, get rid of her. I can't afford these kinds of mistakes."

This didn't sound good. Someone had clearly goofed at the office and she knew better than anyone that Morgan didn't tolerate sloppy work or thoughtless errors.

Morgan turned around and spotted her there. His brooding expression cleared and he lifted a hand, waving her over.

"Handle this," he concluded as she approached

him. "Today." Without saying goodbye, he abruptly hung up.

Winnie dropped down on one of the chaise longues. "Did you have a good run?"

"Yes." He leaned over, kissed her. "Although I have to admit I'm not working at full strength."

She felt herself blush a little but she couldn't help grinning. "What happened? Too much exercise yesterday?"

"Not too much, just right." He moved to the free-standing shower set back from the pool, turned the faucets on and rinsed himself off.

Clean, he grabbed a towel from the pool cabana and rubbed his hair dry. Winnie didn't mean to stare but he was so beautifully made, so tightly constructed of muscle and bone.

Morgan sat down next to her. "Had breakfast yet?"

"No, but I'm not very hungry."

"Well, lunch won't be long now. Here on island time the kitchen's always open and there's always something good to eat."

"Island time. I like that." Leaning back she looked up into the azure sky. She could hear birds twittering and warbling. Sunshine glazed everything with perfect white-gold light. Life here was certainly far removed from the cares of New York.

From the worries of the office and the billions of dollars Morgan managed at Grady Investments. Which reminded her of Morgan's conversation. "Everything all right at the office?"

He sat forward, muscles in his hard abdomen contracting. "There are a couple of problems, but nothing that won't get straightened out."

"Sounds like an administrative problem," she cautiously persisted. "Something happen with one of the assistants?"

Morgan draped his towel around his neck, biceps bunching. "I might have to let someone go."

She mentally went through the administrative assistants that worked for Grady Investments. Most of them had been there for three years or more. "Who?"

"You don't need to worry—"

"But maybe I can help. Maybe when we get back I can put in some time, or help her on training. It could be that she's gotten rusty. I'll sit down with her first thing next Monday."

He ruffled his hair. "It's not quite that easy. She's my new assistant."

Winnie sat there stunned. For the longest moment she couldn't think of anything to say. She wasn't thinking period. Finally she roused herself and scooted to the edge of the longue, put her feet over the side as if she were bracing herself. "You fired me?"

"I didn't fire you."

"But you have a new assistant."

He didn't immediately speak. Then he exhaled slowly, a low rush of air. "Yes."

She felt a rush of emotion, a very painful rush of emotion. "I can't believe you replaced me."

"You were marrying me."

"But you *can't* replace me. I had a job. I liked my job. You can't replace me without discussing it with me."

Morgan stood up, took a few steps and snapped his towel. "We were getting married, Winnie. I thought you'd have enough to do at home—"

"What?" she demanded, jumping to her feet. "Ironing? Cooking? Grocery shopping?"

"No, I have Mr. Foley for all that," he answered impatiently.

"Exactly! If we'd gotten married, what would I do all day?"

Morgan groaned. "I don't want to do this. I want breakfast and coffee. I'm on vacation. Island time. No fights here, no rules, either."

"No!" Her eyes burned. A lump filled her throat. "You can't dismiss the conversation, or me, like this. You've taken my job from me, and I loved my job—"

"You couldn't have loved it that much. You were looking for a new job. You flew to Charleston just five weeks ago and interviewed with Osborne Manufacturing."

Winnie felt a heaviness settle in the pit of her stomach and she blinked hard to keep the tears from falling. "When did your new assistant start?"

"Winnie."

"Tell me!"

"Today."

"When were you going to tell me?"

"We were going to be on our honeymoon. I needed someone at the office. You can't be in two places at once."

She shook her head, hurt and furious. "Well, then I take the job!"

"Bull." He crossed the flagstones, walking to her. "You didn't like the job. You liked being with me."

"Wrong."

He caught her by the waist, dragged her toward him. "Not wrong. I know you," he said, voice deepening. "Maybe you did like your job, but you love me more. You want me more."

His mouth covered hers in a hard, relentless kiss, his hands burying deep in her loose hair. His tongue parted her lips and he drank the air from her lungs. Winnie's head swam, her senses reeling from the explosive contact.

He'd never kissed her like this before, never kissed her with anger or aggression, but she wasn't afraid as much as excited. His emotion matched her own and she answered his kiss, boldly pressing herself against him, and standing on tiptoe to cup the back of his head, her fingers coiling in his damp crisp hair.

She felt him harden against her, felt his arousal through his thin cotton shorts. He groaned deep in his throat as she rubbed her hips across him and with one hand he cupped her breast, kneading the nipple.

Winnie loved the feel of his hand on her breast and when he nudged her legs wider apart she wanted to be naked, wanted to feel him buried inside her.

"Come with me," he said, breaking away

and leading her into the cool darkness of the poolside cabana.

He closed the door behind them, reached under Winnie's sundress and pulled off her panties and then hoisted her onto the slate counter.

The counter's coolness against her hot skin heightened her awareness.

He slid the spaghetti straps of her sundress off her shoulders and then pushed the thin green fabric down so that her dress wrapped around her waist.

"You're gorgeous," he said, bending his head to suck one nipple and then the other.

She was feeling so warm, very excited, yet he wouldn't touch her anywhere but on her breasts. Winnie battled to catch her breath as he alternately lashed and suckled each nipple with his tongue.

She squirmed on the counter, needing, wanting, and feeling completely empty. "Please."

He looked up at her, his jaw thick, his eyes dark with passion. "Please, what?"

"Touch me."

"But I am."

Heat burned in her cheeks. "No, you know."

He shook his head. "No, I don't know."

But he ruined his excellent acting by sliding

his thumbs across her damp, sensitive nipples, creating fresh friction, more tension, more heat.

Winnie shuddered, rib cage expanding as she drew a deep unsteady breath. "Morgan—"

"Yes?"

His thumbs were drawing endless circles on the areolas. His thumbs went around and around, circles that made her belly clench and her insides ache and her knees clamp together to appease the urgent need.

She felt hot. Hot inside her skin. Hot outside her skin. She couldn't stand such bittersweet torment.

Morgan lifted her head forcing her to look deep into his eyes. "What do you want?" he persisted.

"You."

Without letting her go, he pulled her forward, parted her knees and entered her in one smooth, swift stroke. His thrusting was hard, intense, deliberate. He held her hips firmly and with each stroke buried himself more deeply. This was primitive and raw, fierce and possessive. Winnie knew she wouldn't be able to hold back much longer.

As she reached the point of no return Winnie whimpered, dug her hands into Morgan's shoulders and he covered her mouth with his, sucking her cry of pleasure into him.

This lovemaking was different from that of last night. Last night had been gentle, tender, beautiful. This lovemaking was just as intense, her orgasm had shattered her, but today she felt Morgan's drive, his expertise, his will.

It was as if Morgan was showing her how much she wanted him, just how much she needed him, and that *he* was the one firmly in control.

During the next few days they fell into a pattern of eating, playing and lovemaking. Some mornings they'd sail, other afternoons they'd snorkel, but inevitably they retreated from the world, stripped off their swimsuits and spent long hours immersed in a very private world of touch and pleasure.

Over the course of the week Winnie discovered how to touch Morgan and what turned him on. She loved making him hard, loved building the anticipation and loved it even better when she could answer his hunger. She learned to use her hands, her mouth, different positions with her body. It all felt so natural with him. Nothing ever felt wrong.

By the middle of the week Winnie had been

moved into Morgan's bedroom. He said he couldn't stand waking up and not discovering her there and frequently he woke her when the sky was still dark and the night far from over but he'd already be hungry for her warmth, her softness and her skin.

One evening, curled up next to Morgan, their skin still damp from lovemaking, Winnie forced herself to return to the issue that had been bothering her since Monday. "What happens when we go home? What am I supposed to do if I don't have my job?"

His fingers lightly stroked her hip. "Move in with me."

She lifted her head a little, frowning. "I don't get it."

He shrugged. "I want you to live with me. Be with me. I'll take care of the bills."

For some reason his calmness struck her as indifference. Didn't he understand that work was important? That she got a sense of self-worth from working? That much of her self-esteem came from doing a great job?

Winnie rolled away from him and sat up on the edge of the mattress. "As much as I like sleeping with you, Morgan, that doesn't quite constitute a full-time job."

He folded his arms behind his head and looked at her. "We could make it a full-time job."

"This is important."

His expression hardened. "You knew when I proposed that I've had enough of the bachelor thing. I'm sick of being single. I like being with you. I like sleeping with you. I like waking up with you. So this is just as important to me. Move in with me. Make this a permanent relationship."

She drew an unsteady breath, shaken and more than a little confused. Was this his way of saying he loved her? "We're not married, Morgan."

"We don't have to be married to live together."

"But you don't love me."

"Winnie, I don't think I'll ever love anyone…"

"You loved Charlotte," she flashed, interrupting.

He swore. Angry. Really angry. "I learned my lesson. I don't fall in love anymore."

CHAPTER ELEVEN

HE LOVED Charlotte, but he didn't love her. He'd loved Charlotte, but he *wouldn't* love her. Winnie couldn't get the words out of her head and nothing was quite the same after that.

They stayed on the island for another three days and on the surface their physical relationship remained the same but there were new undercurrents between them, friction that hadn't been there before.

It was almost a bitter point for her that Morgan still brought her to the peak of pleasure, still applied his immense skill, but it wasn't a physical release she wanted as much as emotional.

Was this just sex? Would Morgan ever love her? And if it was just sex, wasn't it inevitable that he'd tire of her?

On their last evening on St. Jermaine's, Morgan went for a sail on his own and Winnie stood on her balcony studying the sky, and the horizon. Waiting for the sun to set for the last time.

Heart heavy, she watched the fiery red sun drop, seemingly disappearing into the middle of the ocean, and as the water exploded crimson and gold, tears filled her eyes.

Goodbye, paradise. She was ready to go home.

They reached New York late Sunday afternoon. Morgan had two cars waiting at the airport. One limousine was for Winnie, the other for himself and Mr. Foley.

So it's over, she thought, just like that. One week of great sex and then put the girl in the car and send her on her way.

As her limousine drove over bridges, on and off freeways, through tunnels, and past tollbooths, Winnie had plenty of time to think.

She wasn't entirely sure why Morgan had cooled toward her, but she knew why she'd cooled toward him. It wasn't just his job, or Charlotte, or Annika—it was his complete lack of emotional commitment.

No words of love. No promise of security. Just wink, wink, "I'll pay the bills as long as you continue to take care of me."

Maybe he didn't mean it exactly like that, but it's how it felt, and it felt rather sordid.

Oh, Winnie, she thought, closing her eyes, you didn't have a prayer. From the beginning you were in over your head. You can't substitute sex for love. You can have love without sex, but face it, you're a mush-head, a softie, a born romantic. You don't have a crush on Morgan, you're *in love*. And whatever game you've been playing lately is going to obliterate you.

The driver parked the limousine in front of her Upper West Side apartment building, and carried her suitcase to the door.

"I can manage from here," she said.

"Mr. Grady said I was to see you up."

Hot tears burned the back of her eyes. If only *Mr. Grady* had said something kind to her when they parted! If only he'd said, "Thanks for a great week. Take care of yourself. I'll be thinking about you." But not a word. Not a goddamn word.

She blinked hard. Her chest ached with emotion she was afraid to let out. "Tell Mr. Grady you had no choice," she said, taking her suitcase from the driver. "Tell Mr. Grady I refused to let you in."

Her building didn't have a doorman and she

jammed her key into the lock, opened the front door and closed it behind her.

She crossed the lobby, went to her mailbox and retrieved a week's worth of mail before taking the elevator up to her apartment on the eleventh floor.

Upstairs her footsteps were muffled as she walked the faded green carpet to her apartment at the very end of the corridor. Her apartment was a corner unit and the long silent walk seemed to last forever and each step made her feel even farther from Morgan. Damn him. Damn his beautiful, arrogant, egotistical hide!

By the time she reached her door the tears were falling in earnest. Shifting her suitcase and armful of mail, Winnie fished out her key yet again and leaned against her door to unlock the deadbolt. But as her shoulder hit her door, the door fell open.

Her apartment wasn't locked. The door wasn't even completely closed.

Someone had been here.

It seemed like forever as she stood there, trying to figure out what to do before she forced herself to take a step into her apartment and flick on the light.

With the light on, her heart fell.

Her apartment had been trashed. All her furniture had been upended. Clothes lay in heaps. Broken glass glittered on the floor.

Winnie dropped her mail and suitcase and raced back to the elevator. She was running in slow motion, a raw physical terror stretching time out, distorting reality.

Wildly she punched the down button, begging it to return. Once downstairs, she called the building manager on the house phone. The building manager summoned the police and Winnie sat in the apartment lobby until the officers arrived.

It took the police nearly a half hour to make an appearance and even then they didn't seem overly concerned.

"This is New York," one of the officers said, heading upstairs to check out her apartment. "We can't respond to every break-in call as if it's a homicide."

"But what if the intruder's still up there? What if he's hiding somewhere?"

"Highly unlikely, but don't worry, we'll check it out, and I promise we'll let you know what we find."

Winnie spent another half hour alone in the lobby while the police did their work upstairs.

Finally one of the officers returned to the lobby to take a statement from her.

After filling out the lengthy report, Winnie headed upstairs to inspect the actual damage. Maybe, she told herself, it wasn't as bad as it looked.

But walking into her tiny living room was still shocking. Whoever had been there had done quite a number. Almost everything had been turned over, emptied, or broken.

She didn't understand it. She had no money, no jewelry, no art, nothing of value and yet her apartment had virtually been destroyed.

The police left behind a copy of the report and form with a number where she could call periodically to check on her "case." But Winnie knew nothing would ever come of the "investigation."

Winnie did a slow walk around her apartment, wearily noting that whoever had been here had been very thorough. Her pillows were cut. Her mattress upended. All the clothes dumped from her closet.

What was the point? What did they want, and was it really necessary to slash her couch? Did the intruder honestly think she'd hidden a hoard of diamonds in her cheap sofa cushions?

"What the hell happened?" Morgan's voice thundered through Winnie's apartment.

Winnie jumped and shrieked, whether in fear or relief it was hard to say.

"Why didn't you call me?" he demanded, stripping off his blazer, dropping it on the back of her cushionless couch.

"I...I..." she looked at him, stuttering, utterly helpless. "I..."

"What?"

Her heart pounded. Her stomach churned. "I didn't think you'd care."

Morgan swore a string of violent epithets strong enough to make a hardened sailor blush. "What do you mean you don't think I'd care? I just spent the last week proving to you I care. If that doesn't say anything—"

Winnie's jaw dropped. "Say anything?" she interrupted hotly. "You never say anything. You make love and go to sleep. Make love and go to sleep."

His hands were on his hips. "But that should tell you something. I don't make love with someone I don't like."

"*Like?* I don't want to be liked. I want to be loved."

His eyebrows flattened, his expression as

dark as Winnie had ever seen it. "For Pete's sake, woman, like, love, what's the difference? I want you. I wanted you with me. I asked you to move in with me. I told you I wanted to take care of you. But no, that wasn't good enough for you."

He was making it sound as if she'd been the unreasonable one. "You implied I'd be your *mistress!*"

"I thought you might like the idea."

"Like being your mistress?"

"Well, you sure didn't want to be my wife!" His dark blue gaze was as brittle and cold as black ice. "I'm just trying to figure out what you want, Winnie. You obviously don't want to be my mistress, you *really* don't want to be married to me, so what the hell *do* you want from me?"

Love. But that was the one thing he'd told her he couldn't give.

He could give her things, give her a name, give her pleasure, but he couldn't—wouldn't—give her love.

She bit her lip, fighting tears. "What are you doing here, anyway?"

Morgan snorted, walked away from her, picking his way around the mess but even as he walked she heard glass crunching beneath his shoes. "Your building manager called, let me know what had happened." He turned back, eyes snapping. "Because you sure weren't going to phone me."

Winnie slowly sat down again. He was angrier than she'd ever seen him. "How did my manager know to call you?"

He made a hoarse sound, jaw jutting all over again. "I can't believe you care about details like that at a time like this!"

She'd always thought he was so calm, so controlled, but there was nothing calm or controlled about him right now. He looked like a huge panther ready to pounce. He was stalking, growling, hissing. He wanted blood.

She swallowed, rubbed her hands on her knees. Her knees were cold. She felt chilled straight through. She'd worn a skirt and blouse on the plane, but despite the summer heat, she was freezing now. "I didn't know my building manager knew you."

Morgan muttered another unflattering word beneath his breath before marching back to her and pulling her up onto her feet. "I asked him to look out after you. I gave him money to keep an eye on you. I've been paying him since January if you really want to know."

"January?"

He grasped her upper arms, pulled her closer, head tipping so he was speaking very close to her mouth. "I worried about your neighborhood. I knew you didn't have family in the state, I thought you needed someone keeping an eye out for you. Okay?"

"Okay."

Any fight left in her was gone. She didn't know what to think at the moment and her emotions were scattered. She was tired. She was hungry. She was overwhelmed, really overwhelmed.

He tipped her chin up, stared down into her eyes. "Don't you ever scare me like that again, do you understand?"

Winnie couldn't look away. She could see the navy of his eyes, the reflection of herself, and something else, too, something very dark and shadowed, something which made her think of long-buried pain.

"But I wasn't hurt, Morgan."

"That's not the point." A muscle popped in his jaw. "I told my driver to walk you up. I told him to check out the apartment first—" He broke off, teeth grinding together and, releasing her, he took a step away. For a long silent moment he did nothing but shake his head, a slow furious shake.

"You can't stay here tonight," he said at length. He glanced at his wristwatch, noting the late hour. "I'm going to call Mr. Foley and have him make up a room for you at my place."

The guest *room*, a voice silently taunted. *Not his room, but the* guest *room*.

"That's not necessary. I'll be all right here. It's just a mess. I'll start cleaning things up and it'll be fine by morning."

He snapped his fingers impatiently. "The lock's been jimmied. You need a locksmith. It has to be replaced. Or do you want to argue about that, too?"

He faced her. "Do you want to get anything? Is there anything you want to pack, anything you don't want to leave? This is your chance. Grab whatever you want because there might not be an opportunity to return."

Mr. Foley met them at the door of Morgan's Fifth Avenue apartment. Morgan's elegant apartment was one of the most coveted spaces in all of Manhattan.

"Are you all right, Miss Graham?" Mr. Foley

asked, solicitously taking her travel bag and the stack of mail she'd brought with her.

"I think so."

"You need a hot bath and some dinner in bed." Mr. Foley's tone was very firm. "I've something in the oven for you, a delicious stuffed Cornish game hen and a lovely pear tart for dessert. Now if you'll follow me," he said, bowing slightly, "we'll get you settled for the night."

Morgan watched Mr. Foley usher Winnie away as if she were the most delicate, fragile being on the face of the earth. Well, she might be delicate, Morgan conceded, but she was also damn stubborn. Let Mr. Foley spoil her. His butler was obviously crazy about Winnie and Mr. Foley had never been crazy about anyone Morgan had dated before. In fact, Mr. Foley had never even *liked* anyone Morgan had dated before.

Frowning, Morgan went in a different direction, heading for his study. He'd only just started going through a week's worth of voice mails and business mail when he'd been notified that Winnie was in trouble.

Winnie. In trouble. Winnie. And trouble.

Didn't those two just go together like peas in a pod?

Morgan tried to go through the rest of his voice mail but now he was too tired to concentrate. Heading for his bedroom, he showered, put on a pair of old cotton sweats for bed, but stopped short of turning in for the night.

He had to finish catching up. He forced himself to return to his study.

Leaning over his desk, Morgan flipped on the halogen lamp, and continued playing back the rest of his voice mail messages.

Family. Friend. Family. Sales call. Sailing buddy. Sales call. Morgan sighed, and really hated the phone. It was way too easy for people to leave a dozen messages, but it took forever for him to answer them all.

The next call stopped him cold. It was a voice from the past.

Hello, Morgan, Charlotte here. Darmouth Charlotte— He slowly lifted his head, eyes staring out across his office but seeing nothing. *I think we should talk... We need to talk. I've wanted to call you so many times but I dial your number and hang up before I ever leave a message.*

She drew a small breath and the sound of it was captured on the recording. Morgan's gut hurt. He held his breath waiting for her to finish.

I'm sorry about the wedding, our wedding, I mean. I've always been sorry, but maybe it's for the best. I don't know. Call me. Please. Soon as you can. She rattled off her number before hanging up.

Morgan scrawled the number on a tablet on his desk, numbly deleted the message and played the next.

The next call was from Winnie's parents and they were rather frantic about their daughter's whereabouts as they hadn't heard from her since the day after the wedding that didn't happen.

Mrs. Graham gave him a number where they were staying, said it was a vacation house they'd rented for a couple weeks in the mountains and asked him to make sure Winnie phoned as soon as possible.

Morgan wrote this one down, too, but his thoughts were chaotic and it wasn't until all messages were played, that he hung up the phone and really studied Charlotte's number.

For a long moment he didn't move. She'd called him. She wanted to see him.

He looked away, stared at the shadowed wall, but he could still hear her voice, imagine her face. Glacier blond, glacier beautiful. Impatient, imperious Charlotte.

He'd loved her so much. He'd loved her too much. He'd waited years to speak to her, years to hear from her, but now that she'd finally called, and now that he had her number, he wasn't sure he had anything to say to her.

Abruptly Morgan turned off the lamp on his desk. As a matter of fact, he was certain he had nothing to say to her.

Morgan did not sleep well that night. It had less to do with Charlotte's call than knowing Winnie was in his house, sleeping just down the hall.

He hated not sleeping with her. He hated not being with her. But he also hated not knowing what she wanted from him.

He was still wide awake two hours later when his bedroom door creaked open and he heard a timid voice say, "Who broke into my apartment? What did that person want?"

Morgan propped himself up. "I don't know."

She stood there in the shadows, hanging on to the doorknob, her long hair half hiding her face. "Mr. Foley said that it might have been someone who wanted to know about us. Someone curious about…you."

Morgan silently cursed taciturn Mr. Foley for finally speaking and definitely saying too much. "Maybe."

He heard her sniff. "You know, someone should tell the media that you're really not worth the trouble, and definitely not worth all this fuss." Her voice grew thinner, higher. She was close to breaking down. "People should know that you're not all that interesting, that you prefer numbers and mergers to love and affection, and that you proposed to me because I'm dependable and convenient."

He smiled despite himself and shook his head. She was such a handful. How could he have ever thought her easy, sensible, convenient? "Someone should tell them, and I think it should be you," he agreed, happy to pacify her. "However, it's three in the morning and not even the most tenacious journalist will be at his desk for another hour or two. So let's go back to bed and get some sleep."

But she didn't move. "I can't sleep. I'm scared."

He slid out of bed and walked across the room and gently but firmly closed the bedroom door behind her. "There's nothing to be scared about, at least not here, in this house."

Then he scooped her into his arms, carried

her back to his bed, and set her down in the middle. "We both sleep better when we sleep together," he added, throwing himself down next to her and punching the pillow beneath his cheek. "So close your eyes. Get some sleep."

Easy for him to say, she thought, lying stiff and miserable next to him. She couldn't sleep. Her mind was going a mile a minute. She couldn't forget the mess in her apartment. She couldn't forget the police's indifference. She couldn't forget that Morgan had shown up like a knight on a white stallion.

Suddenly Morgan reached out and scooped her up, bringing her closer against him. "Stop thinking so much," he whispered, his voice raspy in the dark. "Turn your brain off."

"I can't."

"You can. I *order* you to turn your brain off."

She grimaced at the irony. "You can't order me, Morgan. I don't work for you, remember?"

He groaned and dragged her even closer. "Well, I don't want you to work for me. I don't want to be your boss, not when you're my equal." He kissed the back of her head, cupped his hand over her tummy, and immediately relaxed. In less than a minute he began to breathe deeply, evenly.

Winnie turned her head to look at him. His eyes were closed, and his long, dense black lashes rested against his cheek. Even half asleep he was impossibly beautiful.

She felt his breath fan her cheek as he sighed the sigh of a man whose patience was sorely tried. "Close your eyes, Winnie. *Please?*"

"How did you know?" she asked, trying not to laugh.

"Because I know you. Now sleep."

And this time, when she closed her eyes, she did sleep, snuggled deep against Morgan's side.

As tired as he was, Morgan just couldn't sleep. He didn't know how, when he felt completely fatigued, he could still respond to Winnie like this.

She was nestled against him, her cheek on his chest, her hand clenched and buried beneath his ribs. She slept as if he were a mountain, a fortress, her favorite place of refuge and even though he couldn't explain it, it gave him peace.

It was nice to be wanted. He liked being needed. He might even someday grow comfortable with the word love.

For nearly the rest of the night he watched her sleep, and his desire changed as the hours crept by, the hard arousal giving way to something else, a tenderness, a protective instinct.

This, he thought, gently kissing the top of her head, was Winnie, his Winnie. She belonged with him.

Just before five, Morgan finally dragged himself out of bed. He took a cold shower to wake up, then did a cursory shave. The face in the mirror had bloodshot eyes and blue shadows beneath those distinguished red eyes but Morgan felt good. No, he felt great.

But his good feeling didn't last very long. Returning to work was even worse than he expected. The market was down, really down, the big investors were panicking, the traders were running ragged trying to get all the sell orders in. Morgan was just trying to calm the masses, reminding the skittish that markets are cyclical and that even down markets turn around.

But by eleven Morgan couldn't manage his phone and his nonfunctioning executive assistant's. She was on her third coffee break of the morning—although during one break he could have sworn she was in the ladies' rest room painting her nails.

No, he couldn't manage the phones, the e-mails, the massive stack of market reports and the portfolio managers asking him advice on every new market move.

Morgan dialed his home number. Mr. Foley answered and Morgan asked to speak to Winnie.

Morgan didn't waste any time once she got on the line. "I'm sending the car," he said. "I need you down here, Winnie. I have a one o'clock lunch, a three o'clock meeting, and the office is on the brink of disaster. Can you come immediately?"

CHAPTER TWELVE

"You'll be all right here, while I'm gone?" Morgan asked, slipping his black blazer back on and quickly adjusting his tie.

Winnie couldn't help rolling her eyes. "Of course I will," she said, from her position next to Morgan's desk. She'd spent the last twenty minutes sorting through the papers stacked six inches deep on the corner of his desk.

She'd never seen such an untidy, disorganized collection of phone messages, market reports, printed e-mails and travel itineraries before. Morgan's new assistant was desperately in need of a better filing system. Actually, Morgan was desperately in need of a better assistant.

She lifted a handful of pink phone messages. "So where are you going now?"

"A meeting. Lunch meeting." He lifted his black briefcase from the floor. "I'm not sure how long this will take, but I'll be back by three, in time for the conference call."

He headed out and she continued gathering the pink phone slips before putting them into chronological order. On the bottom went the oldest messages, on the top the newest messages, including everything that had come in today.

The third message from the top caught Winnie's eye. *Charlotte called, confirming lunch. She'll meet you at the Russian Tea Room, one o'clock.*

Winnie read the message again. *Charlotte called, confirming lunch.*

It can't be, she told herself. It's not Morgan's Charlotte. It wouldn't be Morgan's Charlotte.

Nonplussed, Winnie stacked the other two messages on top of the one from Charlotte. Her hands shook slightly as she gathered the rest of the messages. She didn't want her imagination to run wild, but she did feel fear. Tremendous fear.

The only woman Morgan had ever loved had been Charlotte. And if Charlotte was back in his life…?

But it's *not* Charlotte.

Don't do this to yourself. Don't make this something it's not.

But her hands were still shaking as she moved on to the next task.

Why would Morgan meet a woman for business at the Tea Room? The Russian Tea Room, now more than seventy years old, was famous for its intimate atmosphere—red leather booths, shiny brass trim, glittering chandeliers. It was a romantic place, a mood place, a place that attracted musicians and artists and actors, *not* businessmen.

Winnie picked up the phone message again. Charlotte. One o'clock. Charlotte. Russian Tea Room. Stomach knotting, she put the message back. It wasn't the old flame Charlotte, it couldn't be. If Morgan were seeing Charlotte at lunch, he'd tell her.

Wouldn't he?

Morgan was late getting back to the office, not returning until quarter past three. Winnie could hardly bring herself to look at him when he finally walked in. He was never late for conference calls, especially not when it involved Shipley's Bank.

She'd agonized about his lunch while he was gone. She'd watched the clock and when two forty-five rolled around and he still wasn't back, she began fretting about his calls. She'd considered phoning him, asking what to do about his calls, but in the end she'd simply rescheduled them both, pushing each call back by an hour.

And that's what she told him when she found her voice. She bit back the reproaches; held in her fear, and acted like the efficient executive assistant he'd once hired her to be. "Morgan, I've rescheduled your three o'clock call to four, and your four o'clock call to five."

But he didn't say thank you. He didn't appear grateful. He simply held out his hand for messages before heading for his office and practically slamming the door closed.

Winnie stared at his closed door. She struggled with her resentment. It wasn't right or fair that he treat her this way. He'd asked *her* to come in today. He'd called *her*, desperate for help.

Give him time, she told herself, fighting for calm. Give him some time and he'll calm down, call you in, and maybe talk about what had happened at lunch.

But he didn't call her in, and he didn't open his door and at a quarter to four, emotions flying high, she opened his office door. "Are you all right?"

He wasn't even working. He sat at his desk but he was facing the window, not his computer. "I'm fine," he said, not bothering to even turn around.

It was like the old days, she thought. The days when he never made eye contact, never acknowledged her, never made her feel like a person.

But things had changed. They were different people now. She knew him, and he wasn't a cold person, or an indifferent person. "Did something happen at lunch?" she asked as gently as possible.

"No."

"But when you left here earlier—"

"Winnie, I really don't want to talk." He swiveled around, his expression closed, eyes shuttered. "No offense, but I'd just like to be alone right now."

Winnie backed out of the office and closed the door. She returned to the desk that had been moved in today for her use and tried to busy herself completing Morgan's expense account, but she couldn't concentrate on the receipts or the form itself. What had happened at lunch? What was he thinking right now?

Suddenly the intercom clicked on. "Winnie,

I know you've just rescheduled the calls, but I need you to cancel them. Try to reschedule for tomorrow. Thanks." The intercom clicked off.

Morgan's new assistant looked at her. "Do you want me to do that, Miss Graham?"

Winnie swallowed, knowing how difficult it'd been to get both calls rescheduled once already. "No," she said, fighting frustration. "Let me handle this."

Winnie rolled forward at her desk, pressed the intercom button. "Morgan, it took a great deal of effort to get both calls rescheduled."

"And?"

"And they're going to be even more difficult to reschedule if you cancel them again."

"So your point is?"

She felt herself grow hot. "My point being that maybe you don't want to cancel the conference calls after all. Maybe you want to go ahead and get the calls done so you don't have to hassle with this tomorrow."

"I see." There was a moment of silence over the intercom. Winnie could feel Morgan's new assistant staring at her. The silence wasn't pleasant.

Finally Morgan cleared his throat. "Did I

miss something?" he asked. "Did I give you a promotion?"

Her stomach did a flip. "No."

"You haven't been made partner?"

He was a jerk. He was such a jerk. Where was her copy of the book? There had to be a picture of him in the book somewhere. "No, *sir.*"

"Then please don't give me career advice." The intercom clicked off.

Morgan's new assistant was staring at Winnie wide-eyed. "Do you still want to handle it, Miss Graham?"

Winnie grabbed her purse, her summer blazer and her keys from the desk drawer. "No. You take over. You're doing just fine."

Winnie spent an hour walking in Central Park before she finally made her way back to Morgan's apartment.

She didn't want to go to Morgan's place, didn't want to be anywhere near him right now, but she didn't have anywhere else to go. Earlier today Morgan had a moving company pack up everything from Winnie's apartment and put it all into storage until he found her a better place.

She hadn't wanted a new apartment. She

hadn't wanted him to send the moving company. But as usual, Morgan won.

Mr. Foley let her in. "Mr. Grady has been phoning every fifteen minutes," the butler said. "He asked that you call when you got in and let him know you're safe."

"I'm safe."

"Well, give him a call. He's anxious to hear from you, and that reminds me, Mr. Grady also mentioned that your mother had phoned. They're staying at a hotel and that number is on a pad of paper in Mr. Grady's study."

In Morgan's office, Winnie turned on the desk lamp and discovered the pad of paper with her mother's name on it, but there were two numbers scribbled down, not one.

Winnie dialed the first number. "Margie Graham, please."

The woman on the other end of the line hesitated. "I'm sorry. There's no Margie at this number."

"No Grahams registered?"

"This is a private residence. I'm not sure who you're trying to call."

"I'm sorry. I've made a mistake," Winnie said, realizing it must be the second number she was supposed to dial.

"Wait, don't hang up!" The woman drew a short breath. "This is Morgan's number, isn't it?"

Winnie stiffened, muscles snapping like rubber bands in her shoulders and neck. This wasn't right. This didn't feel right and she didn't want to know more. "No," she said. "It's not—"

"But I have Caller ID on my phone. It says Morgan Grady on my phone receiver. You're calling from Morgan's house."

Winnie didn't say anything. Her stomach hurt so bad. Her eyes felt gritty.

"Is this Winnie?"

Winnie slowly sat down in the chair at Morgan's desk. "Who am I speaking to?"

"Charlotte."

Charlotte. *The* Charlotte. Winnie knew.

But Charlotte continued blithely along. "I'm an old friend of Morgan's. We were—"

"College sweethearts. Yes, I know."

"Right." Charlotte laughed a little, but it sounded strained. "Listen, Morgan left his briefcase at the restaurant after lunch. Let him know I'll just drop it off later today."

"Here, or at the office?" Winnie asked, hating the tightness in her chest, hating the dull panic. Morgan had only loved Charlotte and Charlotte was definitely back in his life. Peripheral or not, Charlotte was a threat.

"Does it matter?" And Charlotte laughed again, another small brittle laugh that made Winnie feel very cold, and very afraid.

Winnie paced her bedroom, heart racing so fast she couldn't get any air.

God, she was a fool. A dolt. A royal idiot. She couldn't do anything right, couldn't make anything work.

She hated this awful claustrophobic feeling, hated the roar in her head, the crazy adrenaline in her veins. Until the wedding she hadn't had a panic attack in years, and now she'd had two in less than ten days.

All because of Morgan.

Morgan, Wall Street's Most Eligible Bachelor.

All because she'd goofed with him, hadn't been able to get it right, couldn't make the relationship work.

He'd wanted cool. She gave him hot. He wanted reason. She lived in illogic. He used the minimum words and she talked in a steady stream, all words, all the time, words nonstop.

Back in seventh grade Winnie had panic attacks regularly, at least one a week, sometimes one a day. She dreaded everything about school, feared speaking in class, was terrified of P.E.

Softball was the worst. She hated, hated, hated the game. The big hard ball always flew at her face... Her glasses would slip low on her nose and because she couldn't see the ball coming at her, she would swing before the ball smashed into her. Sometimes she would duck before the ball crossed the plate, duck and drop the bat.

The kids all laughed. Even the P.E. teacher laughed.

Ninny Winnie. Winnie Graham who couldn't do anything right.

A knock sounded on her bedroom door and Winnie stopped pacing long enough to answer the door.

"I'm leaving for the evening," Mr. Foley said. He had Monday nights off and usually went to visit his sister on Long Island. He turned a little, noted her suitcase sitting by the door. "You're leaving?"

Her eyes burned. She felt terrible on the inside, just like she used to feel as a girl. "I'm going to go see my mom."

"That sounds like a nice break." Winnie nodded jerkily. Mr. Foley's brown eyes narrowed a little, his expression immensely kind. "Mr. Grady is a very private person, very protective of his personal life. He's never brought anyone here before. You're the first."

"He didn't have much of a choice. My door was pretty well smashed in. He couldn't very well leave me there."

"But he could have taken you to his penthouse just off Wall Street. That's where he usually entertains. But this is his home and he brought you here."

Mr. Foley paused, gave her time to digest this before adding, "I don't know what he's said, or not said, but I've worked for Mr. Grady for a number of years. One thing you need to know is that when it comes to Mr. Grady, actions speak louder than words."

His gaze leveled with hers. "Would you like me to call a cab for you, or are you going to wait for Mr. Grady?"

Heart in her throat, chest filled with longing, she looked away, across her bedroom. He'd put her in the guest room but welcomed her into his bed. Did he love her, or just need her? She didn't know. But she had to find out. "I'll wait."

Morgan brought Chinese food home with

him from a local take-out. They sat in his family room, facing each other at opposite ends of the couch. She didn't know how he knew, but Morgan had ordered everything she liked best. Mongolian beef. Kung Pao chicken. Sweet and sour pork. But she couldn't eat any of it, couldn't even get her chopsticks to work.

"You left early," Morgan said, no problem with his appetite, taking seconds of nearly everything.

There'd be no Valentines with this man. No chocolate-covered cherries. He'd proposed to her because she was the best option. She filled the job. She was the most qualified candidate. No romance there.

"Do you ever think about Charlotte?" she asked, setting her chopsticks down. "Do you ever wonder what it'd be like if you and she were still together?"

"We were talking about work."

She pushed her plate aside. "I'd rather talk about us."

"Charlotte's not 'us.' Charlotte is Charlotte."

Winnie knew she was heading into troubled waters but she couldn't avoid this, couldn't ignore this. She had to understand, had to know why he could love Charlotte but not her. "Just tell me one thing—when you proposed to her, what were you feeling?"

Morgan clamped his jaw tight, battling his mounting frustration. How could he have ever thought Winnie coolly unemotional? How could he have thought her reasonable? "You really don't want to do this—"

"But I do."

"Winnie, I can't play games. I can't make up stories. I don't want to hurt you, either. Why compare Charlotte to you? It's like comparing apples to oranges."

Her chin lifted, hazel eyes bright with tears. "Am I the apple or the orange?"

He couldn't even crack a smile. His blood pressure was shooting up. "You want the truth? Fine. Here's the truth. I did love Charlotte, I loved her a lot. She was my first real girlfriend, my first true love affair. Everything with her had been stormy, passionate, and intense. I thought we'd spend the rest of our lives together."

Morgan drew a deep breath, gritted his teeth. He couldn't believe he was even talking about this out loud, couldn't believe he'd touch this deeply private pain. Seeing Charlotte today had been bad enough. He'd realized all over again how little he'd known her, how little he'd understood how her mind worked.

She'd never loved him, just the idea of him. She'd never wanted him, but the Grady name and the Grady connections. She'd been sickened that he had been adopted at fifteen.

What kind of person gets adopted as a teenager? she'd asked. *You adopt babies, toddlers, you raise them from birth. You can't adopt a teenager.*

Who are your parents anyway? What kind of people give away a fifteen-year-old?

"I thought it was love, Winnie," he said coldly, all emotion bottled inside him, smashed hard into a place he couldn't touch. "But it wasn't love. It was sex."

"Just like us." A tear slid down Winnie's cheek. She batted it away.

She was wrong, Morgan thought, but he didn't have the energy to argue. He'd learned years ago that people couldn't make other people happy. Happiness had to come from within. Happiness had to be a personal choice.

"We have great sex, but we also have a real friendship," he said at last, so glad he'd seen Charlotte today and realized that perhaps the thing he'd loved most about Charlotte was her attitude.

He'd adored her rich-girl diction, her perfect blond bob, her narrow straight nose lifted disdainfully at the world. He'd loved that she, beautiful, regal, rich Charlotte, had wanted *him*. In retrospect, he'd been just as selfish as she. Thank God, Charlotte had broken the wedding off. She'd done them both the greatest favor.

Morgan drew a slow breath. "Even if the sex was bad, the friendship is worth saving. We have a lot here. We have a lot going for us. It'd be foolish to make decisions based on a very narrow definition of love."

Winnie didn't know what to think. She was a romantic. He a pragmatist. She craved bonbons, flowers, violins and he lived in a stark reality minus all those things. She loved the way he touched her, but hated his vision of love. How could this work? How could they ever compromise?

Yet how could she compromise if she didn't trust him? Winnie drew a deep breath. "Who did you have lunch with?"

He looked up at her, his eyes narrowing. There was a strange beat, a moment of silence that felt like a great divide. "Charlotte." There was another silence, this one shorter. "But you already knew that, didn't you?"

When Winnie didn't answer, Morgan sighed. "This is why it won't work, having you as my assistant. A lot of things happened today that shouldn't have happened. I get a lot of calls. I see a lot of people. I need to make quick decisions and I shouldn't have to explain myself, or defend myself—"

"Then don't!" Winnie finally understood why she couldn't continue at Grady Investments. Morgan had his life. He'd always had his own life. She'd just never known about it before.

"It's not an issue of trust, but of energy and time. You're a great executive assistant. The best I've ever had—"

"I got it. Thanks." He didn't need to repeat himself, she thought bitterly. She wasn't stupid. "I already said I understood."

Winnie's nerves stretched, pulled far too taut. She had to get out of here. Had to get some time to herself, needed to get her head back in the right place. "You said you'd given me a three month severance package, well, I think I'll take advantage of it and not work for a while. I might leave the city for a while, go spend some time with my family."

He didn't say anything for a moment. She'd expected him to nod, give his approval. Instead he looked at her, his expression surprisingly bleak. "How long do you intend to be gone?"

She wanted him to say, "No, don't go." She wanted him to say, "Stay here with me." She wanted him to say something emotional, something powerful, something indicating his true feelings. His expression was one thing, but she really needed words.

But he didn't say anything else, didn't try to talk her into staying.

Winnie stared at his eyes, his mouth, the faint lines etched on either side of those remarkable lips. She felt the worst kind of sorrow. Wanted so badly to be with him but didn't know how to make it work anymore. "I don't know. Just depends on what I feel like doing. I'm already packed. I'm heading out tonight."

Morgan's intensely blue eyes met hers. "Well then, I better give you this now."

He reached into his pocket and withdrew a small gold key chain with three shiny keys. "Your new place. I bought it for you. I picked up the keys from the Realtor today, after my thirty-minute lunch with Charlotte. I was late getting back to the office because the paperwork took longer than we expected."

CHAPTER THIRTEEN

WINNIE emptied her bag of groceries in the kitchen of her new apartment, which was part of an elegant brownstone building on a lovely tree-lined street.

She'd been back in the city nearly a week now, after having been gone for a month. She'd spent her first week away with her parents, then a week with her sister Alexis, and then the last two weeks traveling on her own.

She'd told herself she was visiting all the historic places on the southeastern seaboard she'd always wanted to see, but the truth was she was avoiding New York. Avoiding returning. Avoiding, most of all, Morgan.

But she couldn't stay away forever. She lived in New York. Her life was in New York—even if her life wasn't with Morgan Grady.

Winnie put the milk in her refrigerator and

the bread on the counter. She'd bought some fresh flowers, so she cut the bottoms of the stems off and then put them in water. Hard to believe, she thought, arranging the dahlias, that they were already in the last week of August. A late Saturday afternoon and summer was nearly over.

Time to start looking for work. She needed a job. Something to do.

Something other than pining for Morgan.

Because she did pine for him. She felt like a woman from a Victorian novel, felt as if she'd had a taste of heaven and she'd turned around and run the other way.

Someday she'd get it figured out. Someday she'd meet someone like her, someone kind of goofy and absurd, someone sentimental and deeply emotional and they'd make this perfect life together.

But until then, a job would help fill all her empty hours.

Winnie placed the flowers on her dining table and reached for the newspaper. Sitting cross-legged on her couch, she opened up the paper but hadn't even reached the Classifieds when her doorbell rang.

Winnie peered through the peephole.

Morgan. He was dressed in black tie—black tuxedo, elegant white shirt and white silk bow tie.

She unlocked the door and swung it open. "Hi."

Mercy, he was beautiful. She leaned against the door, unable to tear her gaze away. The tuxedo made him look taller, shoulders even broader, and she could smell his cologne. It was rich with vanilla and spice and perfect with a tuxedo.

"I found your glasses," he said. "I thought you might need them back."

She couldn't bring herself to take them, was terribly afraid of what she'd feel if she touched him. "I pretty much only wear my contacts now."

"I liked you in your glasses."

"They're ugly."

"They make you look brainy." His lips twisted, creases at his eyes. "Not that you need glasses to look brainy. You're one of the smartest women I've ever met."

Her heart ached. "Thank you." Winnie shifted her weight from one foot to the other. Her pulse raced. "Where are you going?"

"The Faith Foundation's Charity Ball."

"I thought you hated those things."

His smile turned self-deprecating. "I do, but I'm cosponsor. This is the event each year I have to attend."

"Well, you look incredible," she said, quickly taking the glasses from him, being extra careful so their fingers didn't brush. "If that's any consolation."

His gaze met hers and held. "It's not a consolation if I have to go alone."

Oh, that hurt. She hurt. She didn't want him to go alone. She wanted to go with him. But how would this work? Where would things go? Winnie couldn't bear to think of a future always wondering, worrying, doubting. She needed to be sure of Morgan. Needed to be certain of how he felt. "Where's the party?"

"The Met museum." He reached out, and very gently touched her cheek. "Come with me tonight."

She didn't say yes, she didn't say no. She just stared at him.

"Just a moment," he said, turning around and heading back to the elevator. He returned a moment later and thrust a box at her. The box was slim and taupe-colored and tied with a narrow gold ribbon. "I didn't want you to say you wouldn't come because you had nothing to wear."

"Morgan—" she whispered his name.

"If you're going to say no, I wanted to make sure you were saying no because of me."

She looked away, and her fingers tightened around the slender box. It weighed virtually nothing. That meant whatever was inside weighed even less than nothing. She'd recognized the name printed on the box. It was a very expensive, very exclusive boutique that carried only designer labels from France and Italy.

"I can't," she said softly. "It wouldn't be right." Yet even as she said the words, she could imagine the limo downstairs, probably champagne on ice. They'd have a drink in the car on the way there and then they'd pull up at the museum and…

They'd immediately be surrounded by photographers. The press would be there. The scrutiny would start. The world would pick at her, criticize her, and she couldn't handle it, couldn't endure it if she was just the latest in Morgan Grady's string of lovers.

She wanted more.

She wanted forever.

Winnie tried to hand the dress back. "I'm not black-tie material."

His mouth compressed, deep grooves forming next to his mouth. "You don't even let yourself see the possibilities."

Her eyes burned and she blinked. "It's not that I don't see the possibilities, but I also see the reality. We want different things, Morgan."

His blue gaze searched her eyes. "Not as different as you might think."

She couldn't speak, didn't trust herself to say the right words. She was never concise, or intelligent when she felt so much. Instead she simply shook her head and pressed the box firmly into Morgan's hands.

But he'd have none of it. Swearing, he tossed the box past her, into the living room where it skidded across the floor. And then he just walked away.

Winnie returned to the couch, curled up in one corner and felt absolutely sick.

She felt sick because she knew she was wrong sending him off without her. She felt sick because she was making choices out of fear. She felt sick because she knew she was just a big fat coward.

Just like she'd been a coward most of her life.

She hadn't been confident as a child. Her panic attacks were a testament to that. But instead of ever conquering her fear, she'd slowly let it get the best of her.

She gave up on sports early. She never tried out for cheerleading. She wouldn't audition for a spelling bee or the school plays.

In college she didn't date. How could she? Except for class, she never left her dorm room.

Her very first job interview was botched, and so instead of trying again, she gave up the career she'd really wanted.

And now she was giving up on the one man she wanted.

Tonight Morgan appeared on her doorstep. He'd bought her a dress. He asked her to join him. Yet what had she done? She'd handed the dress back and said no.

She'd said no because she was afraid. She'd said no because she was terrified she'd love him so much and he'd love her not enough and in the end she'd just look like a fool.

How insecure was that? She cared more about her fragile heart than trying to make a relationship with Morgan work.

Far better to be the injured party. Far better to play victim. Far better to be a dreamy romantic than a confident woman willing to take a risk.

Grow up, Winnie. Stop wanting everything to be perfect. You already have the fairy tale!

Winnie stooped and picked up the garment box from the ground. Cradling the box on her lap, she opened the lid, pushed back the thin gold tissue paper and drew out a silk camisole the color of ripe bananas, and a lovely long narrow skirt of matching yellow silk with a pale gold overlay stitched with gold and purple jewels.

She blinked, tears starting to her eyes. The dress looked like a banana daiquiri on a sun-kissed beach.

He'd given her a taste of paradise.

For a moment she couldn't breathe, concentrating hard on not blinking and keeping the tears from falling. She didn't want to get any tears on the silk fabric. Didn't want anything to ruin the most beautiful, magical dress she'd ever seen.

She had to go. She had to be there tonight. She had to show him she was ready for a real relationship with him. One built on friendship, honesty, admiration, and trust. Incredibly dull virtues on paper but extraordinary in real life.

Winnie carried the silk camisole with the beaded straps and skirt to her bedroom, held the two-piece dress against her as she looked at her reflection in her bedroom mirror. Beautiful. How had he known that this was absolutely the most perfect dress for her?

Because he knew her.

Because his actions spoke louder than words.

Winnie pressed her forehead to the painted trim around the door and squeezed back the tears threatening to spill.

Actions, not words.

He'd proposed. He'd taken her to St. Jermaine's. He'd held her every night. He'd hired security for her. Bought her a house.

He was saying as best as he could that she was his, that he wanted her, that he needed her.

And for heaven's sake, wasn't that enough?

Need and want…how was it so different from love?

Morgan said the brief speech he'd prepared, a few positive words about the foster care system and a short but sincere thank-you to those who'd come that night and supported the program.

He was leaving the podium, shaking outstretched hands, and yet his gaze was never far from the door. He hated these things, hated the show and the dress-up and the facade he wore to keep everyone happy. People, he knew, preferred success.

People preferred handsome, rich, polished. Not that he felt that way underneath. Hell, underneath he was one lonely and very alone billionaire.

Almost done, he told himself, seeing a bit of space near the door. Shake a few more hands, pretend to get a drink, and then make a mad dash for the limo.

He was still moving forward, and nearly at the museum's glass doors when he cast one last glance around the perimeter of the lobby, his gaze taking in the tuxedos and black sheathlike dresses, before spotting canary yellow.

Yellow. His yellow.

Her back was to him. She was looking the other way. She'd pinned her long hair partway back, curled the rest, and a few soft tendrils framed her face. The purple beaded straps on her camisole glittered in the party lights and yet he knew the yellow because it was the right yellow, it was the yellow of sunshine, warmth and happiness.

Morgan stood transfixed, drinking her in. He felt the fullness of the summer, the sweetness of the island, and far from urban problems. He felt again the days when he'd just been adopted by the Gradys and he felt such gratitude, and hope.

Hope.

As he watched, Winnie's smooth brow creased. Her eyes narrowed as she searched the room, lower lip caught between her teeth.

She was looking for him.

His chest tightened and Morgan knew without a doubt that he'd never tire of the summer. Or the sun.

And he'd never tire of Winnie.

Quickly, he pushed through the crowd lining up at the bar, lifted a hand in acknowledgment as someone called his name, sidestepped a reporter interviewing a charity patron. Winnie was moving in the opposite direction, heading to the exit, out of the ballroom.

He reached her at the great stone archway, stretched out a hand, and touched the back of her bare warm shoulder. "Winnie."

Heat shot through her, heat and pleasure.

Winnie turned, stomach knotting, lower lip raw from being anxiously gnawed. "I couldn't find you."

"How long have you been here?"

"A half hour. I couldn't find you, and then someone said they'd seen you head to the exit, that you were doing the usual Grady move of sneaking out."

"I was."

"I almost missed you—" She broke off, hazel eyes darkening with silent emotion. "I almost missed everything."

"You've missed nothing."

There was so much tenderness in his voice. Her lip quivered as she fought the intensity of her feelings. "I'm sorry I didn't come with you. I'm sorry I made this whole thing so difficult—"

"You're here now. That's enough. And you look…" He shook his head, pride in his eyes. "Beautiful."

She touched her hips a little self-consciously. The delicate skirt hugged her curves and fell in a shimmer of yellow and gold to her feet. "It's the dress." But she liked the compliment, appreciated the compliment. He made her feel so incredible. "Do you still want company tonight?"

His blue eyes darkened, the navy almost ink. "More than ever."

Winnie woke up to the sound of the sea. Her eyes fluttered open and for a moment she looked at the ceiling not knowing where she was.

Then the waves crashed again, breaking on the sand, and Morgan's arm reached out, extended across her belly before moving up to cup her breast. "I missed this." His voice sounded low and husky. "I missed you."

Winnie rolled over on her side. They'd gone to bed last night with the doors open and now sunlight and fresh air filled the room. They'd left New York Sunday morning to spend a few stolen days on St. Jermaine's.

Winnie loved the feel of his hand on her breast, but more than anything, loved the warmth in his eyes. He did care for her. He cared for her so very much. "You missed me?" she repeated smiling faintly.

"Quite a bit."

"I guess in Morgan speak, that means the same thing as I love you."

His lips twitched. A day-old beard darkened his jaw. His teeth flashed in an easy white smile. "Is there something wrong with Morgan speak?"

Her smile grew; the smile starting on the inside, in her chest, where her heart felt warm, where happiness was made. "There's absolutely nothing wrong with Morgan speak. You say as little as you want. I'll happily fill in the gaps."

He chuckled softly, appreciatively. "You're very funny."

"Absolutely hilarious. In my next career I'll be a standup comedian."

"You remembered."

"I remember everything."

His lips curved, his eyes smiled, a sheen on the gorgeous sapphire blues. "So let's see, regarding your grasp on Morgan speak, if I say, I love pancakes…"

"It really means no one makes better pancakes than Winnie."

"If I say, I like spending time with you?"

"It translates to 'I can't imagine ever living without you.'"

His husky laugh filled the room and leaning forward, he kissed her very slowly. "I love you, Winnie."

Did he just say that? Did he say the words?

Her eyes burned and the ache in her chest was so intense she couldn't distinguish between joy and pain.

"So, Winnie, translate that one for me."

She couldn't.

She, who had a million words at her disposal, couldn't think of one. He'd just blown her away.

"Well, smarty pants," he said softly, reaching out to lift a tendril of hair from her cheek. "I'll tell you what it means. It means, I love you, I love you, I love you. Got it?"

Her lips quivered and a tear spilled over. She didn't want to cry. She really didn't want to cry. This was the best moment of her whole life and tears were for the birds. "I think so. But you might want to say it one more time just to be sure I really, completely understand."

He shifted his weight, moved on top of her. His head dipped, his lips brushed her ear. "I love you, Winnie Graham, and only you, Winnie Graham. Will you please spend the rest of your life with me?"

"Yes."

He gave her a look of mock surprise. "What?

No argument. No questions about my sincerity, or the kind of role you're going to play?"

"No." She blinked and more tears spilled. "No argument. No questions." The tears trickled down her cheek, past her mouth. She could taste the wet salty dampness on the corner of her lips. "And absolutely no doubts. You love me. That's enough for me. It's all I need to know."

Later in the afternoon, after amazing sex, great food served by an extremely chipper Mr. Foley, and more amazing sex, they'd straggled down to the beach to get some sun.

Winnie lay on her beach towel, smiling up at the sky. Paradise. She'd found paradise but she'd discovered something about paradise. It wasn't an island, or a concept. It wasn't a place. It wasn't even being with Morgan.

It was just being okay with yourself. Not being so afraid of yourself. Of accepting the good with the bad and learning to accept others the same way.

"There's an opening at the office," Morgan said from his beach lounge chair, tossing aside his newspaper.

The turquoise water lapped at the white sand, and without a breeze there were hardly any waves in the small crescent bay. Winnie shaded her eyes as she looked at him. "You want me to go back to work?"

"I thought you wanted to go back to work."

She was a bit puzzled by the direction of the conversation. "I do miss the office."

"So call and schedule an interview."

"You're going to make me go through an interview?"

"You think you should get special advantages just because you're the boss's girlfriend?"

She threw her bikini top at him. "I'm not your girlfriend. I'm your mistress. Remember?"

Morgan's dark blue eyes narrowed as they swept over her light gold skin. She was naked except for her yellow bikini bottoms. "Mmm, I'm remembering."

She knew where his mind was headed but she wanted more information from him first. "Tell me about the job. How long has the position been open? Who would I work with?"

Morgan handed her a section of the paper. "It's in here. We've been running the advertisement in Classifieds all week. Résumés are pouring in."

Winnie's gaze swept the narrow columns. "Nothing here for administrative assistants."

"You're on the wrong page. Check under business, marketing."

That's weird, she thought, but she flipped the paper to the page he'd said. Her eyes scanned the ads then rested on one. "It's a market research position."

"The first we've had in nearly five years." His eyes met hers. "The first since you walked out of the interview at Grady Investments nearly five years ago."

For a long moment Winnie didn't speak, her gaze fixed on the tranquil turquoise water and the darker patches of purple indicating submerged beds of coral.

She drew a slow breath. "How did you know I interviewed for an analyst position?"

"It was in your employment file. I discovered it when Mr. Osborne called to check on your references."

He'd known this about her for months and yet he'd never said a thing until now. "Why didn't you tell me you knew?"

"I was waiting for you to tell me yourself." He reached out, clasped her hand and tugged her off her towel and onto his chair.

She felt nervous now, and she scrambled to get her bikini top on. "Told you what? That I panicked in your conference room and made a total fool of myself?"

"You'd make a great market analyst, Winnie. I want you to interview."

Her eyes were burning again. She adjusted her suit, blinked, and focused on the house with its pots of red and pink hibiscus, the trailing purple bougainvillea, and the tall arching coconut trees. "I thought you didn't want me to work at your office. I thought you didn't want to work with me."

"For such a smart girl, you've got it all wrong. I didn't want you to work *for* me. I want you to work *with* me. I know it's only a little preposition, but it's an important one."

EPILOGUE

One month later

THE bathroom was steamy and fragrant with Morgan's aftershave. Winnie rose on tiptoe and leaned across the wide marble counter to grab the toothpaste. But even on her toes it was still out of reach.

Morgan bumped her with his hip. "Hey, stay on your own side."

"I am on my side. My toothpaste just happens to be on your side."

"And how did that happen?"

"Because you borrowed it," she flashed, finally able to scoot past his very solid torso and snatch the tube back. Yet in reaching past him she got a glimpse of his taut abdomen. He hadn't buttoned his dress shirt yet and she was unable to resist the lovely flat bands of muscle cut across his stomach.

Winnie pushed his shirt open wider and pressed a kiss to his warm, toned belly. He inhaled quickly and she smiled to herself and kissed him an inch lower before tracing his hard muscle with the tip of her tongue.

He shuddered at the caress. "Winnie, we don't have time."

She loved the feel of his body, loved the way she turned him on. "Sure, we do," she whispered wickedly before kissing him again, lower this time, her mouth finding him through his Italian-cut trousers.

He caught her head in his heads, his fingers sliding through her loose hair. "You make me crazy."

"Good."

Muttering an oath, Morgan reached down, picked her up from the floor and placed her on the edge of the counter.

She felt a thrill of excitement. "We're going to be late," she mocked, heart racing, eyes shining, loving the adventure of life with Morgan Grady.

"Your fault," he said, parting her knees, pushing up her slim skirt and stepping between her thighs. He slid her body forward and she felt his arousal, his body so hard it made her instantly weak.

Winnie drew Morgan's face down to hers. "Kiss me."

"I'll never stop."

"You'll have to. It's my first day of work."

His lips touched hers and shocks of energy jumped through her. Just one kiss and she felt hot and electric. One touch and she knew she'd always feel wildly passionate about this man.

"You should have thought about that before you started playing dangerous games," he retorted, sliding his hands up to cup her breasts.

She sighed with pleasure, sinking closer to him. "I'm going to get fired before I even get the office tour."

He kissed the side of her neck, just below her ear. "You don't need the office tour. You already know your way around the Tower building's seventy-eighth floor."

Winnie closed her eyes, savoring the feel of his mouth against her skin and she lifted her chin higher to give him better access to her skin. "But how would it look if Grady Investments' newest research analyst showed up late on her first day? Everyone would think I'm taking advantage of my special relationship with the boss."

His lips had found the very secret, very sensitive spot where all her nerve endings seemed to come together. All it took was just one touch there and she forgot everything—duty, reason, responsibility.

Morgan lifted his head, gazed down into her warm, flushed face even as he slid his hands beneath her blouse and unclasped her bra. "Speaking of your special relationship with the boss, I think it's time we changed the status quo."

"You do?" she answered breathlessly, cool air hitting her aching breasts.

"Yes. I can't have all the men hitting on the company's brainy new analyst."

"So, boss, what do you propose?"

"Marry me."

She sat up, stared deep into his blue eyes. They were the most beautiful color she'd ever seen. "Marry you?"

"Unless you're afraid of making me a long-term commitment." His smile slipped and he leaned forward to clasp her face in his hands, his expression serious. "Are you?"

"No. Oh, Morgan, no. You're the love of my

life, the sun in my sky. You're my very own Prince Charming."

"So we try the wedding thing again?"

She wiggled closer and wrapped her arms around his neck. "Can we just skip the big white wedding, have a quiet little ceremony on the island, then jump to the happy-ever-after part?"

His incredible blue eyes, still the sexiest blue eyes in all of Manhattan, creased with love and silent laughter. "You drive a hard bargain for a princess, but you've got yourself a deal," he said, before kissing her senseless.

Happily for all, Winnie still managed to make it to her first day of work as a research analyst on time.

★ ★ ★ ★ ★

Christos's Promise
Jane Porter

DEDICATION

For my husband, Joe. You are my miracle.

CHAPTER ONE

"You'd rather remain locked here in the convent than marry me?"

Disbelief echoed in Christos Pateras's voice. How could this girl—woman, actually, although she didn't look a bit like the twenty-five her father claimed she was—prefer living in the spartan convent over marrying him?

He was no barbarian. Compared to the Greek men she'd been raised with, he was downright civilized.

"You had my answer earlier," Alysia Lemos retorted coolly. "You needn't have wasted your time coming here."

He turned his back on the anxious nun hovering in the background, intentionally making it harder for her to hear. The abbess might have insisted on providing Alysia with a chaperone, but that didn't mean the sister needed to be privy to the conversation.

"You told your father no," Christos answered, his tone mild, deceptively so. "You didn't tell *me* no." He rarely raised his voice. He didn't need to. His size and authority generally were persuasive enough.

But Alysia Lemos's fine dark eyebrows only arched higher. "Some women might find such persistence flattering. I don't."

"So, your answer is...?"

Alysia's incredulous laughter contrasted sharply with the dark blaze in her eyes. "I know you're an American, but surely you can't be this much of an idiot!"

Her cutting dismissal might have crushed a man of lesser ego, but he wasn't just any man, and Miss Lemos wasn't just any woman. He needed her. He wasn't going to leave Oinoussai without her. "You dislike Americans?"

"Not all."

"Good. That should help ease the transition when we move to New York."

Her eyes met his, the dark irises all the more arresting against her sudden pallor. "I'm not moving. And I'd never agree to an arranged marriage."

He dismissed this along with her other protestations. "In case you're worried, I consider myself Greek. My parents were born here, on Oinoussai. They still call this home."

"Oh, happy people, they."

He almost smiled. No wonder her father, Darius, was feeling desperate. She was not an eager bride-to-be. "I don't know if they'll be happy with you for a daughter-in-law, but they'll adjust."

Bands of color burned along the curve of her cheek. "I'm sure your mother dotes on you."

"Endlessly. But then, most Greek mothers live for their sons."

"While daughters are disposable."

He gave no indication that he'd heard the hurt in her voice, the small wobble in her breath as she spat the bitter words. "Not mine. My daughters will be cherished."

At thirty-seven, he needed a wife, and Darius Lemos needed a husband for his wayward daughter. This was no love match, but a match made in a bank in Switzerland. "I'm an only child, the last of the Pateras in my branch of the family. I've promised my parents a grandchild before my thirty-ninth birthday, and I shall deliver."

"No, you hope *I'll* deliver!"

He bit the inside of his cheek to keep from smiling. "I stand corrected."

Alysia's hands balled. She longed to smack his smirk right off his gorgeous, arrogant face. She'd never met a man more sure of himself than he. Except for her father, that is.

She swallowed convulsively, her stomach heaving, as she struggled to understand why her father had reached across the Atlantic for a husband for her. Her father despised the new rich. Her father must be feeling desperate. Well, so was she. He was practically auctioning her off to the highest bidder, his sole heir up for grabs.

Hot tears rushed to her eyes but she held them back. Her mother would never have let her father do this.

"There are worse bridegrooms, Miss Lemos."

She felt the irony but couldn't even smile. "A husband is a husband, and I don't want one."

"Most women want to be married. It's the desire of every Greek woman."

"I'm not most women."

He laughed almost unkindly. "So say you, but I've learned one woman is not so different from another. You all have agendas—"

"And you don't?"

"Mine isn't hidden. I want children. I need children." He scrutinized her as though she were horseflesh. "You're young. You'd be an excellent mother."

She winced. "I don't want to be a mother."

He shrugged, unconcerned. "We can marry today. Here. It'll just be us. Your father is unavailable, I'm afraid."

"What a shame."

His mouth quirked faintly, revealing surprise, even intrigue. "You speak like a sailor."

"The closest I've come to my father's business."

"You're interested in business?"

"I'm interested in my competition." The industry her father loved above all else. Nothing came between him and his ships. Nothing had ever been allowed to interfere with the great Lemos fortune. Not her mother. Certainly not herself.

"I think the business would bore you," he said after a moment, jamming his hands into trouser pockets. "It's talks. Contracts. Number crunching. Tedious stuff."

"For my small brain?"

His eyes glimmered, her mocking tone had made him smile. "You shouldn't listen to everything your father says," he cheerfully drawled. "Only the good things about me."

She could easily have slapped his cheeky face. She knew exactly why Christos Pateras was marrying her. He wanted her dowry. Her dowry and her father's shipping interests. When Darius passed away, Christos would inherit Lemos's empire. "You're overly confident."

"So say my critics."

"You have many?"

"Legions."

She offered him her profile, grinding her teeth together. This was a joke to him and he toyed with her like a cat with a mouse. She struggled to contain her temper, her smooth jaw tightening. "You're mad if you think I'll marry you."

"Your father has already consented to the marriage. The dowry has changed hands—"

"Change it back!"

"Can't do that. I need you too much."

She turned her head, her brilliant gaze catching his. "Despite what you both think, I am neither mindless, nor spineless. Since you appear to have difficulty with your hearing, let me say it again. I will not marry you, Mr.

Pateras. I will never marry you, Mr. Pateras. I'd rather grow old and gray in this convent than take your name, Mr. Pateras."

Christos rocked back on his heels and fought his desire to smile. Her father said she was difficult but he hadn't mentioned his daughter's intelligence, or spirit. There was a difference between difficult and spirited. Difficult was unpleasant. Spirited was something a man quite enjoyed. Like a spirited horse, a spirited chase, a spirited game of tennis. But nothing was more appealing than a spirited woman. "Oh, I think I quite like you," he murmured softly.

"The feeling isn't mutual."

His lips curved, and he watched as she threw her head back, dark eyes challenging him.

With the sunlight washing her face, he suddenly realized her eyes weren't brown at all, but blue. A mysterious, dark blue. Like the sky at night. Like the Aegean Sea before a storm. Honey wheat hair and Aegean eyes. She looked remarkably like the pictures he'd seen of her half-English, half-Greek mother, a woman considered to be one of the great beauties of her time.

"Hopefully you'll grow to tolerate me. It'd make conjugal life…bearable."

A pulse beat wildly at the base of her throat. But her eyes splintered anger, passion, denial. She was going to fight him, tooth and nail. "I'd sooner let you put a bit in my mouth and saddle on my back."

"Now that could be tempting."

Her cheeks darkened to a dusky pink, her gorgeous coloring a result of the Greek-English heritage. Blue eyes, sun-streaked hair, a hint of gold in her complexion. He felt desire, and possession. She was his. She just didn't know it yet.

Alysia fled to a distant corner of the walled garden, arms crossed over her chest, breasts rising and falling with her quick, shallow breathing.

He followed more slowly, not wanting to push her too hard. At least not yet. Furtively he touched the breast pocket of his coat, feeling the crisp edges of the morning's newspaper. She wouldn't like the press clipping. He was the first to admit it was a power play, and underhanded, but Christos wasn't about to lose this deal.

He'd made a promise to his parents that he'd bring fortune to his beleaguered branch of the family, and every decision he'd made since then had been in the pursuit of that goal. Since he'd made that promise, the family fortunes had grown into a different league. Very different.

She must have felt him approach. "Have you no ethics?" Her low-pitched voice vibrated with emotion. "How can you marry a woman against her will?"

"It wouldn't be against your will. You have a choice."

"You disgust me!"

"Then go back inside. Call the nun over. She's dying to be part of the conversation."

Alysia glanced over her shoulder, spotted the nun and pressed her lips together. "You're enjoying this."

"It's my wedding day. What's not to enjoy?"

She took another step away, sinking onto a polished marble bench. He walked around the bench to face her. "Alysia, your father has sworn to leave you here until we exchange vows. Doesn't that worry you?"

"No. You are not the first man I've refused, and dare I say, nor the last. I've been here nearly a year, and the sisters have been wonderful. Quite frankly, I've begun to think of the convent as home."

The convent as home? He didn't believe her, not for a minute. Despite her refined beauty—the high, fine cheekbones, the elegant curve of her brow—her eyes, those indigo-blue eyes, smoldered with secrets.

She did not belong in the convent's simple brown smock any more than he belonged in priestly robes. And God knew he did not belong in priestly robes.

Christos felt a sudden wave of sympathy for her, but not enough to walk away from the playing table. No, he never walked away from the playing table, not that he played cards. He gambled in other ways. Daring, breathtaking power plays in the Greek shipping-industry which so far had resulted in staggering financial gain. He'd been wildly successful by anyone's standards.

"Your home, Alysia, will be with me. I've picked you. You are part of my plan. And once I put a plan into action, I don't give up. I never quit."

"Those admirable traits would be better applied elsewhere."

"There is no elsewhere. There is no other option. You, our marriage, is the future," he said softly, as a warm breeze blew through the courtyard, loosening a tendril of hair from her demure bun. She didn't attempt to smooth it and the golden-brown tendril floated light as a feather.

He liked the play of sunlight across her shoulders and face. The sun turned her hair to gold and copper. Flecks of aquamarine shimmered in her eyes.

"I know who you are, Mr. Pateras. I'm not ignorant of your success." Her eyebrows arched. "Shall I tell you what I know?"

"Please. I enjoy my success story."

"A full-blooded Greek, you were born and raised in a middle-class New York suburb. You attended public school, before being accepted to one of the prestigious American Ivy League colleges."

"Yale," he supplied.

"Which is quite good," she agreed. "But why not Harvard? Harvard is supposed to be the best."

"Harvard is for old money."

"That's right. Your father left Oinoussai broke and in disgrace."

"Not disgraced. Just poor. Hopeful that there would a better life elsewhere."

"Your father worked in the shipyards."

"He was a welder," Christos answered evenly, hiding the depth of his emotions. He was fiercely loyal to his parents, but particularly to his father. His father's piety, unwavering morals and devotion to family had sustained them during times of great financial hardship. And there had been hardship, tremendous hardship, not to mention ostracism in the close-knit Greek-American community.

Quickly, before she could probe further, he turned the spotlight on her. "And your father, Alysia, inherited his millions. You've never lacked for anything. You have no idea what 'poor' means."

"But you aren't poor anymore, Mr. Pateras. You now own as many ships as Britain's entire merchant fleet. Despite your humble origins, it shouldn't be difficult to find a bride a...trifle... more eager to accept your proposal."

"I can't find another Darius Lemos."

"So in reality you're marrying my father."

She was smart. He smiled faintly, again amused by the contradiction between her serene exterior and fiery interior. He found himself suddenly wondering what she'd be like in bed. Passionate as hell, probably.

He watched the shimmering golden-brown

tendril dance across her cheek, caress her ear, and Christos felt a sudden urge to follow the tendril with his tongue, drawing the same tantalizing path from her cheekbone to her jaw, from her jaw to the hollow beneath her earlobe.

His body tightened, desire stirring. He'd enjoy being married to a woman like this. Procreation would be a pleasure.

Alysia leaned back on the bench, her brown shift outlining her small breasts, her dark lashes lowering to conceal her expression. "How well do you know my father?"

"Well enough to know what he is."

She allowed herself a small smile, and Christos noticed the flash of dimple to the left of her full mouth. He'd taste that, too, after the wedding.

"My father must be quite pleased to have you in his back pocket. I can quite picture him, rubbing his hands together, chuckling gleefully." Her head cocked, her lashes lifted, revealing the dark sapphire irises. "He did rub his hands after you made your deal, didn't he?"

Her tone, her voice, her eyes. He wanted her.

Abruptly he leaned forward, captured the

coil of hair at her nape in his hand. Her eyes widened as his fingers tightened in her hair seconds before he covered her mouth with his.

Alysia inhaled as his lips touched hers, and he traced the soft outline of her lips with his tongue. He didn't miss her gasp, or the sudden softness in her mouth.

His own body hardened, blood surging. From the distance he heard a cough. The nun! Wouldn't do to get thrown out of here just yet.

Slowly he released her. "You taste beautiful."

Alysia paled and dragged the back of her hand across her soft mouth, as if to rub away the imprint of his lips. "Try that again and I shall send for the abbess!"

He placed his foot on the bench, on the outside of her thigh. He felt the tremor in her body. "And say what, sweet Alysia? That your husband kissed you?"

"We are not married! We're not even engaged."

"But soon shall be." He gazed at her exposed collarbone and the rise of fabric at her breasts. "Do you like wagers?"

She visibly shuddered. "No. I never gamble."

"That's admirable. But I like bets, and I like

these odds. You see, Alysia, I know more about *you* than you think."

He caught her incredulous expression, and felt a stab of satisfaction. "You won an academic scholarship at seventeen to an art school in Paris. You lived in a garret with a dozen other want-to-be artists, a rather bohemian lifestyle with small children running underfoot. When money ran out, you, like the others, did odd jobs. One summer you worked as a housekeeper. You did a stint in a bakery. Your longest job was as a nanny for a designer and his family."

"They were respectable jobs," she said faintly, blood draining from her face.

"Very respectable, but quite a change from life with a silver spoon in your mouth."

"Is there a point to this?"

His smile faded and he leaned forward, trapping her between his knee and chest. "You've spent eight years of your life trying to escape your father."

Her lips parted but no sound came out.

He watched her closely, reading every flicker in her eyes. "For a while, you were free. You painted, you traveled, you enjoyed an interesting circle of friends. But then you became ill, and your obliging father placed you in a hospital in Bern. Since then, he's owned you, body and soul."

"Body, maybe, but not my soul. Never my soul!"

Again the fire, the spirited defiance. He felt a kinship with her that he felt with few women. He softened his tone, appealing to her intellect. "Think about it, Alysia. In Greece you're powerless. Your father is the head of the household, the absolute authority. He has the right to choose your husband. He has the right to leave you locked up here. He has the right to make your life miserable."

"I'm no prisoner here."

"Then why don't you leave?

She held her breath, exquisitely attentive, her eyes enormous, her lips compressed.

"Now, if I were your husband," he concluded after the briefest hesitation, "you could leave. Today. Right away. You'd finally be free."

She didn't speak for a moment, studying him with the same intentness with which she listened. After a moment she exhaled. "Greek wives are never free!"

"No, maybe not the way you think of it. But I'd permit you to travel, to pursue hobbies that interested you, to make friends of your own choosing." He shrugged. "You could even paint again."

"I don't paint anymore."

"But you could. I've heard you were quite good."

She suddenly laughed, her voice pitched low, her body nearly trembling with tension. She wrapped her arms across her chest, a makeshift cape, a protective embrace. "You must want my father's ships very much!"

Christos felt a wave of bittersweet emotion, unlike anything he'd ever felt before. He saw himself exactly as he was. Driven, calculating, proudly self-serving. And this woman, this lovely refined young woman, knew she mattered only in business terms. Her worth was her name. Her value lay in her dowry. For a split second he hated the system and he hated himself and then he ruthlessly pushed his objection aside.

He would have her.

Alysia slipped from beneath his arm, taking several steps away. She walked to the edge of the herb garden and knelt at the flowering lavender. "Ships," she whispered, breaking off a purple stalk. "I hate them."

She carried the tuft of lavender to her nose, smelling it.

"And I love them," he answered, thinking she should have been a painting.

The bend of her neck, the creamy nape, the shimmering coil of hair the color of wild honey, the sun's golden caress.

He wanted this woman. Deal or no.

She crumpled the lavender stalk in her fist. "Mr. Pateras, has it crossed your mind to ask *why* a man as wealthy as my father must give away his fortune in order to get his daughter off his hands?"

The sunlight shone warm and gold on her head. The breeze loosened yet another shimmering tendril.

"I'm damaged goods, Mr. Pateras. My father couldn't give me away to a local Greek suitor, even if he tried."

More damaged than he'd ever know, Alysia acknowledged bleakly, clutching the broken lavender stalk in her palm. Unwillingly memories of the Swiss sanatorium came to mind. She'd spent nearly fourteen months there, all of her twenty-first year, before her mother came, rescuing her and helping her find a small flat in Geneva.

Alysia had liked Geneva. No bad memories there.

And for nearly two years she'd lived quietly, happily, content with her job in a small clothing shop, finding safety in her simple flat. Weekly she rang up her mother in Oinoussai and they chatted about inconsequential matters, the kind of conversation that doesn't challenge but soothes.

Her mother never discussed the sanatorium with her, nor Paris. Alysia never asked about her father. But they understood each other and knew the other's pain.

Alysia would never have returned to Greece, or her father's house, if it hadn't been for her mother's cancer.

The mournful toll of bells stirred Alysia, and she tensed, lashes lowering, mouth compressing, finding the bells an intolerable reminder of her mother's death and funeral.

The bells continued to ring, their tolling like nails scratching down a blackboard, sharp, grating. Oh, how she hated it here! The sisters had done everything they could to comfort her, and befriend her, but Alysia couldn't bear another day of bells and prayers and silence.

She didn't want to be reminded of her losses. She wanted to just get on with the living.

Sister Elena, a dour-faced nun with a heart of gold, signaled it was time to return inside.

Alysia felt a swell of panic, desperation making her light-headed. Suddenly she couldn't bear to leave the garden, or the promise of freedom.

As if sensing her reluctance, Christos extended a hand in her direction. "You don't have to go in. You could leave with me instead."

It was almost as if he could feel her weakening, sense her confusion. His tone gentled yet again. "Leave with me today and you'll have a fresh start, lead a different life. Everything would be exciting and new."

He was teasing her, toying with her, and she longed for the freedom even as she shrank from the bargain.

She could leave the convent if she went as his wife.

She could escape her father if she bound herself to this stranger.

"You're not afraid of me?" she asked, turning from Sister Elena's worried gaze to the darkly handsome American Greek standing just a foot away.

"Should I be?"

"I know my father must have mentioned my… health." She gritted against the sting of the words, each like a drop of poison on her tongue. Unwilling tears burned at the back of her eyes.

"He mentioned you hadn't been well a few years ago, but he assured me you're well now. And you look well. Quite well, if rather too thin, as a matter of fact."

Her lips curved into a small, cold self-mocking smile. "Looks can be deceiving."

Christos Pateras shrugged. "My first seven ships were damaged. I stripped them to the hull, refurbished each from bow to stern. Within a year my ships made me my first million. It's been ten years. They're still the workhorses of my fleet."

She envisioned him stripping her bare and attempting to make something of her. The vivid picture shocked and frightened her. It'd been years and years since she'd been intimate with a man, and this man, was nothing like her teenage lovers.

Hating the flush creeping through her cheeks, she lifted her chin. "I won't make you any millions."

"You already have."

Stung by his ruthless assessment, she tensed, her slender spine stiffening. "You'll have to give it back. I told you already, I shall never marry."

"*Again,* you mean. You'll never marry *again.*"

She froze where she stood, at the edge of the herb garden, her gaze fixed on the ancient sun dial.

He knew?

"You were married before, when you were still in your teens. He was English, and six years older than you. I believe you met in Paris. Wasn't he a painter, too?"

She turned her head slowly, wide-eyed, torn between horror and fascination at the details of her past. How much more did he know? What else had he been told?

"I won't discuss him, or the marriage, with you," she answered huskily. Marrying Jeremy had been a tragic mistake.

"Your father said he was after your fortune."

"And you're not?"

Lights glinted in his dark eyes. It struck her that this man would not be easily managed.

He circled her and she had to tilt her head back to see his expression. Butterflies flitted in her stomach, heightening her anxiety. He was tall, much taller than most men she'd known, and solid, a broad deep chest and muscular arms that filled the sleeves of his suit jacket.

Her nerves were on edge. She felt distinctly at a disadvantage and searched for something, anything, to give her the upperhand—again. "Good Greek men don't want to be the second husbands."

"We've already established I'm not your traditional Greek man. I do what I want, and I do it my way."

CHAPTER TWO

IT STRUCK her then, quite hard, that two could play this game. All she had to do was think like a man.

Christos Pateras wanted her to further his ambitions. He was marrying her to accomplish a goal. This wasn't about love, or emotions. This was a transaction and nothing more.

Why couldn't she approach the marriage the same way? He wanted her dowry; she wanted independence. He wanted an alliance with the Lemos family; she wanted to escape her father.

Greece might be part of a man's world but that didn't mean she had to play by a man's rules.

She sized him up again, assessing the odds. Tall, strong, ridiculously imposing, he exuded authority. Could she marry him and then slip away?

No more Alysia Lemos, poor little rich girl,

but an ordinary woman with ordinary dreams. Like a small house in the country. A vegetable garden. An orchard of apple trees.

She stole a second glance at Christos's rugged profile, noting the long, straight nose, line of cheek, strong clean-shaven jaw. He looked less ruthless than determined. Assertive, not aggressive. If she ran away from him, what would he do?

Chase her down? She doubted it. He'd have too much pride. He'd probably wait a bit and then quietly annul the marriage. Men like Christos Pateras wouldn't want to advertise their failure.

He turned, caught her eye, his dark gaze holding hers. "Everyone thinks you've already married me."

"How can that be?" she scoffed.

Opening his coat, he drew a folded newspaper from the breast pocket and handed it to her.

Not certain what she was supposed to find, she unfolded the paper and pressed the creased pages flat. Then the headlines jumped out at her, practically screaming the news. Secret Wedding For Lemos Heir.

Anger, indignation, shock flashed through her one after the other as the headlines blinded her. How could he do it? How could he pull a stunt like this?

And then just as quickly as her anger flared, inspiration struck. For the first time in months she saw an open door. All she had to do was walk through it.

Marry him, and walk away.

It was all in place. The husband, the marriage, the motivation. She just needed to go along with the plans and then leave.

Perfect. Her heart did a strange tattoo.

Maybe too perfect. Christos Pateras didn't seize control of the Greek shipping industry by luck. He was smart. No, rumor had it that he was brilliant. A brilliant man wouldn't marry a young woman and then just let her slip away. He'd be prepared. He'd be alert.

She'd have to be very, very careful.

Alarm and eagerness tangled her emotions. She could do this, she could escape him, it was a matter of being just as smart as him.

Her heart began to pound faster and she felt heat creep beneath her skin. Excitement grew but she dampened her enthusiasm, not wanting to overplay her hand or reveal her true intentions.

She frowned, feigning surprise and shock. "You can't be serious."

"It's front page news."

"There's no wedding. How can there be a story?"

"Read it for yourself."

She obliged, skimming the front page story where her father had been quoted as saying he couldn't confirm or deny reports of the secret wedding, only that he knew that Greek-American shipping tycoon, Christos Pateras, had visited Oinoussai in the past several days and had visited his daughter at the convent. Other sources confirmed that Pateras had been seen in town, while another source mentioned the convent as the secret wedding location.

Her father's work, no doubt. The puppet and the puppeteer. Incredible. But this time, she was the puppeteer. She was in control.

She crumpled the paper for show. "You and my father make a spectacular team."

"Your father's idea, not mine."

"No one will believe this drivel."

"Everyone believes it. Media has descended on the harbor. They're expecting to see the blushing bride and groom board the yacht later this afternoon."

He looked so damn smug, as if he'd thrown a net around her, trapping her in his scheme. *Sorry, she silently apologized, but I win this one. Hands down.*

She was going to marry him. And then she'd leave him. He could pick up the pieces. The fall-out with her father wouldn't be her problem. If Christos Pateras wanted to make deals with her father, then fine, let him experience her father's wrath firsthand.

Guilt briefly assailed her. Then she ignored the voice of conscience, reminding herself that Christos and her father were the same kind of man. Selfish. Unthinking. Lacking compassion.

Not once during her mother's horrible last year did her father slow his schedule, put off a meeting, change his travel plans. He never once attended her radiation treatments. Never held her hand during the chemo. Never checked on her at night when she lay huddled with pain and fear.

Her father acted as if nothing bad had happened, ignoring the terminal diagnosis as though it were a spate of bad weather and simply charged ahead with his plans for new ships, new routes, new alliances.

Damn her father, and damn Christos Pateras.

Alysia knew of no fate worse than that of being a Greek tycoon's wife.

But she hid all this, focusing instead on her goal. Independence. Peace. A life far from the wealthy Greek shipping families. Maybe back to Geneva. Maybe a little house south of London.

"When would we marry?" she asked, her pulse leaping in anticipation.

"Today. We'd marry here, in the chapel, and then sail this afternoon."

"And just what are your expectations?"

His dark gaze studied her, his expression blank, giving away nothing. "As my wife, you'll travel with me. When I entertain, you shall perform the duties of the hostess. And for my family functions, we'll appear together, behaving like a real couple."

"Versus a business liaison?"

"Precisely."

"For your parents sake?"

"Right, again."

He didn't want to disappoint his parents. She could almost admire him for that. Almost.

But fortunately, she needn't worry about his family, or his expectations. She wouldn't be around long enough to fulfill any such duties. If they married today, this afternoon, she was just hours from freedom, hours from starting a new life for herself far from Greece and the influential Lemos name.

"Anything else?" she demanded coldly, conscious that she could never let Christos Pateras know her intentions. Christos might dress fashionably, move with athletic ease and speak eloquently, but underneath the gorgeous veneer he was the same man as her father. And her father, ruthless, critical, unyielding crushed those close to him, destroying family as indiscriminately as he destroyed friends. No one was safe. No one was exempt.

"I expect us to have a normal relationship." He, too, had become detached, businesslike.

It struck her they'd moved to the negotiation stage. The deal would take place. It was just a matter of formalizing the details. He knew it. She knew it. A bitter taste filled her mouth, but she wouldn't back down now. "Define normal, if you would."

"I expect you to be faithful. Loyal. Honest."

She felt something shift inside of her, another whisper of conscience, but she dismissed it with a small sneer. Men had controlled her all her life. For once she'd take care of herself. "That's it?"

"Should there be more?"

He was testing her, too. He knew there should be more, would be more. They hadn't even discussed the physical aspect of the marriage and it loomed there between them, heavy, forbidding.

"This is a marriage of convenience, yes?" She cast a glance at him before looking too quickly away, but she caught the predatory gleam in his eyes. He wasn't nervous. He seemed to enjoy this.

"Marriages of convenience don't produce children. I need children."

Before she could speak, he continued.

"I'll do my best, Miss Lemos, to ensure you're satisfied. I want you to be happy. It's important we're both fulfilled. Sex is a natural part of life. It should be natural between us."

Fingers of fear stroked her spine, stirring the fine hairs on her nape, even as blood surged to her face, heating her cheeks, creating a frisson of warmth through her limbs. "We hardly know each other, Mr. Pateras."

"Which is why I won't force myself on you. I'm content to wait until some of the newness wears off and we've grown more…comfortable with each other before becoming intimate."

Another surge of heat rushed to her cheeks. His voice had deepened, turning so husky as to hum within her, warm and intimate. For a split second she imagined his body against hers, his mouth against her skin.

The very thought of making love with him made her inhale sharply. Every nerve in her body seemed to be alert, aware of this man and his potent masculinity.

Crossing her arms over her chest, Alysia tried to deny the tingle in her breasts, and the longing to be real again. It'd been forever since she'd felt like a woman.

She wouldn't look at him. "You're willing to commit to a loveless marriage?"

"I'm committing to you."

Oh, to have someone want her, to care for her…

She drew a ragged breath, hope and pain twisting in her heart, seduced by his promise and the warmth in his voice. What would it feel like to be loved by this man?

She drew herself up short. He'd never said anything about love, or wanting her. He wasn't even committing to her. He was committing to the Lemos house, committing to her father, but not to her. How could she allow herself to daydream? Hadn't she learned her lesson by now?

This is how Jeremy had broken through her reserve. This is how she'd offered up her heart. Well, she couldn't, wouldn't, do it again. Experience had to count for something.

Hardening her emotions, she reminded herself that Christos Pateras did not matter. His promises did not matter. The only thing that mattered was escaping the convent and her father's manipulations. It was what her mother would want for her. It was what her mother had wanted for herself.

Glancing up, her gaze settled on the high, whitewashed wall. All convent windows faced inward, overlooking the herb garden and potted citrus trees. None of the windows faced out, no glimpse of the ocean, no picture of the world left behind…

But she hadn't left it behind. Her father had ripped it from her just weeks after her mother's death. There had been no mourning for him. Just business, just money and deals and ships.

A lump filled her throat. For a moment her

chest felt raw, tight. "If we are going to do it," she said after a long painful silence, "let's not waste time."

They were married in the briefest of ceremonies in the convent chapel. Rings, exchange of vows, a passionless kiss.

In the back of the limousine, Alysia clenched her hand on her lap, doing her best to ignore the heavy diamond-and-emerald ring weighting her finger. Christos had already told her it wasn't a family heirloom, three carat diamonds had never been part of his family fortune. No, the ring had been purchased recently, just for her. But she wouldn't wear it long. By this time tomorrow she'd have it off her finger, left behind on a dresser or bathroom counter, she promised herself.

A strange calm filled her. For the first time in years she felt as if she were in control again, acting instead of reacting, making decisions for herself instead of feeling helpless.

With a swift glance at her new husband, she noted Christos Pateras's profile, his strong brow creased, a furrow between his dark eyes. He wore his black hair combed straight back, and yet the cowlick at the temple softened the severity of his hard, proud features.

He'd be surprised—no, furious—when he discovered her gone. He didn't expect her to deceive him. It wouldn't have crossed his mind. Just like a Greek man to assume everything would go according to his plan.

He sat close to her, too close, and she inched across the seat only to have his hard thigh settle against hers again.

She became fixated on the heat passing from his thigh to hers, panic stirring at the unwelcome intimacy. She wasn't ready to be touched by him. Wasn't ready to be touched by anyone.

She scooted closer to the door, pressing herself into the corner, willing herself to shrink in size.

"You're acting like a virgin," he drawled, casting a sardonic look in her direction.

She felt like a virgin. Years and years without being touched, not even a kiss, and now this, to sit thigh to thigh with a stranger, a tall, muscular, imposing stranger who wanted her to bear his children.

Stomach heaving, Alysia pressed trembling fingers against her lips. What had she done? How could she have married him? If she didn't escape him, surely she'd die. Despite her mother's wisdom, despite the gentle counsel of the sisters, Alysia didn't want family. No children, no babies. Ever.

She couldn't ever give Christos Pateras a chance. She wouldn't let him make a move. No opportunities for seduction. First chance she could, she'd leave.

"Relax," Christos uttered flatly. "I'm not going to attack you."

She opened her eyes, glanced at him beneath lowered lashes. He looked grim, distant. Gone was the laughter, the fine creases fanning from his eyes.

The luxury sedan bounced down the narrow mountain road, the street unpaved, lurching across a deep pothole. Despite the seat belt, Alysia practically spilled into Christos's lap. Quickly she righted herself, drawing sharply away. Christos's mouth pressed tighter.

The silence stretched, tension thick. Squirming inwardly, aware that she'd helped create the hostility, Alysia searched for something to say. "You like Oinoussai?"

"It's small."

"Like America."

The corner of his mouth lifted in faint

amusement. "Yes, like America." The amusement faded from his eyes, his features hardening again.

She felt his dark gaze settle on her face, studying her as dispassionately as one studied a work of art hanging on a museum wall. "Have you ever been to the States before?" he asked.

"No." She'd always wanted to go, was curious about New York and San Francisco, but she hadn't had time, nor the opportunity. Thanks to her father, she'd been too busy enjoying the special pleasures of the sanatorium and the convent.

"I have a meeting in Cephalonia, which we'll sail to from here. And then I thought we could conclude our honeymoon someplace else, someplace you might find interesting before returning to my home on the East Coast."

Honeymoon. She tensed at the very suggestion. He'd said he wouldn't force himself on her, said he'd be content to wait. Honeymooning conjured up lovemaking and intimacy and…

She shuddered. This was a mistake. She'd made a mistake. He had to turn the car around, take her back to the convent now.

"We're not going back to the convent," he said, still watching her, dark eyes hooded.

Her head snapped up. She stared at him, shocked that he knew what she'd been thinking.

"My dear Mrs. Pateras, you're not difficult to read. You wear your emotions on your face, they're all there, right for me to see."

He tapped her hands, knotted in her lap. "Try to relax a little, Alysia. I'm not demanding sexual favors tonight. I'm not demanding anything from you just yet. You need time. I need time. Let's try to make this work, learn a little about each other first."

Angered by his rational tone, finding nothing rational in being coerced into marriage, she lifted her head, temper blazing. "You want to learn about me? Fine. I'll tell you about me. I hate Greece and I hate Greek men. I hate being treated like a second-class citizen simply because I'm a woman. I hate how money empowers the rich, creating another caste system. I hate business and the ships you treasure. I hate the alliance my father has formed with you because my father detests America and American money—" she drew a breath, shaking from head to toe.

One of his black eyebrows lifted quizzically. "Finished?" he drawled.

"No. I'm not finished. I haven't even started." But her outburst had leveled her, and she leaned heavily against the leather upholstery, exhausted, and suddenly silent.

She wasn't used to this, wasn't used to fighting, to speaking her mind. Her father had never allowed her to say anything at all. Her father never even looked at her.

"What else is bothering you?" Christos persisted, his attention centered on her and nothing but her.

She shook her head, unable to speak another word.

"Perhaps we should leave our philosophic differences for a later date. Those big issues can be overwhelming, hmm?" He smiled wryly, his expression suddenly human. "Why don't we start with the small things, the daily routines that give us comfort. For example, breakfast. Coffee. How do you take yours? Milk and sugar?"

She shook her head, eyes dry, gritty, throat thick. "Black," she whispered.

"No sugar?"

She shook her head again. "And yours? Black?"

"I like a touch of milk in mine." He spoke without rancor, the tone friendly, disarmingly friendly. "Are you an early riser?"

"A night owl."

"Me, too."

"Lovely," she answered bitingly. "We should be perfect together."

His expression remained blank, yet a hint of warmth lurked in his dark eyes. "A promising beginning, yes, but I do think a week or two alone should help rub some of the edges off, take the newness away. And with that in mind, I've cleared my calendar and after this meeting on Cephalonia, will have the next couple weeks free."

"How accommodating."

"I try."

Her exhaustion fed her fear. She felt a fresh wave of panic hit. What if she couldn't break away? What if he stayed too close, paid too much attention, to allow her to leave? She'd be trapped in this relationship, forced into marriage. The possibility made her almost ill, and a lump lodged in her throat, sealing it closed.

She couldn't afford to wait. She had to escape, and soon. Before boarding the yacht. Before appearing in public together.

He must have sensed her panic because he suddenly lifted her hand, examined the ring on her finger, before kissing the inside of her wrist. "You don't have to hate me."

A tremor coursed through her at the touch of his lips, her blood leaping in her veins. She tried to disengage but his mouth caressed her wrist in another sensitive spot.

"Please don't," she said, pulling at her wrist, attempting to free herself from his clasp.

"You smell like lavender and sunshine."

Anger hardened her voice. "Mr. Pateras, let me go."

He released her arm and she buried her hand in her lap. Her inner wrist burned, the skin scorched, her pulse pounding.

She hadn't realized she'd become so sensitive.

Alysia forcibly turned her attention back to the rocky landscape, watching the rough road as they snaked down the hill, kicking up dust and loose gravel. They were nearing the outskirts of town.

An unwanted thought suddenly crossed her mind. "Will I see my father in town?"

"No. He flew out this morning for a meeting in Athens."

Relief washed over her. At least she wouldn't have to deal with him right now.

"You don't care for him much, do you?" Christos asked, checking his watch and then glancing out the window again.

"No."

"He seems like a decent man."

"If you like maniacally controlling men."

His eyebrows lowered, his brow creasing. "He's tried to do what's best for you."

A lead weight dropped in her stomach. Christos Pateras didn't know the half of it! Her father had never done what's best for her. It'd always been about him.

She could forgive her father many things, but she'd never forgive him for neglecting her mother in the final weeks of her life. As her mother lay dying in that marble mausoleum of a house, Darius never once reached out to her; no acknowledgment of her pain, no interest in bringing closure, no awareness of her needs.

He should have been there for her. He owed that much to her. How could he not have cared?

A lump formed in her throat, and narrowing

her eyes, Alysia concentrated very hard on the rocky landscape beyond her closed window.

"I wish I'd had the pleasure of knowing your mother."

The lead weight seemed to swell in size, pressing against her chest, making it hard to breathe. Gritty tears burned at the back of her eyes. "She was beautiful."

"I've seen photographs. She once modeled, didn't she?"

"It was a charity event. My mother was dedicated to her causes. I think if my father had let her, she would have done more." Her voice sounded thick with emotion.

"You must miss her."

Dreadfully, she thought, struggling to maintain her control. She was finding it almost impossible to juggle so many contradictory emotions at one time. The whole last year had been like this, too. The loss of her mother on top of the others...

It was too much. She sometimes didn't know where to go for strength and had to fight very hard to reach inside herself for the courage to continue.

"Your mother liked Greece?" Christos persisted.

"She tolerated it," Alysia answered huskily, patting her shift pocket for a tissue. Her eyes were watering, her nose burned, she felt like an absolute mess. And to top it all off Christos was looking at her with such concern that she felt as though she were covered in cracks, threatening to break in two.

"Too oppressive?" he mused.

"Too hot." She smiled for the first time all afternoon. Mother had hated the heat; she positively wilted in it. "Mum pined for the English grays and cool greens the way some pined for lost love."

Christos laughed softly, his expression surprisingly gentle. But his gentleness would be her undoing. Alysia stiffened her spine, reminding herself that she couldn't trust his smile, or his warmth. He wasn't just any man; he was a man handpicked by her father and tainted.

Christos Pateras married her for money.

He was as bad, if not worse, than her father.

Flatly, no emotion left, she asked about her things. "Will I have any of my books or photos sent to me? And my wardrobe? What's happened to that?"

"Everything's already been transferred to the

yacht. Your entire bedroom was boxed up and put in the ship's storage."

Shock rivaled indignation. "You're quite sure of yourself, aren't you?"

"I had your father's support."

"Obviously. But what I want to know is *how?* And why?" Her father had never liked Americans, and detested foreign money. "Why did he go to you? What made you so special?"

"I had what he needed. Money. Lots of it."

"And what did he give you in exchange?"

Christos's dark eyes gleamed at her, a faint smile playing his lips. "You."

"Aren't you lucky."

He shrugged. "Depends on how you look at it. Anyway, your father is happy. He won't bother you anymore." He turned a smoldering gaze on her. "I won't let him."

She heard the promise in his voice, and a hint of menace, too. For a moment Christos Pateras sounded like a street-boxer, an inner city thug, but then he smiled, a casual, relaxed smile, and she felt herself melt, her chilly insides warming, her fear dissipating ever so slightly. Truthfully she'd welcome a buffer between her and her father. He'd made her life nearly unbearable. She needed to get away.

Elegant whitewashed villas came into view, along with the sparkling harbor waters. The late-afternoon sun illuminated the bay. "There's my yacht," Christos said, leaning forward to point out a breathtaking ship of luxurious proportions.

She leaned forward, too, her breath catching in her throat. The yacht might prove to be just as confining as the convent and it crossed her mind that she might have bitten off more than she could chew.

No, she'd be fine. She'd figured a way out. She simply needed time.

Numerous fishing boats dotted the harbor, as did several yachts, but one moored ship dwarfed all others. The glossy white, sleek design only hinted at the elegant state rooms inside. The yacht would have cost him dearly.

She didn't realize she'd spoken the thought out loud until he chuckled softly, a twisted smile at his lips. "She was expensive, but not half as much as you."

Indignation heated her skin, hot color sweeping through her cheeks. "You didn't buy me, Mr. Pateras, you bought my father!"

But he was right about one thing, Alysia thought darkly as the limousine pulled up to the harbor. The media were out, and out in force. Reporters and photographers crawled all over town, jostling each other to take better position.

They surged forward when the car stopped and she sucked in a panicked breath. All those cameras poised…all the microphones turned on…

"It'll be over in a minute," Christos said, turning to her.

She felt his inspection, his dark eyes examining her face, her dress, her hair. He startled her by reaching up to pluck pins from her hair. The heavy honey mass tumbled down and he combed his fingers through it with unnerving familiarity.

"That's better," he murmured.

Just the touch of his fingers against her brow sent shivers racing through her. Repulsion, she told herself, even as the tight core of her warmed, softened. She didn't want him. Couldn't want him.

But when he tucked one long silky strand behind her ear, his hand caressing the ear, then the tender spot below, her belly ached and her limbs felt terrifyingly weak.

No one had touched her so gently in years.

Her need shocked her. She felt like a woman starved for food and warmth. Helplessly she gazed at him, hating herself for responding to him. "Are you quite finished?" she whispered breathlessly.

"No, not quite," he murmured, before his dark head lowered.

She stiffened as his head dropped, drawing back against the leather upholstery. *No!* No, no, no. He couldn't do this, couldn't kiss her, especially not here, not when she felt like this. Everything was too new, too strange, too crazy.

If he felt her resistance, he ignored it, clasping the back of her head, fingers twining in her long hair. She caught the glint in his dark eyes and a hint of rich, sweet spice. Not vanilla, not cinnamon, but some other fragrance so deep, and familiar, that it tantalized her memory.

His mouth took possession of hers and she breathed him in again, reminded of almonds, sweet baby powder, the heady musk of antique roses...

Somehow it all fit, he, this, the kiss. His mouth, the warmth of his skin, the strength in his arms. Tremor after tremor coursed through her veins, creating an intense craving for more sensation.

Even as his lips parted hers, another electric current shot through her, sparking awareness in every nerve in her body. More, her brain demanded, her lips moving beneath his, her tongue answering the play of his, more, more…

The kiss deepened, and unconsciously she moved against him seeking to prolong the contact, relishing the hard plane of his chest, the warmth of his skin, the heady sweet spice of his cologne.

As his tongue sought the sensitive hollows in her mouth, the inside of her lip, the curve of cheek, blood pooled in her lower belly, her veins pulsing. This felt, he felt…

Incredible.

Muffled voices penetrated her brain. Voices. People.

Her eyes flew open, reality returning.

Cameras pressed against the limousine windows, dozens of lenses, shutters snapping. "Mr. Pateras, we have company."

He raised his head, his mouth curving into a satisfied smile. He didn't even give the throng of reporters a second glance. "Let them watch. After all, this is what they've come for."

Panicked, she tried to bolt from the car,

lunging out thinking only of running from the crowd and the cameras and Christos—

A hand clamped at her waist, biting into her skin, holding her still. "Mrs. Pateras—" Christos's husky voice pierced her panic "—smile for the cameras."

CHAPTER THREE

LEAVING the noisy media throng behind, Alysia stepped aboard the yacht, late-afternoon sun glinting off the water in the purest form of golden light.

Christos swiftly introduced her to his staff and crew, rattling off the dozen names, even as the yacht gently swayed in the harbor waters.

The emotionally intense afternoon, the numerous introductions, the strangeness of her new surroundings suddenly exhausted her. Or was it the stark realization that until they touched land, she was really and truly caught in this pretend marriage?

She might never get away.

She might be trapped forever.

Her head swimming, she gulped air, panic overriding every other thought. What had she done? What in God's name had she done?

"I can't," she choked, searching for the exit,

her gaze jumping from wall to door to patch of blue sky outside. "I can't do this, I can't, I can't—"

"You can," Christos softly countered, stepping closer to her side. "You already did."

He cut the introductions short and took her by the elbow, steering her through the formal salon to an elegant stateroom decorated in the palest shades of blue. Just beyond the wide French doors, the ocean shimmered a brilliant royal-blue. The effect was calming, indescribably peaceful, and she relaxed slightly.

"Do you need a drink?" he asked, sliding his suit jacket off.

"No."

"Brandy might help."

Nothing would help, she thought, not until she got off the yacht. But she couldn't say that, and she couldn't allow him to become suspicious.

Christos tossed his jacket across the foot of the bed. "Maybe a long hot bath would feel good. I can't imagine you were allowed such indulgences in the convent."

"No, definitely not. Cold showers were de rigueur."

He began unfastening the top button on

his fine dress shirt. "Think you'll be comfortable here?"

Her gaze took in the massive bed with the bolsters and mountain of pillows. Soft silk drapes hung at the French doors. The same ice-blue silk covered a chaise lounge. Her fingertips caressed the silk chaise, the down-filled cushion giving beneath the weight of her hand. Her room at the convent had been so spartan. "Yes."

"Good." He continued unfastening one small button after another, revealing first his throat and then his darkly tanned chest with the crisp curl of hair.

Alysia sucked in a breath, the glimpse of his chest hair so personal she felt as if she'd invaded his privacy. Yet she found herself turning to watch him again, half-fascinated, half-fearful. Christos appeared utterly at ease as he slipped the shirt from his shoulders, the smooth muscular planes of his chest rippling.

"Your wardrobe's in the closet," he added. "Do change into something more comfortable. We'll have a light meal now on the deck and then supper later, closer to ten."

The typical Greek dinner hour. But not the

typical Greek man. She quickly averted her gaze again.

Then his words registered. *Your wardrobe's in the closet.* "We share this room?"

His expression didn't change. "Of course."

She took a defensive step backward, bumping the edge of the writing table. She glanced down at the desk's polished surface, noting the neat arrangement of paper, inkwell, pen. "Mr. Pateras, you know the terms of our agreement."

"Sharing a bed isn't a sexual act, Mrs. Pateras."

"It's close enough."

"Surely you've shared a room before."

He didn't mention her former husband. He didn't need to. She knew exactly what he was thinking and she didn't like his presumption. "Regardless, I'd like a room of my own, please."

He walked toward her. She leaned back, her bottom bumping the desk. Without apology, he took her in his arms, his mouth covering hers.

Heat flooded her veins, heat swept through her middle, into her belly and deeper still. She felt hot and weak and when he parted her lips with his, she didn't resist. If anything she opened her mouth wider, arched closer, straining against the emptiness since her mother's death, and the years before.

His palm found her hip, pressed her more tightly against him. She felt the thrust of his arousal and her breasts ached, nipples hardening. This was too close but not close enough, too much sensation and yet too little, everything felt hot and flushed and yet it was wrong.

But she didn't pull away, couldn't pull away, riveted by the tumult of her feelings.

His tongue flicked against her inner lower lip before exploring the recesses of her mouth. Teeth grazed teeth, and then he bit once into the softness of her lip. Her protest sounded like a whimper, more desire than denial, and Christos made a sound low in his throat, rough, hungry.

He was tasting her, exploring, setting her body and limbs on fire. No pretend marriage for him. He'd have her naked and beneath him in no time.

Her legs were trembling and she felt the fire lick her ankles, her knees, between her thighs. It was, she thought wildly, a fire she didn't want, wouldn't be able to control.

Christos broke the kiss off, lifting his dark head to gaze into her eyes. He trailed a finger down her flushed cheek. "Separate rooms?" he said hoarsely. "I don't think so."

Christos left to speak with the captain and Alysia fled to the shower. Inside the glass stall, water streamed from the showerhead and she soaped her face vigorously, determined to wash away every trace of Christos's kisses.

Who did he think he was, kissing her, touching her, treating her like one of his possessions?

He might have made a deal with her father, but he hadn't made a deal with her! With another swipe of the soapy washcloth, she scrubbed her mouth again and then her neck, shoulders, breasts.

It had been ages since she'd indulged in a long, hot shower and she lathered her hair in the fragrant shampoo provided. The rich scent reminded her of a fruit cocktail with its fragrance of citrus, mango, papaya. It formed billowy suds and rinsed easily.

Christos Pateras spared no expense of anything. Yachts. Wives. Or bath necessities.

Suddenly the yacht hummed to life, the engine's vibrations shooting through the white ceramic floor tiles into the soles of her feet. They were leaving Oinoussai at last!

With one towel wrapped around her body, and another twisted turban-style around her head, she padded quickly to the bedroom.

Ambivalent emotions whirled within her, her breath catching in a mix of excitement and dread. She'd waited so long to leave Oinoussai, but to leave as an American's wife!

As the yacht pulled anchor she felt momentum shift in her own life. Anything could happen now.

Everything could happen now.

In mute satisfaction, she watched Oinoussai recede, the small island shrinking small, smaller, smallest until miles of water lay between the yacht and the rocky sweep of land.

Finally the island became just a speck in the sea, and then disappeared altogether. When the island was gone, and the horizon blue, just endless blue water and a low, gold sun starting to set, Alysia released the bottled air in her lungs in a rush, her eyes stinging, her heart thumping, lungs raw and bursting.

She inhaled another breath and suddenly it all became easier, freer, as if a weight had toppled from her chest.

Free. She was free. She might have been back on Oinoussai only two years, but those years felt like forever. It had been forever. Not just her mother's death, but the sanatorium, the horrible marriage to Jeremy, the baby...

The baby.

Alysia sank onto the bed, crushing the ice-blue silk coverlet. Groaning, she covered her face with her hands, pressing the heel of her palms to her eyes. Miniature yellow dots exploded against the blackness of her lids.

Her heart felt as if it were on fire and the pain consumed her. With a strangled sob, she rocked back and forth, stricken with need, tortured by the memory.

Alexi, I miss you, I miss you, I miss you.

It was too much, too sharp, too horrible.

She couldn't do this, couldn't give in to the terrible grief again. The doctors at the sanatorium had taught her to fight back, to keep the memories at bay. Grinding her palms against her eyes, she pressed until she could see nothing, hear nothing, remember nothing.

Little by little she calmed, still rocking herself on the bed, unconsciously mimicking the motion she'd used to soothe Alexi when he couldn't get comfortable, when sleep seemed impossible. Back and forth, back and forth, until at last the monster inside her slept.

And slowly the grief receded until it lay still and silent, a great hulking giant at memory's gate.

Drawing a painful breath, she slowly lifted her head, catching a glimpse of herself in the large gold-framed mirror hanging above the antique chest of drawers.

Wide, wild eyes. Trembling lips. Terror there, hatred, too.

How could she not be full of hate? She'd done a terrible, unforgivable thing. She hated no one more than she hated herself.

Christos watched her appear on the deck, a vision in the palest shade of pink. Her long thin sleeveless dress clung to her breasts, brushed her ankles, sliding over her slim hips. With her long wheat and honey hair pulled into a knot at her nape, she looked incredibly feminine, very fragile, and he felt a wave of possession sweep through him. She was his now. She belonged to him.

He'd seen her before, years ago, at a gathering in Athens. She was young, even more blond, and she'd entered the room to tearfully whisper something to her father.

The men had hushed, the meeting interrupted, and Darius Lemos reacted in anger. He slapped his daughter in front of everyone, the sound of his palm loud, too loud in the suddenly silent room.

Christos had been twenty-seven and the foreigner, the interloper, alienated at the back of the room. Although he spoke fluent Greek, he hadn't understood all the innuendoes tossed his way. All he knew was that he'd had his fill of poverty, and powerlessness, and he'd never let anyone dictate to him again.

He'd been shocked when Darius struck his daughter, the savagery of the blow leaving a vivid handprint on the girl's face. But the girl hadn't made a sound. She simply stared at her father, tears swimming in her eyes, before wordlessly leaving the room.

The meeting resumed and all continued as if nothing happened.

But something happened. Something happened to Christos.

Alysia approached him now as slowly, as hesitantly as she'd approached her father all those years ago.

Silently he handed her a glass of champagne, noting as he did the spiky tips of her sooty lashes, the dampness at the corners of her startling blue-green eyes. She'd been crying.

"Second thoughts?" he murmured.

"And thirds, and fourths." She turned her head away, revealing more of her creamy nape.

Again he felt the urge to take her in his arms, to kiss her soft skin and make her warm in his hands. He'd know her better than anyone one day. He'd discover all the secrets she kept buried within her.

She rested her slender arms on the railing, the glass of champagne ignored, dangling in her fingers. The yacht was moving swiftly through the water and the wind lifted tendrils of hair from her smooth knot.

"Where are we going?" she asked.

"Where do you want to go?"

"Away from Greece."

"Done."

She turned her head just enough to glance at him over her bare pale shoulder. Her skin gleamed. Her blue eyes were dark, mysterious. "I don't even know where you live."

"We'll live outside New York most of the

time. But I also have houses in London, Provence and on the Amalfi Coast."

"You sound restless."

Amusement curved his mouth. "See, you know me already."

The uniformed cabin steward stepped onto the deck, signaling that the light meal was ready. Christos held out a hand, gesturing for Alysia to follow the cabin steward to the table set on the far end of the deck.

Christos held her chair as she took her place at the small table on the deck. "You look beautiful in pink."

She set her champagne glass down, pushing it across the linen cloth toward the floral centerpiece. She waited until the steward stepped away to speak. Very carefully she kept her gaze fixed on the yellow and white roses. "Let's not pretend this is anything but a business arrangement, Mr. Pateras."

"By its very nature, marriage is a business arrangement." He sat down across from her and leaned back in his chair. "But that doesn't mean it has to be sterile, or cold and intolerable. Nor does it mean we can't celebrate our union."

She grasped the stem of the champagne flute between two fingers. "And what are we celebrating, Mr. Pateras? Your new financial gain? Your alliance with Darius Lemos?"

"All of the above."

She made a move to set her glass down. "Then I'd rather not."

"What if we celebrate your beauty then?"

"I definitely won't drink to that."

"You don't think you're beautiful?"

"I know I'm not."

"I find you breathtaking."

"Perhaps you've lacked for company, lately."

He smiled, almost indulgently. "I've had exceptional company. But you, I must admit, fascinate me. You're a tormented beauty, aren't you?"

She paled, her eyes growing enormous, her blue irises dark and flecked with bits of bottle-green. "This conversation makes me very uncomfortable."

"Sorry."

But he didn't sound sorry, she thought, fighting fresh panic, feeling increasingly trapped.

While dressing tonight she'd determined to keep her distance, to remain detached, to do everything in her power to keep him at arm's length but his power was insidious.

She found herself drawn to him in ways she couldn't fathom.

He was a stranger. He'd been bought by her father. He only wanted Lemos money. So why did her heart stir and her emotions twist, why did she want what was absolutely wrong for her?

She half closed her eyes, reminding herself that he was a spider and he'd woven a web and if she weren't careful he'd eat her, the same way a spider ate a little fly.

This was about survival.

Alysia crossed one ankle behind the other, as if to fortify herself, become impenetrable. She'd shut him out, draw the line here. He wouldn't cross it. She wouldn't let him.

Christos stirred, lazily stretching out one long arm to drag her chair toward him. He had no intention of letting her escape. "No need to be frightened."

"I'm not." Good, frost glittered in her voice.

"Your pulse is racing. I can see it there, at your throat."

Her heart was racing. She felt breathless, dizzy, on edge. If he touched her, she'd scream. If he drew her any closer, she'd leap out of her skin. This was all going wrong, terribly wrong and there was nothing she could do now but play the cards she'd been given.

"It's not. I'm quite calm. You probably need glasses."

His lips tightened and then eased and she realized he was grinning. "My vision is perfect. Twenty/twenty. Neither my father nor mother wear glasses, either." His smile faded, eyebrows pulling and suddenly all laughter was gone and he looked hard, focused, determined. "Why do you think so little of yourself?"

The swift change of subject knocked her off balance. Alysia felt as though she'd run smack into a wall and she shook her head once, dazed by the contact with a reality she resisted.

Why, he asked? Because she'd committed an act so terrible, so vile that her husband had left her, her friends abandoned her, her mind had shut down. It had taken her time in the sanatorium to begin to recover.

"You're intelligent, beautiful, sensitive, possibly charming," he said, touching her on the cheek with the back of his hand. She averted her head. He took her chin in his hand and turned her back to face him. "Why so little pride?"

The kindness in his voice almost undid her.

No one except her mother, and maybe the abbess, had spoken to her so softly, so gently, in years. He made her feel like a…human being.

Tears started in her eyes and she blinked them back. Clutching the champagne flute's slender stem even more tightly, she tried to break the intensity of his gaze. "Please, no more."

"I want to understand."

"There's nothing to understand. I am what my father says I am. Reckless. Disobedient. Rebellious."

His dark gaze moved searchingly across her face, examining every inch of her profile before dropping to her breasts and lower still. "Are you?"

"Of course. I'm my father's daughter."

She'd meant to be flippant but it came out dreadfully wrong, more despair than arrogance in her husky voice. Suddenly she felt completely naked, her dress no more protection than a sheet of plastic kitchen wrap.

Alysia clutched the champagne flute as though her life depended on it. What if he discovered the truth about her? What if he realized the kind of person she really was? "Let me go, please. You can keep the dowry, my jewels, my savings. I don't want anything."

"You couldn't survive poor. You've never tasted poverty. It tastes as bad as it looks."

"I'd rather be poor and free. *Please,* just let me go."

His dark gaze bored through her. He didn't speak for a long, tense moment. Finally he shook his head. "I can't. I need you too much."

Her slim body jerked, her hand convulsively tightened on the goblet and with an ear-splitting pop, she snapped the crystal stem in two. The champagne flute crashed in pieces to the table. A shard of glass lodged painfully deep in her thumb.

It was like slow motion, she thought, watching the blood suddenly spurt in a brilliant red stream. Christos swore violently, sounding every bit a native Greek, as he grabbed a linen napkin and covered the arc of blood.

"I'm fine," she protested weakly.

"You're not. You're a bleeding fountain." He lifted the napkin briefly to inspect the damage. "You might need stitches."

"It'll stop."

He cast her a scathing glance. "There's glass in it. Hold still."

Eyebrows flat, expression grim, his lips compressed, he probed the wound, gently working the sliver from her tender thumb. She winced at the pressure and he caught her grimace. Suddenly his expression changed. His eyes were so dark, so deep they looked bottomless. "I don't want to hurt you."

"You didn't hurt me. I did it myself."

"Still."

Still. As though he had the power to somehow heal all wounds, restore her peace of mind and soothe the cuts and bruises. Not just a groom, but a miracle man. Wouldn't that be something? Tears sprang to her eyes and she bit into her lower lip overwhelmed by the intensity of her longing to feel whole and rested, more herself again.

Christos tossed the glass shard onto the tablecloth. "That should do it," he said, wiping away the drying blood and bandaging her thumb.

She held her breath as he tucked the ends of the linen cloth beneath the edge of the bandage. Something about his touch made her feel too warm, too liquid. He made her feel so...safe. What an illusion. Could anything be more unjust?

"Your father told me you're not to be trusted," Christos glanced up into her face, black lashes only partly lifting, his expression concealed. "But I didn't know he meant with my crystal."

His lips quirked, a black eyebrow arched, but beneath his ironic tone, she heard concern, then immediately chided herself. *This is a deal, a marriage deal and you are a very expensive bride.*

Her throat sealed shut. Unable to speak she stared at his hands, the backs very broad and tanned, his fingers long and well-tapered. His touch was so light, so deft, he could have been a carpenter, or a surgeon. Legally he was her husband. *Husband.* A shiver raced down her spine, and yet it wasn't fear creating havoc, it was anticipation. Her imagination was running riot. Nervously she glanced up into his face and her heart skittered sideways, as if she was a frightened country mouse instead of one of the wealthiest women in Greece. But money didn't equate with confidence, or happiness. No one knew that better than she. "My father…he told you I wasn't to be trusted?"

"Mmm."

A blush of shame rose to her cheeks. What

else had her father told him? She knew too well that her father's honesty could be brutal. He had hurt her, and her mother, countless times with his cutting appraisal. No one was good enough for him. Certainly not his family.

"Don't," Christos said, his voice unusually husky as he reached up to brush her flushed cheek with the tip of his finger.

A strange pain flickered through her and she pressed her bandaged hand to her belly. Everything felt so raw just then, so exposed. She could smell the sharp pungent salt in the air, the warmth of the night, the motion of the ship as it surged through the waves. "Don't what?"

"Think." Grooves formed on either side of his mouth, small creases fanned from the corners of his eyes. "You're torturing yourself again."

"Better me than you." She smiled as carelessly as possible, a devil-be-damned smile that hurt in every pore of her body. She'd fought her demons before and won. She'd win again. And she'd do it without Christos's help, or interference, whatever it might be.

"One more quick check," he insisted, taking her hand and lifting the edge of the napkin to examine the cut as if it were a wound of significance. "Maybe you won't need stitches after all."

"Thank you, Doctor."

"My pleasure."

He should have laughed, grinned, said something lighthearted. Instead he stared into her eyes, earnest and focused, deep furrows marring his high bronze brow. She swore he could see right through her. See her fears, her shocking secrets.

The blood drained from her face, the intensity of his gaze unnerving. What did he see when he looked at her like that? What did he possibly know? She felt threads of panic, hints of the past. "Really, Christos, I won't fall apart over this." She'd meant to be funny, to ease the tension, but he didn't even crack a smile.

His jaw flexed, a small muscle pulling near his ear. "First time you've used my given name."

What was he doing to her? Softening her stony heart, breaking through her defenses, that's what he was doing. She couldn't allow it, wouldn't let him dismantle the high, hard wall she'd built around herself. No one came inside. Ever.

The sooner they reached Cephalonia, the

better. Alysia pushed back her chair, and rose unsteadily. "I don't think I'm hungry. If you'll excuse me, I'd like to return to my room."

"Certainly. Why don't you go to our room and rest. I'll have dinner sent to you later."

CHAPTER FOUR

AFTER her solitary dinner, Alysia changed into her satin lilac pajama set, the wide trousers and loose jacket style top covering her from ankles to collarbone. Of all her pajamas these were the least figure-flattering and not at all bridelike.

Bride. Even the word stuck in her throat, making her gag. But she wasn't a bride. She was an impostor and this time tomorrow she'd be gone. Christos could have the marriage annulled and they'd both put this embarrassing episode behind them.

Alysia crawled into bed and tried to sleep, but sleep didn't come. Moonlight flickered through the gap in the curtains and the rocking of the yacht was doing funny things to her insides. She felt deceptively warm, and alive, nerve endings alert, senses sharp. Turning onto her side, she closed her eyes and listened to the slap of waves against the yacht's hull, the groan and creak of wood and the low hum of the engine. Would Christos put in an appearance? Did he intend to share the bed?

How could she think she could manage a man like Christos Pateras? She must have been out of her mind. He might not be exactly like her father, but he was close enough. He'd get what he wanted and he wanted children.

Her stomach cramped and she squeezed her eyes shut. Don't panic, she soothed. Tomorrow they'd dock in Cephalonia, the largest of the Ionian islands, and mountainous Cephalonia was diverse enough, busy enough, to allow her to escape and hide. She just had to wait for the right opportunity.

Calmer, Alysia relaxed, and gave herself over to the gentle roll and sway of the ship. The rocking motion soon lulled her to sleep.

Warmth permeated her dreams, as well as the realization that a very solid, very real presence was taking up more than half of the bed.

Opening her eyes she discovered Christos next to her, his long muscular body inches away, his arm outstretched, practically touching her.

Alysia stiffened, held her breath, as his palm moved slowly across her head to tangle briefly in the long strands of hair. As quietly as possible, she scooted away, creeping to the bed's edge and listening with satisfaction as his hand fell to the mattress.

Alysia gathered her hair, moving it from harm's way. His deep, steady breathing reassured her and little by little she relaxed. Just when she was close to drifting off again, Christos stirred.

Suddenly he moved against her, pressing his thighs to the back of her legs. Total body contact, hip to ankle, his knees fitting behind hers, his groin pressed to her bottom.

Despite the clamor of protest inside her head, her body came to life, nerve endings screaming as if electrified.

Opening her eyes, she gripped the downy comforter, and stared at the edge of the bed, then down at the carpet. There was nowhere to go. She bit her knuckle to keep from shouting out loud.

She wasn't ready for this kind of intimacy. She didn't know Christos, and couldn't bear to be pressed limb to limb with him.

As her senses flooded, responding to his heat and strength, her fear grew. She'd never met a man who aroused such contradictory emotions in her before. Awareness, mistrust, desire, dread.

Using her elbow, she pushed against his chest, trying to prod him backward. He didn't budge. She pushed again. And still nothing but his deep, even breathing, his warm breath bathing the back of her neck.

Damn him. Damn his incredible nerve. Damn his empire, too.

He had her trapped on the edge of the bed. She couldn't move forward, she'd fall on the floor. If she wiggled backward, and she tried, she came up square against his groin.

Suddenly she realized not all of him was asleep.

Part of him was definitely awake and his thin cotton pajama pants did nothing to contain his impressive length.

Mortified, she pressed a forearm across her eyes, trying to block out the pressure of his arousal against her bottom. But the more she denied the existence of his erection the more rigid his shaft became, enflaming her tender skin, creating heat and liquid desire between her thighs.

The tip of his erection strained against her nightwear, her thighs tingling, her innermost muscles tightening, clenching at air and nothing when he lay so dangerously close.

She'd never admit it in a thousand years, but she wanted him, wanted to feel more of him, and the carnal want was more than she could bear. She'd never been physical, never felt sexual in her life, but Christos Pateras was changing all that. He was making her ache for things she'd never fully experienced.

Alysia writhed. She couldn't help it. She only prayed he was so deeply asleep he didn't know the effect he was having on her. Wriggling, her hips shifted, and she brushed the tip of his shaft, tormenting herself.

In the dark, with her arms around herself, and his arousal square against her, she could imagine making love to him, imagine him inside of her, imagine the pleasure of being filled by him.

It was all she could do to not whimper aloud.

And still, he slept on.

Suddenly one of his arms snaked out and clasped her around the waist, holding her firmly against him. His chest pressed to her back. His hips formed a cradle for her bottom. His taut thighs shaped hers. His shaft nearly pierced her through the satin of her pajamas.

Her heart stuttered, her breath caught in her throat. Digging her teeth into her soft lower lip, she muffled a groan. This was torture. Exquisite torture of the best and worst kind.

"Go to sleep," Christos growled in the darkness, his voice pitched deep and rough.

"I can't."

"You can. Just close your eyes. Stop thinking."

Thinking! She wasn't thinking. She was feeling, and every nerve ending begged for more sensation. She felt wired for action and nothing was happening. Absolutely nothing. So how was she supposed to sleep?

It seemed as if she lay awake for hours, her lower belly aching, her inner muscles clenching at nothing.

Easy for him to say sleep, he wasn't the one about to explode out of her skin. But finally, painfully, she drifted off. When she next awoke, the sun was shining and Christos was gone.

Dressing in a slim taupe linen skirt and matching knit top, Alysia tried to deny the nervous thrill she felt at seeing Christos again. He'd made her feel desperate last night, his hard muscled body a torment, and yet he'd also been warm. And solid. And real.

She thrust her feet into strappy tan sandals and hurried upstairs to the deck. A steward met her, greeted her with a bow and showed her to the breakfast table overflowing with lavish platters of fresh fruit and sweet rolls, yogurt and coffee. But no sign of Christos.

She felt her excitement plummet, anticipation turning inside out. The disappointment was so strong that she felt furious with herself for caring so much about someone she knew so little. For heaven's sake, he was a stranger. She married him to escape her father, not for a stab at domestic tranquillity.

Alysia nearly dropped her china coffee cup. She wasn't falling for him, was she? She didn't really expect a happy-ever-after with him… did she? This wasn't a real marriage. It wasn't a honeymoon.

Wake up, she snapped at herself. *Grow up!*

Halfway through her croissant, her appetite well and truly gone, she spotted gleaming white bobbing next to the ship on the water. Pushing back from her chair she moved to the railing and looked down. A speedboat.

Sleekly designed, painted a glossy white and

maroon, the speedboat hadn't been there before. Had someone come on board? Or was Christos planning a trip out?

Either way, there was a boat, and means for escape.

Her fingers tightened on the railing, the wood warmed by the sun. She felt a whisper of regret, but mocked her weakness and her attraction to a man so potentially dangerous. This wasn't the time to rely on her emotions. She needed to act.

Swiftly descending the flight of stairs that joined the two wraparound decks, Alysia slid over the bottom rail and into the low-slung speedboat. She reached past the steering wheel toward the gauges. A key dangled from the ignition. *Yes*.

A shadow darkened the deck, filtering the bright morning sun. "Going somewhere?" a husky voice drawled.

Christos.

Her stomach fell so fast and hard she leaned against the speedboat's dash, fingers compulsively flexing.

Go, just go, a terrified voice screamed inside her head. Get out of here.

But she couldn't move, paralyzed by fear.

She stiffened, expecting him to grab her, haul her from the boat. He'd be enraged. He'd be physical.

"You like the Donzi?" he asked, his voice husky, almost amused.

How could he be amused? She'd tried to run away.

"The Donzi?" she choked, her breathing ragged, her body weighted with fear, and dread. Her father would have broken her in two if she'd tried this with him.

"My speedboat. It's an American boat, made in Florida."

Tensing, she dragged her gaze up, an inch at a time. He was wearing faded khaki shorts that exposed every sinewy muscle in his thigh and calf and a white cotton T-shirt that had obviously seen better days.

He looked fearless, careless, distinctly American. A frisson of warmth shot through her. There was no anger in his eyes. No anger in the twist of his lips.

"Get your swimsuit," he said, stepping down into the boat, one long bare leg grazing hers. "I've got a favorite beach I like to visit whenever I'm near Cephalonia."

She almost tripped in her haste to escape

him. "I'm not much for the beach," she fibbed, scrambling out of the boat, away from him, cursing her slim-fitting skirt that hindered her movement.

Christos watched her struggles with interest, arms folded across his chest, the white T-shirt pulled taut at the shoulders. "This isn't an elective, Mrs. Pateras. It's a requirement. Get your suit. We're going swimming."

Heaping Greek curses on his head, Alysia changed in the bedroom, stepping out of her panties and bra and into a two-piece bathing suit she hadn't worn in years. Except for the bare midriff, the tank-style suit was cut conservatively, a little high on the thigh, but not indecently so, the top more like a soft sports bra, ample coverage there, too.

This shouldn't do much for Mr. Pateras, she thought, glimpsing her slim pale limbs in the mirror, her arms too long, her legs too thin, her head looking ridiculously doll-like on her fragile body.

She didn't look much like a Greek woman anymore, her curves melting away. Nursing her mother had taken its toll, the long exhausting hours decimating what little remained of her appetite. No wonder the sisters were always telling her to eat. She wasn't just slender anymore, she was skinny.

Alysia resolved to eat better starting immediately. No more cups of black coffee and nibbles of croissant for breakfast. She'd eat more fruit and vegetables, take bigger portions, make sure she was getting enough of the healthy foods.

The telephone by the bed rang and Alysia started. It rang again and she reached for it.

It was Christos. "Are you coming up or do I need to fetch you?"

"I'm coming," she retorted grimly before slamming the phone back down. She was definitely going back up. The last thing she needed was to be alone with Christos in the bedroom again.

Christos untied the speedboat from the yacht and within minutes they were jumping the white-tipped waves, sending streams of water into the air. The wind whipped Alysia's long hair into a frenzy, and she grabbed at it, futilely trying to bring it under control.

The speedboat hit a big teal-green wave and Alysia threw her hands out to steady herself.

Grinning, Christos shot her a quick glance. "Too fast?" he shouted.

"No!" The speed dazzled her, nearly as much

as the brilliant sunshine and intense sparkle of blue water. She felt immersed in sensation—the speed of the boat, the surge of the engine, the wind whipping through her hair. Could she feel any more alive?

"You must have spent a lot of time on the water with your father," Christos said, his voice breaking up in the wind.

"Not really. He doesn't really like sailing. He usually flies everywhere he needs to go."

They were flying over the water now. Salty spray coating her skin, droplets dancing in her hair. The daring capabilities of the Donzi left her breathless. "This is incredible," she confessed. "I could get addicted to this."

Christos laughed, the sound deep, husky and something turned over in Alysia's chest. She could see herself cradled in his arms, snuggled against his chest as she'd been last night. He'd been so warm and strong, his hard body a refuge.

Fiercely she squashed the image, reminding herself that he'd forced her into this marriage, manipulated her into taking vows. This wasn't a real relationship. He'd *bought* her.

Her pleasure in the boat ride faded and she sat numbly for the remainder of the trip. When

Christos slowed the Donzi to steer into a protected little bay, Alysia felt tears prick her eyes. He made everything seem so interesting. His voice resonated with warmth and she found herself responding to him over and over again.

It made her mad. No, furious. And not just at him, but at herself. Didn't she have any sense? What about her self-control?

The boat motored closer to shore. The bay, shaped by massive rocks and backed by rugged vegetation, looked utterly private. No roads, no other boats, no people. Just the crescent beach with powdery ivory sand and the gentle lapping of waves.

They were alone. Completely alone.

Panic shot through her. Panic because this secluded little beach was nothing short of a lover's paradise. Picnic lunch, leisurely swim and exquisite lovemaking on the pristine sand.

Christos shifted and turning she caught a glimpse of him pulling his T-shirt over his head. His lifted arms tightened his chest, his rippled abdominal muscles contracted. His flat stomach was so lean and hard she itched to trace each sinewy muscle with her finger. A peculiar sensation rippled through her.

More desire, fresh desire flooded her, her

breasts lifting with her swift intake. She felt an ache at the juncture of her thighs, her body suddenly hot and weak all over. She wanted something from him no man had ever given her. Wanted something that until now she didn't even know existed.

Tossing his T-shirt down, Christos looked at her, their eyes meeting. His dark gaze locked with hers, and in his eyes she realized he knew what she was feeling, and that he was feeling it, too.

Her tummy clenched, her nipples hardened, her mouth full and sensitive. All from just one look.

If he touched her she'd melt. She'd puddle at his feet and beg for release. She'd clutch his wrist and move his hand across her body, across her stomach, to cup her breasts and then down again, over her hips to her thighs. She'd show him every spot that tingled. She'd press her mouth to his, taste his skin, drink him in—

Good God, what was happening here?

Jerkily Alysia rose, turned, covered her parted lips and shook her head. No, no, no. Not like this, not here, not with him.

She felt the boat rock and then heard a splash. Christos was in the water. He waded to the beach, tied the speedboat to an iron ring drilled in one of the massive rock formations.

He returned to the boat and reach for her. "Let me give you a hand."

"Don't touch me!" Color washed her cheeks. She sounded absolutely terrified.

His eyes narrowed, thick black lashes concealing his expression. "You okay?"

No. She wasn't okay. She was anything but okay. Her heart felt strange and her emotions were wild and she didn't know what was happening to her but she was losing control, felt sickeningly out of control, and this wasn't supposed to happen. Not with him.

It'd been over four years since her marriage to Jeremy ended and in all those years she hadn't been with another man. Four years had passed since she'd last been touched, kissed, caressed. Four years of nothing and now she felt absolutely crazy with sensation.

"I can manage," she choked, resenting the fact that he stirred her up, that he *mattered*.

Christos shrugged, his lips compressed, and without a word gathered the picnic basket and towels from inside the boat and headed back to shore.

Alysia sat in the tethered boat, hands knotted in her lap and watched him drop the basket and towels into the sand before he returned to the water to swim. As the boat bobbed she followed his progress. He was a strong swimmer, his long, toned arms slicing through the waves, his dark head turning at regular intervals for air.

He'd covered the bay, reached the far end of the cove and prepared to turn around. Alysia pulled off her skirt and top and dived over the edge of the boat, swimming quickly to shore. The water actually felt wonderful, not too warm or too cold, just refreshing.

On the beach she toweled off, and then spread her towel to dry. She sat down on her damp towel and watched Christos's approach. He was on his back now, lazily swimming along the shore. His dark head was thrown back, his muscular arms rotating in impossibly smooth arcs.

Poseidon. God of the Ocean.

Suddenly another boat motored into the bay and anchored not far from Christos's Donzi. The group piled out, several families it seemed, mothers spreading blankets and towels on the sand, while the children splashed in the surf. The fathers sat together, a circle of male authority and Alysia darkly noted that while the men sat, the women did all the work. Typical.

Christos waded out of the ocean, water streaming, dark hair curling wetly on his muscular chest. He dropped to the sand next to her. Instinctively she scooted over, needing more space. Christos gave her a peculiar look. "Nervous?" he asked.

"No!"

"Good. Because we are married, Alysia. This is going to be a real relationship."

Her pained expression didn't go unnoticed. Christos's jaw tightened as he watched her from beneath lowered lashes. Her face was like a canvas, storm after storm crossing the finely drawn features.

He scooped a palm of sand, letting the warm grains trickle between his fingers. "Why did you marry me? What changed your mind?"

Her head jerked up, long blond hair wet, clinging to her slim shoulder. "What?"

"You changed your mind about marrying me. Why?"

She didn't answer and he reached out, opened his palm, trickling the soft sand to fall onto the inside of her arm. Alysia snatched her arm away and the warm grains slid to her inner thigh.

The pale grains of sand on her taut thigh were too irresistible to ignore. He lightly brushed the trail of sand from her thigh. Alysia gasped and jerked her knees closed, trapping his hand. He felt the smooth plane of muscle in her thigh, the heat of her body, the silky satin of her skin.

A faint tremor coursed through her. He felt it ripple through him and glancing at her, he arched one eyebrow. "This is nice."

Pink color darkened her cheeks, a blush of mortification. Her knees opened and she shoved his hand away from her leg.

"I rather liked it there," he drawled.

"Keep your hands to yourself."

"I want a marriage, Alysia. I want you."

"You said you'd give me time."

"I am. I have. But how much more time is necessary? You're attracted to me—"

"You've quite an imagination, Mr. Pateras, if you honestly believe that!" she interrupted, her head lifting, scorn flashing in her dark blue eyes.

He grinned, enjoying the flash and fire in her eyes. He liked it when she was angry, liked the fury and the challenge he saw buried there. "I do have a rather vivid imagination and I've a number of ideas I'd like to try with you."

"I might not be a virgin, Mr. Pateras, but I'm afraid I lack your level of sexual expertise. You might be better off finding a partner that could better satisfy your needs."

"I don't want a mistress. I want you."

"No."

"Why can't I want you?"

"Because you don't even know me." She dug her hands into the sand, burying her skin to the wrist. "And you can't want someone you've only just met."

"Why not?"

"Because. It's just not right."

"Ah, your morals. I see. You'll marry a man to escape your father but you won't stoop low enough to want him."

"No, that's not it."

"That's exactly it. You'd find it a whole lot easier to accept our arrangement if you were forced to endure my touch, then you could blame it on me. But the truth is, you want my touch and that makes you angry."

Alysia jumped to her feet and began brushing the sand from the back of her legs with tangible violence. "I'm not attracted to you, I don't want you and I want nothing to do with you."

"Little late for that, don't you think?"

Suddenly she stiffened, and raised a hand to shield her eyes as she stared out toward the water. Her lips parted in a silent oh, her focus entirely fixed on the tide. He felt her tension, her slender body taut, her breath bottled. She stood like that another couple of seconds before running frantically to the water's edge.

Alysia saw the small body floating face down, arms outstretched, legs apart. She heard a scream, someone was screaming and she lunged into the water, grabbing at the child, flipping him up.

Breathe, she shouted, breathe.

The little boy wiggled, blue rubber mask framing his dark startled eyes. The sea-green snorkel fell from between his clenched baby teeth.

He wasn't dead. He was swimming. Snorkeling.

Her legs turned to jelly and she nearly collapsed into the water, still clutching the little boy to her chest.

People surged towards her. Women, men, the other children, everyone yelling at once.

"Down," the little boy imperiously demanded, no longer frightened, just angry. "Put me down now."

Above the commotion she caught Christos's gaze, his dark eyes fixed on her. There was no anger in his eyes, no expression at all. Weakly she set the child down, placing him on his feet.

A woman, his mother most likely, yanked him into her arms, turning on Alysia in a tirade of angry Greek. Alysia saw the woman's mouth move, flapping, flapping, flapping, but heard nothing the mother said, her brain dazzled by silence, stunned to stillness by the wretched memory of death.

Christos worked through the crowd, circling her shoulders with one arm, pushing the others away. "Shall we go?"

She nodded, her brain dimly aware of the pressure of his arm around her body, his size shielding her from the others nearby.

Her mouth felt parched, dry like the sand. They walked across the beach, leaving the others behind. Christos stopped briefly, bending over to gather their towels and shirts.

At the boat he undid the knotted rope. She waded to the boat, water surging around her thighs, swirling to her hips. She climbed up the boat's ladder and moved toward the driver's seat.

Christos glanced at her as the speedboat sliced through the ocean on the way back to the yacht, but he said nothing, and for that, she was grateful.

She couldn't look at him, couldn't talk to him, too mired in grief. Her stomach cramped, pain contorting in her belly. She clutched her hair in one hand and hunched over the side of the Donzi, throwing up into the saltwater.

Alexi.

Christos had seen the look on her face as she'd pulled the little boy up, snorkel, mask and all, it was a look of dread and terror, the expression of one who has seen a ghost.

Toweling off after his shower, Christos quickly dressed, donning black trousers and a fine white dress shirt.

She hadn't wanted to talk about what happened on the beach and he hadn't pressed for an explanation. It was enough that they both knew she'd run for the boy, seeing something else, thinking something else.

Christos saw enough today to feel worry of his own. Alysia's ghost would haunt her forever if he didn't try to help. He had to do something. But what?

He slid his arms into his black tuxedo jacket, grateful they'd be dining out tonight. They were dining on Cephalonia tonight, joining Christos's closest friends at Constantine Pappas's elegant villa, and he thought the party atmosphere would be good for Alysia, especially in light of what happened on the beach today.

He'd told her that dress for dinner was formal and while knotting his tie, Christos found himself wondering what she'd wear.

He imagined the long gowns she might pick from, beaded fabrics, velvet fabrics, delicate silk fabrics, but nothing he thought, could be more seductive than the conservative two-piece swimsuit she'd worn at the beach today.

Her suit, a pale pink tank-style with thin spaghetti straps, clung to her breasts and hips like a second skin. And wet, the fabric revealed the contours of her nipple, the cleft in her derriere, the protruding hipbones. He'd wanted to take her right there in the warm sand, pull her down beneath him and bury himself inside her.

Jutting his jaw to better see his collar,

Christos knotted his black bow tie, then snapped off the bathroom light. Time to check on his bride.

CHAPTER FIVE

"You didn't tell me we were joining other shipowners for dinner!" Alysia stared at Christos in dismay, her thin silk shawl folded over her arm, her small beaded purse clutched in her fingers. She'd imagined a quiet dinner alone with Christos. Instead they'd be spending the evening with old, powerful Greek families, families that knew too much of her family history.

"I thought I'd mentioned it."

"No, you did not."

He inclined his head, his black hair gleaming like polished onyx, his white shirt a perfect foil for his dark, hard features. "I apologize, then. It must have slipped my mind. We've been invited to Constantine Pappas's for dinner. You know him, I believe?"

Oh, she knew Constantine Pappas very well. Not only had he once been her father's best friend, but he'd created tremendous, and lasting, controversy in the Greek shipping industry by inviting foreigners to invest in his company, investors like Christos.

Suddenly it dawned on her, that Christos might very well be Constantine's silent foreign investor. "You're not…you don't…with Mr. Pappas?"

"Are you asking if I'm his business partner? The answer is yes. I've backed his business for nearly ten years."

"Constantine and my father are enemies." But she saw from Christos's expression he already knew that. "But my father doesn't know that, does he?"

"No. I've always been a silent investor. And I've had my own business. Your father only knows me as an American holding company."

"He doesn't really know you, does he?"

"We're business acquaintances. Not friends."

She felt a bubble of hysteria. "So how did you make the deal? Did he ask to see your stock portfolio? Your savings accounts, what?"

"I sent him some income tax statements."

"Income tax statements. Amazing. You had money, he had a daughter, a deal was struck." Shock made her tongue thick. Tears welled in her eyes. "How many men did he go through trying to find one rich enough?"

"I don't know, Alysia, it doesn't really matter anymore, does it?"

"Not to you, because you won. You got Lemos's name, Lemos's ships, Lemos's business and Lemos's daughter." The shame of it made her skin crawl. What kind of man sold off his only child? What kind of man would sell her to a virtual stranger? Christos wasn't even Greek. He was American. He was everything her father despised and yet it didn't matter because Christos was rich, filthy rich, appallingly rich.

"I hate you!" She swung her beaded purse, swiping him in the chest. "I hate that you'd do this to me. To *us*."

The moment she'd said "us" she'd realized why she felt so crazy the past few days. If she'd met Christos anywhere else, in any other situation, she would have fallen in love with him, fallen for his impossible good looks, his strength, his sensuality. Instead marrying him like this destroyed everything. He was a mercenary and all the charm in the world couldn't change that one horrible fact.

"I'm sorry." There was no emotion in his deep voice, nothing at all.

"I'm not going with you tonight," she said, blinking away the tears, her chest tender, her throat sore. "If you want to celebrate your victory, you go without me."

"Constantine is throwing the party for us. It'd be a slap in his face to not show up."

"I can't go there. I can't face everyone."

"Why not? Because you feel like an outsider? Guess what, darling, I've spent my life on the outside. I know what it's like to be the subject of constant speculation. I've heard the criticism about my past. But I don't care what others think. I don't need to please anyone but myself."

"Obviously," she flung back. He might consider himself Greek, but he was still an American. He'd been born in another country, raised with another society's values. As much as he wanted to think of himself as Greek, he was still alien, would always remain alien, despite his marriage to her. "I'm not going tonight. I want no part of this. You've made your deal with my father. Now leave me alone."

He shrugged, unmoved. "You made a deal with me, too, and I expect you to hold up your end of the bargain."

"It's not a fair bargain!"

"You should have thought about it earlier. But since you are a Pateras now, you shall do I as ask."

"Ask?"

"Insist." His dark eyes narrowed, his jaw jutting harshly, hinting at emotions he so far hadn't revealed. "As my wife you will go with me tonight and treat Constantine Pappas with respect, indeed, reverence. Is that clear?"

The yacht slowly motored into the harbor, pulling up alongside the dock. Alysia and Christos didn't speak as they stepped ashore, and the silence continued once they were seated in the waiting Rolls-Royce.

In the car Alysia wondered how much Christos actually knew about her father's relationship with Constantine. The two had once been best friends, growing up together on Oinoussai and attending college together. It wasn't until they'd both gone to work in the shipping industry that their friendship changed. Always competitive, they grew suspicious of the other. Suddenly a lifelong friendship turned into a bitter rivalry, exploding one summer into wild accusations of cheating, stealing, lying, and petty crime.

The chauffeured car pulled up in front of

Constantine's enormous villa, the white marble building glimmering with light, and Alysia brought herself to speak. "Mr. Pappas must be shocked by our marriage."

"Everyone's a bit intrigued," he answered.

And that was putting it mildly, she suspected. Alysia gripped her pale blue silk shawl and drew the fringed edges to her breast, her dress the color of aquamarine. "People will gossip."

"They do anyway."

"Yet everyone knows he was trying to find a husband for me. He'd practically advertised in all the Greek papers!"

Christos's white teeth gleamed in the darkness. "You forget, everyone believes ours is a love match. We had a secret wedding. Most people will assume we've gone behind your father's back."

"My reputation."

"Is in tatters," he agreed, reaching out to touch the slender sapphire-and-diamond bracelet encircling her wrist.

The chauffeur swung the back door of the Rolls-Royce open and stepped back, silently attentive.

But Alysia couldn't bring herself to move.

She felt tricked somehow, outwitted into this game. All her life she'd been manipulated by her father and now she was married to a man who intended to do the same. A lump formed in her throat. "I thought you might have been different."

Christos's jaw tightened, a small muscle popping. He ignored the chauffeur, his full attention on her. "Sometimes we have to bend the rules to get ahead."

"Bend the rules? You mean, break them, don't you? You play every bit as underhanded as my father."

She felt the weight of his gaze. "Perhaps, but my motives are different."

"So you say!"

"I guess you'll just have to trust me."

"Trust you?" Slowly she shook her head, disbelief coloring her speech. "I'd trust my father before I trusted you. At least I've known him all my life. You, I just met."

Christos's large, callused palm clasped her clenched fists, gathering them into his hands. He kissed her clenched fists and then released them. "Sometimes strangers can be blessings in disguise. Now come, it's time we went inside."

Alysia had to admit that Constantine was a

better host than her father would have been. He greeted her warmly, kissing her on both cheeks, congratulating her on her marriage. If he felt acrimonious toward her, there was no sign of it. She found herself struggling, though, to answer his polite inquiries about her father with equal enmity. Clearly Constantine sought to put past tensions behind them. She could do no less.

"Well done," Christos whispered into her ear, as they moved from Constantine and his wife to another couple.

She tried to hold herself aloof as Christos discussed business with the other man, but he snaked an arm around her waist and drew her firmly against his side. His fingers kneaded softly into her waist, moving down slightly to caress her hip.

Alysia attempted to draw away, and his arm only tightened, holding her more firmly. An escape was impossible.

Throwing her head back, she parted her lips to protest but caught the warning light in his eyes. *Remember where you are,* his expression said, *remember who we're with.*

Men. Businessmen. And Christos was conducting business.

She swallowed the bitterness in her mouth, unwillingly flashing back to a time she'd impulsively interrupted one of her father's meetings to ask if she could join a group of teenagers heading to an Athens disco. She'd never been to a disco, never been dancing. It had sounded exciting and despite her mother's warning, she'd gone to her father, desperate for permission. Her mother had been right. Her father was furious at the interruption, slapping her sharply across the face in front of a dozen men. He'd slapped her and sent her to bed.

Instead of dancing she'd wept for hours, trapped in her loneliness, and her shame.

Her father had crushed her feeble attempts at independence, refusing to permit her even the smallest of freedoms, wanting the traditional Greek daughter.

The slow circle of Christos's thumb against her hipbone permeated the cloud of memory and with a small jolt, her attention returned to the business discussion and the warmth of Christos's hand on her hip.

Heat shimmered within her, a spark of awareness that made her tingle from head to toe. And again she felt desire stir, languorous need awakening, threatening to possess her rational mind.

As Christos and the other man discussed the European market and the American economy, Alysia's head began to swim, dazed by the tension flooding her limbs. As the conversation continued, she heard fewer words, too aware of the blood surging through her, the tightening in her belly making her thoughts race in a dangerous direction. She'd never felt desire like this. It made her desperate to answer the emptiness aching inside her.

Just when she thought she couldn't stand it anymore, the couple moved on and she caught his fingers in one hand, lifting them from her hip.

"Don't," she gritted, undone by the intimacy, overwhelmed by her hungry response.

"We're supposed to be happy. We're newlyweds in love."

She stiffened in silent protest, hating how powerless she felt, helpless with needs she couldn't control. If he could make her feel this way in public, what would happen tonight when they were alone?

She couldn't let him make love to her. She wasn't on birth control, she doubted he'd wear a condom. He'd made it clear that he wanted children and he wanted them soon. One of these nights he'd push to consummate the marriage. Maybe even tonight.

She had to leave, couldn't afford to wait for another opportunity.

She had to go. Immediately. The party was the perfect cover. So many beautiful people coming and going, music playing, a hum of activity. Christos wouldn't even know she'd gone until too late.

Afraid she'd lose her resolve, she turned to him, murmured an excuse, a pretense of needing to use the ladies' room. Quickly she moved away, out of the white-and-gold ballroom, down the hall, continuing to a narrower passage, one that cut through to the kitchen.

She ignored the kitchen staff, her head high, her purse dangling carelessly from her wrist. She didn't run. Just kept her gaze fixed on the door before her.

The driveway, lined with a dozen expensive imported cars, Bentleys and Rolls-Royces, Mercedes, Jaguars and Ferraris, looked like an exotic car show. Alysia passed the parked cars with barely a glance, nodding briefly at the cluster of drivers who stood in front of a marble lion smoking.

One driver—her driver?—called out to her, asking if she needed a ride. She shook her head and continued on, knowing that a taxi would be the safest option.

She flagged the taxi, a four-person Mercedes, not far from the Trapano Bridge at the south end of Argostoli. Close to the harbor, she could smell the pungent salt in the air, and the hum of the ocean.

"Where to?" the driver asked.

"Sami," she said, directing him to the island's other port, a small village with ferry access to other islands, as well as the mainland. And Sami lay miles from bustling Argostoli with its community of wealthy shipowners who knew too much about her and the Lemos family. No one in Sami would know her.

Alysia pawned her diamond-and-sapphire bracelet in Sami for necessary cash. Out of the money she'd gotten for the bracelet she paid for her ferry ride to Lefkas, and then on Lefkas, was able to buy a one-way plane ticket on Olympic Airways for Athens.

How ironic, she thought with a small twist of her lips, that the bracelet, a gift from her father on her sixteenth birthday, should now buy her freedom.

If only she'd taken the bracelet to Paris, pawned it there. She could have used the money. It might have saved Alexi.

Suddenly she saw Alexi's perfect face, his silvery blond curls, his small arms outstretched, floating.

Floating.

Alysia squeezed her eyes shut, pressed her knuckles against her mouth and fought to erase the memory. For a long moment she sat hunched, her insides frozen, her body rigid with endless, wordless grief.

To think that a bracelet could save her baby's life.

To think that a bracelet could have saved her sanity.

But, no, she couldn't think like that. She'd promised her mother she wouldn't think like that. Those thoughts were the dark ones that ate her alive. Those thoughts nearly destroyed her before. She had to live in the moment. There was only the moment. The past was gone. And the future lay ahead.

In Athens she called an old childhood friend, Lalia, to see if she couldn't perhaps stay with her for a few days until she arranged for a new passport.

Lalia, who'd always been very modern, so far forgoing marriage to pursue a career as a textile designer, was more than happy to accommodate Alysia, especially as she was preparing to fly to London on business and was anxious to find a housesitter for her high-strung cat.

"Zita's very sensitive and he hates disruption," Lalia said, gathering her travel bags and taxi fare together. "Don't be disappointed if he won't play. He'll probably hide until I come home. Just feed him and pretend everything's normal."

Alysia checked her smile. "How like a man."

"Speaking of men, I thought you were married?"

"Rumors." Alysia held the door open for her friend. "Now go, before you miss your flight. And don't worry about a thing. Zita and I will get along just fine."

The first day alone Alysia did nothing but sleep, and read, and sleep some more. The second day she made some calls. The government office handling passports couldn't help her without a copy of her birth certificate, which would require her coming into the office in person to fill out the necessary paperwork.

She hung up the phone and reluctantly conceded that she'd have to visit the government building in person. She'd hoped to avoid going out in public but perhaps if she donned a hat and sunglasses she'd pass unrecognized.

Zita, the onyx-colored, tailless cat, poked his head out from beneath the lace curtains at the window and gazed at her through narrowed eyes.

Alysia imagined she saw disapproval in Zita's slitted eyes and turned her back on the cat. Everything's fine, she firmly told herself. Don't let a cat put your nerves on edge.

The labyrinth of government offices exercised Alysia's strained patience. An afternoon spent waiting in long lines, filling out paperwork in duplicate, only to be sent to another endless line, turned a beautiful autumn afternoon into sheer torture.

Three hours after entering the government building, Alysia left, having been informed that the passport, even if rushed, would take two weeks to process.

Two weeks.

Alysia let herself into Lalia's apartment. Closing the door with one hand, she kicked off her leather loafers and dropped her purse on top of the shoes.

Barefoot she padded down the hall and into the kitchen, opening the refrigerator door for a bottle of chilled mineral water. "Zita," she called. "Hungry?"

The cat didn't answer. Of course, she hadn't expected it to answer, but people were supposed to take to their cats, right?

With her bottle of water in hand she headed toward the living room, richly patterned rugs—all Lalia's design—beneath her bare feet. "Zita! Where are you? Still hiding?"

She stopped short. A man, a tall, broad-shouldered man, sat on the sofa—no, dominated the sofa—with a tailless black cat curled in his lap.

Christos.

CHAPTER SIX

"Hello, Mrs. Pateras," Christos said, his tone disarmingly conversational as he caressed Zita's dark head. "How was your day?"

She stared at the broad tanned hand cupped over the cat's head, strong fingers slowly, deliberately scratching behind Zita's short, pointy ears, and began to tremble. Her legs suddenly went nerveless, turning into mush.

The bottle of water almost slid from her fingers. "Christos."

"You remembered," he retorted with a savage twist of his lips. He rose so swiftly from the couch that he nearly dumped Zita on his feet. "I wasn't sure if you would. But then, I'm only your *husband*."

He smiled at her, and yet there was nothing remotely kind in his expression, his features granitelike, his dark eyes glittering.

Zita meowed a protest at being so unceremoniously dumped from his comfortable resting place, but Christos ignored the cat, and clenching his fists, took a quick step toward her before checking himself.

She felt his anger, his barely controlled temper, and a sick tremor coursed through her. "Ahh…"

"What was that, sweetheart? Cat got your tongue?"

His joke went in one ear and out the other. She couldn't speak, her tongue wooden, her jaw taut, fear turning her inside out. Instead she helplessly shook her head, her gaze darting to the door and then back at Christos.

"I wouldn't try it. You won't get away and you'll only make me angry."

"And you're not angry now?" she flashed, finding her voice, and simultaneously stunned by the weakness in her knees. She felt as if her legs would buckle beneath her any moment now.

"Oh, I'm angry all right, I'm fit to be tied. But my father has persuaded me to show you mercy."

Mercy. What an odd, terrifying, and yet incredibly Greek thing to say.

Christos moved toward her, closing the distance between them. She was forced to tilt her head back to see his face, realizing belatedly she'd forgotten his height, and the sheer size of him.

"How did you find me?"

"You didn't think I would?" A black eyebrow lifted, expressing surprise.

"You didn't know I was on the mainland. You don't know Lilia."

"But I know you." His eyes gleamed, dark and hard, fixing on her face with predatory instinct. His smile deepened and it was the coldest, most malevolent smile she'd ever seen. "I knew you'd apply for a passport. I knew you'd try to leave Greece."

Her tongue thick and heavy, wouldn't form words. Instead she stared at him, dry-mouthed, wide-eyed, unable to think a single coherent thought. Fear pummeled her brain, melted her bones. "No…" she whispered helplessly. "It couldn't have been so easy."

"Sweetheart, it was too easy. Like taking candy from a baby." He stopped in front of her, reached out and lifted one gold strand from her shoulder, sliding the tendril through his fingers as if silk. "You see, sweet Alysia, I have a home here in Athens. I spend a great deal of time here. New York may be my headquarters, but I maintain offices in Athens, too. I have employees in Athens, and they've been watching you, from the moment you flew into the airport to the moment you just walked in the door."

Horror filled her. He'd had her followed the past few days. She'd been under surveillance. A prisoner, his prisoner, and she didn't even know it.

Slowly he coiled the tendril around his finger, wrapping it into a honey ribbon. He wrapped it tighter then gave a little pull, making her wince.

"You made a fool out of me," he murmured with another small tug. "In front of my colleagues and friends. You humiliated me at the Pappas's, created quite a stir. You should be punished. How shall I punish you? Any suggestions?"

Her tongue continued to cleave to the roof of her mouth. Her heart hammered. "No."

One of Christos's thick black brows lifted. "No suggestions, or no to punishment?"

All this time she thought—believed—she was free. These past several days had felt like heaven. Instead she'd been his, remained his possession. It made her want to weep with frustration. "Why did you think I'd want to leave Greece?"

"You hate Greece. You feel trapped here. I imagine you wanted to fly to England, look up your mother's family." Carefully he unwound the tendril.

"You're awfully clever, aren't you?"

"No. You're just awfully predictable."

"Go to hell!"

Almost absently he caressed her cheek. "Don't be childish, Alysia. It's not becoming."

She flinched at his touch, drawing sharply away. "I can't believe you had me followed."

"How could you think I wouldn't protect my investment?"

The softness in his voice, the husky tone, contrasted cruelly with his expression. His eyes said it all. She'd betrayed him.

He reached into a pocket and withdrew the diamond-and-sapphire bracelet she'd recently pawned. "Here. Put it back on."

She cringed at the bracelet, hating the reminder of the power Christos held over her. "No."

"Do it. Or I will." Without waiting for her to answer he took her hand, flipped her wrist open and snapped the glittering bangle onto her slender arm.

It looked completely incongruous with her leather loafers and casual clothes yet it felt heavy, like iron, he was shackling her to him, taking control of her life again.

"Do not take it off," he said curtly, "and do not think of running away again."

"I refuse to be an object, Christos!"

"You're no object. You're my wife." He tilted her chin up with one of his fingers, his dark eyes searching her mutinous expression. "I erred in judgment once, but I won't make the same mistake again. It's time I exerted my rights in this marriage and time you behaved like a proper Greek wife."

She knew, a split second in advance, that he was going to kiss her. Yet there was no escaping him. His mouth crushed hers, grinding her lips apart, his tongue boldly thrusting inside her mouth, stabbing at the softness with ill-concealed contempt.

But even as his tongue lashed at her sensitive contours, her body warmed, her innermost muscles tightening in anticipation. Despite everything, she wanted him.

Christos's dark head lifted and he gazed into

her eyes, a mocking smile etched on his lips. "I'm beginning to understand why your father found it necessary to keep you locked up. You're wild. You're utterly wanton."

Heat burned in bands across the tops of her cheekbones. She tried to take a step back but his hands clasped her at the waist, fingers dipping into the small of her spine.

Again his mouth crushed hers, his tongue raking the sensitive contours of her mouth, thrusting at the hollow of her cheek, beneath her tongue, even tracing the roof of her mouth.

She clung to him, clasping his arms, her legs without strength. She felt mindless with wanting and helplessly opened her mouth wider to him, her tongue finding his, teasing.

He moved to strip her of her jeans, but his hand stilled on her tummy. "Stop me, now—" he muttered thickly, but she didn't speak, and she didn't answer him.

With a groan he tugged her jeans down and then her panties, pulling them off her ankles and casting them to the ground. She felt him grind his hips against hers, his erection creating friction between her thighs.

He worked his zipper down, dropped his own trousers even as his fingers slid between her legs, finding her heat and to her shame, her eager moisture.

Christos dropped her to the ground and parted her legs with his knees. He held her bottom in his hands and without a word, drove into her.

She gasped at the thrust, her body forced to accommodate his size, and she buried her knuckles into his back, overwhelmed by the intensity of his body filling hers, joining them intimately together.

He shifted, easing slowly out of her and then with a kiss on her neck, entered her again, filling her once more, making stars sputter against her tightly closed eyes.

And he made love to her without a word, without another kiss, just moving inside her slowly, deeply to pull out and enter again, and again, and again.

He felt long, hard, thick, and yet his skin was as smooth as silk, his hips hard and narrow, in her hands. She clung to him as he moved inside her, scarcely daring to breathe, caught up in the pictures he was painting in her head. Him, her, the constellation of stars.

She felt him tense, a soft groan coming from his lips, and as he surged forward, deeper into her, she felt herself step out into the darkest night and fall, silently, blindly into waves of sensation. She rode the waves with desperation, clasping Christos's shoulders, burying her face against his broad chest.

There was no one but them. No place but now. Nothing but this.

Him, her, his body still straining, his hands now cradling her head.

She'd never come before. Never had an orgasm.

"I'm sorry," Christos said thickly, untangling his limbs, his skin still damp, his black hair disheveled. He drew away, rubbed his face with one hand, stood up.

He was sorry and he was done. So that's how he felt. It wasn't what she'd imagined, wasn't what she'd experienced. Nothing beautiful for him. Just a physical act. A form of exercise.

She sat up slowly, realizing they both still wore their shirts but not pants.

Thank goodness she'd just had her period. Thank God she shouldn't be fertile now. She couldn't, wouldn't, conceive.

He stepped into his underwear and then his pants. "Did I hurt you?" he demanded, his voice pitched low, almost rough.

"No." She wanted to tell him it had been incredible, that even without love, it was the most sensual experience of her life. She'd answered each of his thrusts by lifting her own hips, wrapped her arms around his neck to draw him even closer, wanting it all, wanting him. But now...no pants, the dampness of him inside her, the obvious disgust on his face...

Good thing there was no love between them, no love lost, either.

What had they done? What had she been thinking?

Christos raked a hand through his dark hair, attempting to comb it into submission. "Dress. It's time to go. My driver is downstairs waiting."

He didn't speak on the short drive home. He felt Alysia's revulsion. It mirrored his own.

He was appalled by his actions, stunned that he'd forced himself on her. He'd taken her without regard to her feelings, or her needs.

Christos was grateful when the limousine drew in front of his estate, the palatial marble villa rising from behind iron gates and exotic greenery.

The gates magically slid open and the car continued up the driveway, the powerful engine vibrating like a great beast. He couldn't wait to get out of the car and as far from Alysia's accusing eyes as possible.

He'd promised to respect her, promised to never force himself on her, and yet what did he do but throw her onto the ground and bury himself inside her?

Alysia cast a desperate glance behind her at the high wrought-iron fence and gatehouse before turning to face the dozen employees gathered on the villa's front steps.

Christos nodded at them and then gestured toward Alysia, his expression grim. "The wife," he announced curtly, before continuing up the sweeping circular staircase, leaving her to follow like a child in disgrace.

She flushed, and wordlessly trailed after him, aware of the cool scrutiny of his employees.

Reaching the top of the stairs Christos showed her into a lofty room that was obviously his own private quarters. Desk, leather armchairs, reading lamps.

He closed the door, motioned her to one of the leather chairs. She sat gingerly on the edge of one, wondering what would come next.

"I'm sorry I lost my temper. I behaved like a brute. It won't happen like that again." His speech was sharp, and short. He leaned against the shut door, his arms crossing over his chest, muscles tight, tension emanating from him in great silent waves. "Your father warned me you'd try to run away. He said you'd go the first chance you got. I thought I was prepared. Yet I let down my guard at the party."

She squirmed inwardly realizing how humiliated he must have been at Constantine's. Everyone looking for her. Everyone aware that his new bride had deserted him.

"Your father called," he continued. "He offered his services, apologized for your behavior."

She ducked her head, even more mortified. Her father calling to offer *his* services!

"I told him no thank you, of course." Christos's dark gaze met hers, his expression flinty. "I said you'd be back in no time and soon fulfilling your duty, providing me with sons."

Her heart beat faster. Her throat threatened to seal close. And still she didn't speak so he plunged on. "We will make love until you conceive. We will start that family. You will prove to your father—and the other Greek ship owners—that my faith in you isn't misplaced, that you know and accept your responsibility."

"No."

Her voice was but a whisper and yet he heard it. "No what, Alysia?"

"No, I will not give you children." She lifted her head, looked him in the eye. "No sons. Not even daughters. No heirs."

"Is this a philosophical issue for you? Part of your rebellion against Greek society?"

"A personal issue."

"Ah, then we can work through this."

"No, we can't work through this. You married the wrong woman. You chose the wrong wife. A hundred women could have filled my position. A hundred women would have begged to bear your children. I, on the other hand, will not."

His smile had all but disappeared and she slid instinctively backward, hips hugging the chair, even though he hadn't moved from the door. "I have tried to be patient, Alysia, tried to understand your feelings, but my patience is about gone. We need to move forward. We need to start our future."

He approached her quietly, crouching at her feet, his palms sliding up her shins, over her knees, electrifying her legs. Awareness exploded in her middle, tension coiling in her lower belly making her thighs tremble.

Christos's dark gaze momentarily met hers and he smiled—if the slight twist of lips could be called a smile—acknowledging her unwilling response.

His palm shaped her outer thigh and followed with his body. She felt the press of his chest against her knees as he parted them, moving between her legs.

Blood pumped through her veins, heat searing her face, shredding countless nerve endings beneath her skin. It shocked her that she could still want him, shocked her that she could feel so raw and physical even after what had taken place at Lilia's apartment.

"Not again," she gritted as his thumbs caressed the lean line of her thigh.

"And just what do you think I'm going to do?" he drawled, his voice never more husky, never more American than now.

Her mouth felt so dry that it cleaved to the roof of her mouth. She stared into his face, drowning in sensation, painfully aware of the size distinction between them.

"You're going to want more...sex," she retorted, her voice more breathy than angry, her body so traitorously warm she despised herself.

"I'll take more time, this time, I'll take it slow." He dropped a fleeting kiss against the side of her neck, just beneath her earlobe.

She tried to kick him again. He held her tighter. "You are the worst kind of man."

"The worst kind? Lower than your father?" He pressed another equally brief, equally tantalizing kiss to the outline of her breast, just brushing the taut, aching nipple. "That is a shame."

Warmth surged through her, traitorous warmth and she wanted to weep with frustration. She couldn't believe she'd want a man she hated so much, and yet her body, her stupid wretched, needy body was responding to him in hungry, wanton desperation.

His lips found her nipple again, closing around the exquisitely sensitive bud, suckling it through her blouse. She squirmed helplessly, fire and need rolling through her in great waves. For a half second she clung to him, closing her eyes and giving herself over to the pleasure of desire. She allowed herself to feel it all—the throb of his muscular body, the heat simmering beneath her skin, the insistent need between her thighs—and then when the craving became too strong, she wrenched away, rolling out from beneath Christos's arm to stand across the room, facing the window.

"You don't like me, I understand that," he said quietly, his voice devoid of all emotion, "but we're married. We have to make this work."

She squeezed her eyes closed as if to shut out his voice. "You will never get what you want from me."

He rose, yet he didn't leave. She felt his presence as if he still held her in his arms. "I don't know what happened between you and your first husband, but Jeremy Winston did something to you—"

"*No.*"

"He put a curse on you, froze your heart, trapping you like Sleeping Beauty in the tower."

"You don't know what you're talking about."

"I know enough. I know your marriage ended with heartbreak. I know you spent nearly two years in Switzerland, after you left the Sanatorium, trying to find yourself again."

Alysia's head felt light, so light that it tingled at the top. "I can't talk about it."

"Why not? What happened, Alysia?"

"Nothing happened."
"Something did—"
"No!"
"Something so dark, so terrible—"

The words surged around her, words sweeping, blurring until the room spun with words and she heard nothing more.

Christos had called a doctor and the doctor, after a thorough exam, recommended rest, vitamins and more iron. Women, the doctor said, are often anemic and if they wanted to conceive, it would be wise for Alysia to increase her iron intake.

"I'm not that anemic," she protested, a day after the doctor had been called, and facing her third steak in a row. "I can get iron from spinach. I don't have to eat a platter of steaks."

"We can't have babies if you're not strong."

"I am strong, and I don't have to gorge on meat to conceive. Now back off with the bully routine. I won't be intimidated."

Christos visibly fought to control his temper. "I'm not trying to intimidate you. I just want you to be careful."

"I am careful. I'm also bored. I'd like to get some fresh air. If that's all right with you, of course."

He muttered something beneath his breath and shook his head, obviously eager to end the discussion. "You may go to the pool. I'll have the maid put towels on a lounge chair for you. But don't stay out in the sun too long. You don't want to burn."

Alysia dragged the chaise lounge from beneath the umbrella closer to the pool where she could enjoy the sparkle of the sun on the clear, aquamarine water. She'd brought a book downstairs with her but it turned out to be a rather dry historical account requiring more concentration than she could muster at the moment. After a half hour of reading, she tossed the hardback aside and gave herself over to the pleasure of nothing.

The sun felt wonderful on her back and unhooking the bikini top, she wiggled into the towel, drinking in the steady warm sunshine and promptly fell asleep.

Sometime later, she had no idea how long, she felt a touch, a lovely caress, like feathers or velvet dragged gently across her bare spine.

Sighing she nestled into the towel, not wanting to lose the delicious sensation. The leisurely caress repeated itself, and her lower tummy tightened, warming. She breathed in slowly, not wanting to open her eyes and lose the dreamy sensation.

The velvetlike touch played at the edge of her bikini bottoms, lingering over the line of skin just above the patch of fabric. She wiggled a little, teased by the touch and yet disappointed by the brevity.

Suddenly it clasped her bottom, no tentative touch, but a large hand firmly cupping the curve of cheek.

This was no dream.

Alysia leaped up, snatching her bikini top even as she struggled to cover herself. "Christos!"

The tall shadow shifted, creating a sliver of sunlight where darkness had been. He sat down on the lounge chair next to her. "You should have put lotion on. You've been out here hours and burned yourself to a crisp."

She glanced at her wrist, no watch, and then up at the sun. It had moved. A great deal, actually. A quarter of the way through the sky. "What time is it?" she demanded, struggling to get her bikini top back on without exposing herself.

"Quarter to four."

"What?"

He watched her fumble with the flimsy fabric with interest. "Perhaps I should help you."

"I don't need your help."

"You need to put something on the burn. You don't want the skin to blister."

"It's never blistered before." Yet her trembling fingers made it almost impossible to adjust the scrap of fabric across her chest. She had a horrible sensation that one nipple, or the other, would pop out at any moment.

"Alysia, I have seen breasts before."

"But never mine."

His lip curled, a black eyebrow winged. Laughter tinged his husky voice. "I'm sure I can handle the shock."

Of course he'd say something smart like that. He was a born wit. Jumping to her feet, she grabbed her towel and slid into her robe with just the briefest flash of flesh. "Unfortunately I don't think I can."

The silk robe felt ice-cold against her hot back and she winced as she tied the silk sash around her waist. "What time is dinner?"

"Drinks at seven. Dinner at nine."

She'd promised to be there, had planned on meeting him, but Alysia hadn't counted on the extent of her sunburn. It was a livid sunburn.

The warm bath had helped, at first, but as soon as she'd lightly toweled off, her entire backside, from shoulders to her insteps, felt like fire.

She couldn't even pull a pair of panties on without tears starting to her eyes. Her bra straps sliced into her now-blistering shoulders. Nothing in her closet looked comfortable. She stripped off the bra, stripped off the underwear and carefully crawled between cool bed sheets.

To hell with dinner. She'd stay in bed instead.

Too proud to summon Christos, she simply didn't show up downstairs at seven.

Quarter after seven, he arrived at the bedroom door.

He didn't bother to knock. He just walked straight in. "Knowing your penchant for running away, I thought I'd check to see if you were still with us."

Alysia drew the bed sheet toward her chin. "As you can see, I'm still here."

"But in bed."

"Yes."

"Is that, by happy chance, an invitation?" His teeth flashed whitely in a crooked grin.

"No."

"But you appear naked."

"Because I'm too sunburned to dress."

"Show me."

Her stomach did a slow, peculiar curl. Heat prickled across the curve of her cheeks. "You want proof?"

"Please."

CHAPTER SEVEN

Prickles of awareness touched her spine, contrasting with the fever raging in her skin. Alysia struggled to deny the feeling. "I'm not going to pull the covers down just so you can see a sunburn."

"You haven't been in the sun for over a year. You could have second- or third-degree burns."

"You're exaggerating. I might be a little sore, but it's just a sunburn."

"I'll be the judge of that." Christos stalked to the edge of the bed and wrenched the covers from her clenched fingers, peeling the sheet back.

Alysia rolled over onto her stomach to protect her front, humiliated by his impersonal scrutiny. "Just a sunburn," she gritted, "I told you. Now will you please allow me some privacy!"

"You're fried to a crisp," he answered, touching the middle of her back.

She couldn't help wincing. It hurt, badly. "*Please*. The covers."

"Not until I put something on your skin first. I've some aloe gel with a topical anesthetic in it that should help."

"Can you at least let me cover my…bottom." She felt his gaze move to the aforementioned and she blushed from head to toe, acutely embarrassed.

"You are modest," he drawled, heading to the bathroom and returning with a hand towel and tube of ointment.

He spread the small towel across her bottom, going to great lengths to adjust it just so, his long fingers brushing the curve of her cheek not just once, but repeatedly, as he slid the small towel up, before tugging it down. To the left. Up a hair. Down a bit, and over to the right.

He was manhandling her and she found it degrading. But that didn't seem to keep her from responding, each brush of his fingers, each slip of the towel sending fiery arcs of feeling through her veins, coiling need in the deepest part of her, a need so strong, so insistent that she throbbed from the inside out.

"That's enough!" she snapped, finding his touch nearly as unbearable as the ache spreading from her womb into her limbs.

His fingers trailed across the dip in her spine, and tugged the small towel higher on her cheek, leaving the underside of her bottom exposed to air. "Are you sure? I wouldn't want to deprive you of your modesty."

"Then perhaps a bigger towel would have been more helpful," she gritted from between clenched teeth.

"I was afraid a bigger towel would irritate the burn."

The cool air seemed to caress her exposed bottom and it took every bit of her self-control to not wiggle. Part of her felt humiliated and another felt shamelessly excited. "You're the one irritating the burn."

He merely laughed softly, the husky sound reverberating from his chest. Unscrewing the cap from the ointment tube, Christos took a seat next to her on the bed.

His thigh brushed her hip and she tensed, shoulders hunching around her ears. She was aware of Christos in every nerve in her body, feeling his strength and warmth as if he were the sun and she the moon.

He rubbed the aloe between his hands and she could hear the slick lotion slurp against his skin. It struck her as an indecent sound, sexual and raw, and the ache in her lower belly intensified. Pressing her inner thighs together, she tried to control her breathing and yet her heart raced, her senses enflamed. She wanted him to touch her even as she feared it.

"Lie still," he commanded, leaning forward, his sinewy thigh pressing against her own. "This might sting a bit."

Sting? The ointment felt like ice. Helplessly she bucked against his hand, wriggling to escape the prickly hot and cold sensations. But he didn't let her escape. He pressed her down against the sheet and continued applying the aloe gel in slow, steady strokes.

Little by little the anesthetic went to work, numbing the worst of the pain and again making her hopelessly aware of Christos's hands stroking her spine. His hands moved over her body, down the length of her spinal column, into the dip of her lower back, and then up, over the flare of her hips.

Heat coursed through her, but this warmth

had nothing to do with the sunburn and everything to do with his sensuous caress.

His fingertips explored the hollow just above the cleft in her cheeks and she wiggled, telling him to move away. He did, but only to move to her flare of hips, caressing up her waist, to the curve of her breasts.

Alysia couldn't breathe. His thumbs stroked the soft swell. Her nipples hardened, the soft flesh prickling with awareness. She wanted more sensation than feathers and butterflies, more than just this soft teasing touch.

His hands returned to her rib cage and then lifted altogether. She drew a short, shallow breath. "Thank you," she choked.

"Not quite done," he answered, lightly massaging her shoulders and nape.

"It's good," she replied, her voice sounding thick and slow.

But how could it be otherwise? His touch sent blood coursing through her veins with dizzying speed. She couldn't catch her breath. Her heart raced too fast. Her body quivered from head to toe, but the greatest tension coiled in her middle, hot and heavy, her inner thighs almost dancing with need.

"I haven't covered everything," he replied,

squeezing another dollop of gel onto the middle of her back.

She wanted to protest but no sound came from her mouth. Instead she closed her eyes, her lips parting, attuned to every shift of his body, every press of his thigh against her own.

Again his palms fanned the width of her rib cage and curved down to cup her breasts, thumbs flicking across taut, swollen nipples.

Mercy.

If there was purgatory, she'd found it. Caught between heaven and hell and she wanted him to stop just as much as she couldn't let him.

Swept away by touch, sensation, raw physical hunger. Years of being nothing but skin and bones and suddenly she was all nerve endings. Alive, humming, hot liquid desire.

Forget prayers and penance, she'd take sin any day.

He stroked down again, his warm, hard hands moving beneath the towel, shaping the curve of her bottom. The liquid heat between her thighs threatened to consume her. She pressed her legs together tighter, trying to deny the tingle in her flesh, but Christos applied more pressure, deeply kneading the muscles in her bottom and she felt equal waves of shame and craving.

"Don't," she muttered, humiliated and yet sinfully aroused.

"Do you want me to stop?"

"N-n-no." The confession cost her but it was the truth.

Even without being able to see his face, she could feel his smile. But for once she didn't care. The sensations filling her body were too lovely, too consuming to interrupt.

His fingertips discovered the sensitive line between bottom and thigh and he caressed that, too, awakening a river of longing in the only place that hadn't been burned. The teasing of her sensitive flesh created the most awful awareness of her body and needs. She felt huge in that moment, voracious.

She ought to have more control, ought to tell him in scathing tones that she wouldn't put up with such liberties, but oh, liberties had never felt so wonderful. She was quite dizzy with want, and she took in air in short, shallow gasps, afraid to breathe, afraid to distract him, afraid that this pleasure would end.

Pressing her open mouth to her forearm, she shuddered as Christos's fingers slid inward, tracing the cleft of her bottom down, until he'd discovered the tight protective curls and her hot, wanton dampness.

She was on fire, truly, but this had nothing to do with her sunburn and everything to do with need. Suddenly she'd become all liquid and hunger, like molten lava.

No one had ever touched her with such tantalizing intimacy, not even Jeremy who'd been a timid—and dare she admit?—unsatisfying lover. For Jeremy sex had been just that: a brief coupling and then uncoupling. It hadn't crossed her mind to assert that she had physical needs.

When Christos's fingers slid across her slick, sensitive flesh, she trembled, biting her arm to keep from arching against his hand. She couldn't lose control, couldn't betray herself with him. But when he stroked the engorged bud, a thousand nerve endings danced and her hips lifted, as if of their own volition.

He caressed her again, and again, and each time he touched the acutely sensitive bud, she felt as though he was winding her tighter and tighter like an old-fashioned wood top.

More, faster, tighter.

Brilliant color filled her mind, painted

stripes of red and green and white against the polished wood.

Stroking her, he wound her tighter still, drawing her in and out of herself, aware of his hands, his warmth, her heat, her labored breathing.

She couldn't catch her breath and the intensity of it made her long to scream. And then when she felt quite mad and mindless, he put her over the edge, setting the coiled wooden top on the ground, fingers stroking faster, faster, faster.

He let her go. And suddenly she was flying, flung across the floor, spinning wildly out of control.

The speed and strength of the climax stunned her. She bit her forearm, choking back a scream, muffling the intensity of her response.

Hell, hell, hell!

She'd thought she'd had an orgasm yesterday, but that…that was nothing like this. This… it was unreal. Incredible. Unbelievable. One could get addicted to feeling this way.

Her open mouth pressed to her arm drew her back to the moment. Christos stirred and she suddenly remembered him, and his part in this.

He'd brought her to a climax with his hand. Good God, how impersonal. How crude. She longed to bury her face in the pillow and hide but that wouldn't exactly work. He was waiting for her to speak. Waiting for something.

Slowly she turned her head, her eyes feeling heavy, sleepy, and she stared up at Christos. His own gaze looked slumberous, his dark pupils almost black.

He'd enjoyed this, she realized, startled, overwhelmed. He'd enjoying making her fall apart in his hands.

She dampened her bottom lip, overwhelmed by her weakness. And still he waited for her to speak. She grasped at the first thing that came to mind.

"That was nice."

His lashes lowered, concealing his emotions. "I must be out of practice. I'll have to work on that." And with a nod in her direction, he left, leaving her naked and alone in bed.

Sleeping that night was excruciating, her skin so hot she felt as though a fire had been lit beneath her skin. Once she woke to find Christos at her side, aspirin in his hand. She gratefully accepted and allowed him to spray a topical pain relief across her back. He avoided mentioning what had taken place earlier and after he left she fell into a deeper, more restful sleep.

A maid brought a breakfast tray to her in bed and Alysia ate her melon and sweet roll sitting up in bed, moving gingerly, if at all.

Christos appeared briefly, dressed in a suit and tie, dark hair slicked back, accenting the hardness of his features. "How are you feeling?"

"A little better."

"I'd warned you about the sun."

Of course he did. He was the font of all wisdom. She gritted her teeth, resisting the urge to reply sarcastically.

"If you need me, you can reach me at my office."

"I won't need you."

He shrugged. "You say that, but your actions contradict your words." And with that, he was gone.

He was right, she realized, sinking back into bed. She felt completely split, two personalities inhabiting one body. One part of her craved purity, denial, discipline. Another hungered for heat and passion. It'd always been this way, too. As a child she'd felt so emotional, so hungry for affection, and her father's coldness, his critical manner, had made her ashamed of her feelings, turning a little girl's needs into something dirty and wrong.

Daughters were to serve. Daughters were to be silent. Daughters were to sacrifice.

Her father made it clear Alysia failed on all three accounts.

The older she grew, the more she struggled against her passionate nature, fighting to deny herself, fighting to be what her father demanded of her. She'd always had a knack for drawing and she turned to her giant sketch pads, pouring her energy into endless charcoal drawings, portraits of the family servants, sketches of neighbor children, landscapes of the sea and rocky terrain.

Earning the art scholarship had been an answer to prayer. Her father had been furious that she'd even applied, but her mother somehow persuaded him to let her go. Once in Paris she embraced everything new, relishing the eclectic circle of artists and writers who talked about everything but making money. They were passionate and interesting, clever and original. Jeremy was one of them, always the life of the party, charming, handsome, completely irresponsible. She'd loved that about him. Loved the fact that he couldn't hold a job. Wouldn't hold a job. He was the least controlling person she'd ever known.

They didn't date long. A couple of nights after first making love he suggested they move in together. But deep down she was still a good Greek girl and she couldn't just live with a man. She needed to be a wife, and then a mother.

And so she had been. Both.

Alysia curled on her side, smoothed her hand across the cool cotton sheet. Paris seemed so long ago. Jeremy was just a name of a man she'd once known.

It was strange she thought, she'd lived lives that didn't exist anymore. The good Greek girl was gone. Only the hedonist remained.

And the hedonist had decided she wanted Christos, wanted to remain with Christos, even if she had to bend the rules to make the relationship work.

He wanted a wife. She'd be his wife. She just wouldn't get pregnant. The doctor had given her a blue plastic case with a six month supply of birth control pills, to give her time to build up her strength before trying for a baby. So for the next six months she was safe.

And then she'd see another doctor, and renew the prescription.

Late in the day, Alysia managed to bathe and dress, slipping on a soft cotton sundress and low-heeled sandals. She ate dinner alone in the formal dining room and wandered the garden grounds, hearing the distant horn of a car.

Footsteps sounded on the flagstone path. She turned, discovering Christos behind her. He'd changed from his suit into pale linen trousers and a smooth cotton shirt the color of butterscotch. The caramel color suited him, enhancing his bronze complexion and the gleam of his black hair.

"I'm sorry to have kept you waiting," he said. "There's been a problem at my head office in New York."

He sounded quietly ironic, as if everything between them was a joke. Hurt unfolded inside her chest, hurt because she understood that there was something intrinsically good in him, in them, but they couldn't seem to get around the obstacles.

"I've been all right. I'm quite good at entertaining myself."

He nodded slightly, comprehending her implied reference at learning to stay busy and out of her father's way. "I need to be in New York tomorrow. We'll leave tonight."

She felt a leap of excitement, and a peculiar sense of hope. Cynically she mocked her expectations. Starting over in a new place wasn't exactly starting fresh. The problems would follow. The conflict remained.

But maybe it didn't have to. Perhaps away from Greece they could start over, make something new. Here everything felt tainted. She felt tainted. But in America they could change, she could change. She would try harder. She'd please more.

"I've already instructed Housekeeping to pack. We'll be leaving soon." He hesitated, his expression grim. "There's something else. Your father wanted to stop over tonight, to say goodbye. I told him no. I hope that's all right with you."

Christos's private jet landed so gently that there wasn't even a bump as the plane's wheels touched the tarmac. They taxied to the executive terminal and immediately deplaned, exiting the jet only to be handed into the back of a waiting limousine.

Despite the early hour, dawn just breaking,

Christos returned phone calls during the short drive to his country house in Darien, Connecticut.

Once during his conversation, he covered the receiver and leaned forward, pointing out a series landmarks to Alysia.

In the dim morning light it was difficult to see much, but she made out the shapes of ornate iron gates, stone walls and extensive grounds with endless manicured lawns. Although she'd grown up surrounded by wealth, the vast American country estates impressed even her.

Christos's house, rather than dominating the verdant landscape, nestled into a green knoll as if to take comfort in the undulating land with its views of the water and grove of majestic hardwood trees.

"It's not what you expected," Christos said, noting her expression as he hung up the phone.

And it wasn't. She'd expected something grandiose, another opulent mansion built of polished marble. Instead this rambling two-story country house had been fashioned from clapboard and stone, featuring big beautiful bay windows and discreet covered doorways. The soft morning light outlined the shingled roof, the sharp gables, the cascading roofline. It was a fairy-tale house, the entry marked by a profusion of climbing roses.

An older woman answered the door, dressed simply in a black jersey dress, her steel-gray hair coiffed in a severe knot. The housekeeper, Alysia assumed. She assumed wrong.

"Mother," Christos said, clasping the woman by the shoulders and kissing both cheeks. "What are you doing up at this hour?"

"I've been waiting by the door."

"So I see."

Alysia went hot, then cold. Not a housekeeper, but his mother. Abruptly the stone and whitewashed clapboard house lost its fairy-tale charm.

Christos made the introductions and his mother, greeted Alysia cordially, if coolly, which didn't surprise Alysia in the slightest. In Greece, mothers-in-law were notoriously hard on daughters-in-law. No woman was ever good enough for another woman's son. Greek mothers lived for their sons and considered it their duty to instruct new wives how to run the household, perform domestic duties.

The elder Mrs. Pateras turned to her son. "She's sick?"

"No, mother, she's just slim."

The gray-haired matron cast a skeptical glance over Alysia's slender figure and wan complexion. "You called a doctor in Athens, no?"

"Yes, Mother, but the doctor assured me she just needs iron. He prescribed some iron tablets and those will help."

Mrs. Pateras's dour expression grew darker. She tossed her hands in the air, gesturing with impassioned emphasis. "I thought you wanted family, Christos. Babies, no? A skinny wife isn't good for making babies. You need a good Greek girl, not a Lemos!"

Alysia expected a mother-in-law who'd been cool, perhaps even critical, but Mrs. Pateras's vocal attack left her speechless, the blood draining from her face, her body cold.

"Mama, gently, please," Christos quietly remonstrated. "You must give Alysia a chance."

"I know all about her. I know she's not the one for you. A good Greek girl, Christos, a *good* girl."

Christos glanced at Alysia, their eyes briefly meeting. "She is a good Greek girl," he answered, his expression blank, his dark eyes shuttered, before turning back to his mother.

"But she's Lemos's daughter."
"Yes."
"So how can she be the right one for you?"

CHAPTER EIGHT

His mother gone, Christos shut the door. "She'll be fine. She just needs time," he said flatly.

Alysia didn't dare contradict him, but knew better than most that time didn't always heal. Time just made some more bitter, but she couldn't say that to Christos, and she couldn't criticize his mother, either. Mothers, especially Greek mothers, were above reproach.

Aware that he felt awkward, she sought to alleviate some of the tension. "Would you like coffee?"

"Yes, but let me make it. You're the guest."

The guest. Not his wife, but the guest.

In the kitchen she watched as he ground the beans and filled the machine's filter. He glanced at her as he turned the machine on, his expression brooding. "Alysia, it would be best if you do not discuss your father here, or in front of my parents."

"I don't understand. Is there something I should know?"

"Yes. No. It doesn't matter. Just do as I say."

Alysia could hear his mother's scathing tone echo in her head. *A good girl, not a Lemos.* She shivered. "This is personal," she said numbly. "What happened? What did my father do?"

Christos shrugged, obviously uncomfortable. "It's a long time ago."

"Not so long ago if your mother can't look at me without cursing."

"It wasn't that bad."

"Close enough." She lifted her chin, horrified to discover she was on the brink of tears. She was suddenly scared. She'd begun to feel things for Christos that she'd never felt for any man, not even Jeremy. Christos had broken through that chink in her armor. Pulled the stone from around her heart. If his family hated her they were in serious trouble. "I have a right to know. As your wife, Christos."

"Your father made it impossible for my father to get employment on Oinoussai, resulting in my father being blacklisted. He couldn't get work on the island, not ever again."

A lump lodged in her throat. "How? Why?"

"Your father was engaged in unethical business practices—"

She closed her eyes, not needing to hear another word. So Christos did know. Her father, desperate to get ahead, hired men to damage other ship owners' vessels, sabotaging sailings. When the ships couldn't sail, her father rushed in and gathered the business. "Constantine told you?"

"No. I knew long before I ever went into business with Constantine. My father was one of the welders hired to dismantle Constantine Pappas's ships."

"He should have gone to the police," she whispered, sickened at the horrible things her father had done in the name of business.

"He wouldn't, out of respect to your mother."

She felt a cold knot form inside her. "Actually I think my mother would have thanked him."

"Don't worry. Constantine and I settled our debts with your father. That's why he and I went into business together. We both needed each other. And with his help, I've had my revenge." He leaned against the counter, and smiled, but there was no warmth in his eyes, no tenderness in the twist of his lips. "I have you."

And her father's fortune.

She closed her eyes, swaying. She felt like a fool. Here she was, falling in love with Christos, while he was exacting his revenge. What an idiot she was! She never had been able to separate her body and her heart.

"Your father desperately wants grandchildren," he added tightly. "And he'll get them, but they'll be Pateras, not Lemos. Never Lemos."

Freezing inwardly she wrapped her arms around herself. "What children?" she taunted. "And from where?"

"I know you've said you can't have children but you've never been to specialists. Doctors can perform miracles these days. There are procedures—"

"Stop telling me about doctors and procedures, and listen to me!"

"I'm listening but you're not saying anything."

"Yes, I am, but you just don't want to hear it. You want me to be like your mother, you want me to stay home and take care of things here."

"Yes. Exactly."

"But that's what you want, not what I want.

You can't dictate my life, Christos. I've a mind. I want to use it."

"Use it by creating a home for us, a family for us—"

The back door opened, silencing him, drawing them both up short. A cheery voice shouted out a bright hello. Christos drew in a ragged breath, his hard features brittle with anger. "Mrs. Avery," he announced, his voice clipped.

They stared at each other, visibly shaken. Christos drank from his coffee cup and Alysia smoothed a hand across her skirt, trying to steady her nerves.

He married her for her body. For her ability to bear him children.

Children she wouldn't have. Seven years ago, maybe. Now? Never.

The housekeeper's low-heeled shoes clicked briskly on the hardwood floor as she entered the kitchen. Her small, plump hands busily tied her apron over her bright red dress. "Breakfast?" she asked, before catching sight of Alysia.

"Yes, please," Christos answered grimly.

The woman's round face suddenly wreathed in smiles. "The new Mrs. Pateras?"

Christos shot Alysia a dark glance. "Yes, indeed, Mrs. Avery. And now that you're here,

I'll leave the new Mrs. Pateras in your capable hands."

Alysia heard the front door slam in the middle of Mrs. Avery's house tour. Alysia stiffened, turned toward the sound.

"Don't worry. It's just Mr. Pateras leaving for work." And with a bright smile Mrs. Avery continued showing Alysia around.

The original house was over two hundred years old and had been greatly expanded and remodeled at the turn of the last century. The rooms were all large and well proportioned, the ceilings eleven and a half feet high with enormous paned windows providing spectacular views and welcoming light.

But it was hard to feel the sun's warmth when she felt so cold inside. Hard to enjoy the comfortable luxury when she couldn't forget her last conversation with Christos.

What he wanted, she realized wearily, was a traditional wife. A wife like his mother. A wife to carry his children.

Just like she'd failed her father, she'd fail Christos. The things he wanted she couldn't give.

Christos called and left a message with Mrs. Avery, telling her he wouldn't be home until seven-thirty. Mrs. Avery usually left at six, but tonight she offered to stay and serve the dinner she'd already prepared. Alysia assured the kindly housekeeper that she could dish and serve just fine and sent Mrs. Avery home.

Alone, Alysia slowly set the table, using the good china and crystal, carefully folding the linen napkins. All afternoon she'd replayed the scene in the kitchen through her head, reliving Christos's revelation that his family had suffered at the hands of her father, reliving his own revelation that he'd married her not simply for her fortune, but to exact a price on the Lemos family, to take the Lemos name and make it his.

She'd paid the ultimate price for being her father's daughter.

Numbly Alysia lit the tall tapered candles on the table, shaking her hand to extinguish the match, even as Christos appeared in the dining-room doorway.

She turned, caught a glimpse of the fatigue etched in deep lines at his mouth and eyes. His gaze took in the fresh rose centerpiece and elegant place settings. "Mrs. Avery must think we're enjoying the honeymoon."

She heard the cynicism in his voice but refused to be baited. "Would you like a glass of wine? I've opened a bottle. Mrs. Avery said you enjoy wine with your dinner."

Reluctantly he nodded. "All right, then."

She poured him a glass, handed it to him. He avoided touching her fingers.

Christos wandered around the dining-room table, sipping his wine, studying her arrangement of flowers, the linen cloth, the gleam of crystal in the flickering candlelight. "We're not celebrating anything, are we?"

"No." She felt herself begin to flush, self-conscious and embarrassed. She'd tried to please him. "You don't like the table?"

"Seems like a lot of trouble."

"It was no trouble. Growing up we always set a formal table for dinner. Nice linens. Candles."

"Ah, yes, the lives of the rich and famous."

His sarcasm stung, sending blood surging to her face. "I can't change who I am."

"Just as I can't change who I am." He sipped from his goblet.

"It was not easy being Darius Lemos's only child."

"No, of course not. It must have been awful being rich."

"Spoiled rotten, I was." She smiled at him, her jaws aching with the effort. "Dining every night with crystal and candlelight."

"We couldn't afford crystal. Candles were frivolous."

She felt wound so tightly, her body so tense she was trembling inwardly. Jerkily she leaned forward, blowing out the candles she'd just lit. The blackened wicks smoked. "Better?"

"You didn't have to do that."

"I didn't have to do that, but it's what you wanted. You're going to punish me now, every chance you can get. You're going to use every opportunity to impress upon me how desperate you were growing up and how revoltingly rich we were. You, working so hard, making something out of yourself, and me, just a spoiled little rich girl in need of a hospital and doctors to fix my self-esteem."

"Is that why you were there? Low self-esteem?"

She laughed, even as her chest tightened with hurt and pain. "Wouldn't you like to know!"

"I would, yes."

"So you can figure out why my father couldn't marry me off to a real Greek?" She caught sight of his expression, his jaw jutted, eyes narrowed in anger.

She rushed on, fueled by his coldness and her acute loneliness. "You think you have the upperhand here, but I have news for you. You were bought, Christos, you were bought because you could be bought. A self-respecting Greek wouldn't have me. A self-respecting Greek would sooner put his eye out than look upon me. But you, hungry for ships and money and power, made a deal with my father, and now you're curious, dying to know why Daddy Darius couldn't get rid of me."

"I do have some questions."

"I bet." She trembled with rage. "You, Christos Pateras, like my father, love to play God."

He said nothing, his back rigid, his dark eyes narrowed, thick lashes lowered.

"But I'm tired of you and my father making choices for me, deciding who I am, what I'll do, how I should think. I've had twenty-five years of men making decisions for me and I will not put up with it anymore."

"You're making me out to be a monster."

"Aren't you? My father was a monster. He

couldn't love, or forgive. Tell me, how are you different from him?"

He said nothing, his jaw popping, his body so tense she feared he might reach for her, punish her insolence with a quick backhand the way her father used to do. But he didn't move. Didn't lift a finger.

Suddenly her anger deflated, and she felt wretched. She didn't understand why she had to lash out at him and what she'd hoped to accomplish.

This wasn't the way to his heart, that much she knew.

But she'd never have his heart. Just as she'd never have his respect.

Fighting tears, she fled to her room.

Unable to calm herself, Alysia tackled her stacks of luggage, finishing the unpacking job Mrs. Avery had begun. She was still filling the drawers in her dresser when Christos opened the bedroom door.

She'd felt him in the doorway, felt him watching her, but he didn't speak and she didn't turn around.

Her eyes burned and she blinked hard, concentrating on her task.

She'd said terrible things to him, called him

terrible names, and he didn't deserve it, not all of it, at least. She was angry with him because she wanted more from him but fighting wouldn't bring him closer. It would only push him farther away.

"I've dished up dinner," he said quietly.

A lump filled her throat. "I'm really not all that hungry."

"You need to eat. Come," he repeated, extending a hand. "Let's not waste Mrs. Avery's meal."

She didn't have the strength to fight him, nor the energy to resist. She was hungry, and tired, jetlag catching up with her, and she followed, if only to avoid further conflict.

In the dining room the candles glowed on the table, the lightbulbs in the grand crystal-and-silver chandelier dimmed. The room shone pale yellow in the flickering light and the plates on the table were filled with Mrs. Avery's roasted chicken and buttery new potatoes.

They ate in silence, each contemplative, studiously avoiding conversation.

Finally Christos pushed his plate aside. "Fifteen years ago I made a choice," he said quietly, not looking at her, but at a fixed point on the table. "It was a difficult choice."

She looked across the gleaming table, her gaze fixing on his mouth, unable to meet his eyes. He undid her. He made her want things she thought she'd given up long ago.

"I had to choose between school and sports. I'd got into Yale on an athletic scholarship."

"Baseball," she murmured.

He nodded. "I loved the game, loved being outside, on the grass, and the camaraderie of being part of a team. But I wasn't a great player. I was good, and I might have made it to the pros, but I couldn't take the risk."

He lifted his wineglass, took a sip and set the goblet down again. "If I stuck with baseball there was a good chance I'd struggle for years. I wouldn't be able to take care of my parents, and I knew without my help, my mother would spend her life scrubbing other people's toilets. I couldn't bear it. My pride couldn't bear it. My family had been through so much. I wanted more for them, more for all of us."

"So you pursued business instead."

"I pursued your father," he corrected softly, self-mockingly. "Every decision I made, every contract I signed, every investment had one purpose—to get me closer to the day I'd crush your father."

"You hated him that much?"

"I hated what he did to my father. As you can see, I'm not a very forgiving man."

"You don't strike me as ruthless."

"I wasn't always."

Had there been a different Christos then, a younger Christos who wanted less, and perhaps loved more? "I might have liked you then."

His dark head lifted and he gazed at her from beneath a furrowed brow. His cheekbones jutted, his jaw at an angle, and even though he stared at her, she was sure he was looking inward, seeing not her, but himself, and his expression haunted her. "Maybe," he answered in a deep, strangled voice. "Maybe."

She rose from her chair, wanting to go to him, but halfway around the table realized he wouldn't want her, didn't need her, not that way.

Torn, she gathered the dishes, stacking the bread plate on the dinner plate and pushing the cutlery to the middle.

"There is one other thing." His deep voice stilled her jerky motions. "I wouldn't mention it except I know my mother, and I know she will."

She glanced at him over her shoulder, waiting for whatever would come next. He smiled, but the smile didn't warm his eyes. "I was engaged earlier this year, before I married you."

Dishes cradled to her tummy, she struggled to make sense of what he was saying. "Engaged to whom?"

"A local girl."

"Someone from a family like yours."

His dark head inclined. "Our mothers arranged it."

With a flash she intuited what he was really saying. "Your mother was the matchmaker."

His gaze held hers. "Yes, and our families were thrilled. They made quite a big fuss."

"I can imagine." And she could. Christos Pateras, an American-Greek tycoon, a dazzling American success story, marries local American-Greek girl. It would have been a perfect match. Even the gods would have been smiling.

"You loved her?" she whispered, hating how her body responded with pain. Why did she care? Why did she have to feel so much?

"I loved her sweetness. I loved her gentleness."

"She wanted children."

"She dreamed of a big family."

Jealousy consumed her. Alysia didn't even know this other woman and she felt wild with envy. To be the woman Christos would cherish…

But she couldn't leave it at that. She had to know more. "Was there an accident?"

"No." Christos's black brows knitted, his expression grim. "I broke it off a couple of months ago, realizing she wasn't the one for me."

Sweet relief flooded her limbs. "What changed your mind?"

"Your father."

Alysia didn't know if she dropped the dishes or if they simply fell. Either way, they came crashing down, plates rolling, cutlery clattering, one fork bouncing. Nothing, she dimly realized, broke. How fortunate.

She struggled to gather the dishes but her fingers wouldn't cooperate.

All she could see was her father, pen in hand, scribbling staggering figures on paper, promising Christos ships, wealth, more power.

She sucked in air, scalding tears filling her eyes and grabbed blindly at the fallen silverware, unable to see, unable to think.

Her father cutting a check and Christos taking it all. The deal, the marriage, the business. Not for love. But for money. For revenge.

Christos's chair scraped back. He took her arm and she jumped back, his touch setting her skin on fire.

If only she'd been the poor girl from a poor emigrant family, engaged to Christos. To be chosen for one's goodness, to be chosen for one's rightness, to be chosen and loved!

"Don't," Christos said roughly, taking her arm again.

She opened her eyes, looked at him, unaware of the tears filling her eyes. Emotion darkened his own beautiful features. "Don't what?" she whispered.

"Don't say it. Don't want it. What we have is what I wanted."

"Is it?"

"Yes."

"But what we have is nothing."

"That's not true. It's no better, no worse than any other arranged marriage."

"I can't live like this."

"Sorry. You don't have a choice."

"Don't I?"

"No. Not anymore. Not as my wife."

CHAPTER NINE

BEFORE he'd taken a step, she knew he was going to touch her, to take her into his arms and create havoc within her again. She wanted his touch as much as she dreaded it, fearing the loss of control, especially to him.

Alysia tried to escape but Christos was too quick, catching her by her arms and drawing her against his chest. His hands cupped her bottom, pulling her firmly against his hips. "All your life you've been the poor neglected Alysia. No one to love you. No one to want you."

He pressed her even closer to his hips, making her vividly aware of his arousal. "But I want you, I want you more than I've ever wanted anyone."

"You want me to punish my father—"

"I couldn't care less about your father. I want you." He kissed the side of her throat, his breath warm, his lips making her skin tingle.

His lips felt incredible, his mouth sending torments of feeling racing up and down her spine. He was turning her into something hot and dangerous. Her body felt electric, her nerves overly sensitized.

Helplessly she slid a hand across his chest, dazed by the warmth he created within her, and her desire to feel him, be a part of him, capture the passion she'd felt in his arms before.

"Careful," he mocked her, his voice deepening, "I might actually think you want me."

The warmth of his breath against her cheek, the mockery in his voice, the heat of his body against hers made her crave more.

As Christos's dark head dipped, she reached up, clasping his nape, a soft moan escaping her lips. She slid her fingers through his crisp, damp hair and inhaled his clean male scent.

His mouth parted hers, his tongue teasing the softness of her inner lip until her lips opened wider. She felt the core of her melt. Shameless in her desire, she shifted, rising slightly, encouraging him.

He pressed her backward, against the dining-room table, his kiss deepening, drawing her tongue into his mouth. He sucked on the tip of her tongue, creating a tight friction that echoed the throbbing in her belly and the ache between her thighs.

He sucked harder on her tongue before finding the inside of her lip. He bit the softness of her lip and she gasped, arching into him for relief.

"I do want you. I want you to make love to me," she begged, her voice thick, husky with passion.

It was all the encouragement he needed. Christos swept her into his arms and carried her up the stairs, pushing open the bedroom door, through the darkened room to his bed.

He found the warm, smooth flesh of her abdomen, unbuttoning her blouse with quick, sure fingers. His palms caressed the length of her torso, tracing the edge of her lace bra beneath the weight of each breast. Her nipples tightened, peaking with feeling, yet he grazed the nipples, bypassing them to kiss the hollow beneath. She squirmed, reaching for him, struggling to unbutton his shirt.

He helped her with his shirt, peeling the fabric from his shoulders to reveal the taut planes of his chest. Her palms slid down his hard abdomen to his belt buckle and with shaking hands she unfastened the buckle and then his trousers.

He sucked in his breath when she found him, her hand wrapping around his hard satin length. He drew her hand away, whispering, "Not yet," and lowered his own head to savor the sensitive hollow between her breasts, his tongue drawing circles of fire, around and around until she clamped her knees together in futile desire.

He finished off her blouse, pushing the silk fabric aside, and then unhooked the lace bra, sending that to the floor as well. The air felt cool against her heated skin and she reached for him, drawing him back down to her.

When his mouth covered one tight bud, she responded blindly, helplessly dragging her nails down his torso, lightly raking the carved plane of his chest, and small hard nipples.

She was slick with need by the time he knelt between her thighs. "No more anything," she whispered, "I just want you."

He entered her slowly, trying to give her time to adjust to his body, but she didn't need much time, welcoming the exquisite sensation of fullness.

Her body felt lovely and alive, her muscles

suffused with warmth, her skin incredibly sensitive. Every place he touched her glowed. Every kiss made her crave more.

"Am I hurting you?" he demanded hoarsely.

"No," she answered, pressing a finger to his lovely lips, stilling his speech. "Just love me."

And he did, bracing himself on his hands, thrusting deeply inside, first slowly and then faster, creating alternating torments of fullness and need, drawing them together, building the tension, building the reward.

His mouth returned to hers, and she answered his kiss with near desperation, lifting her hips to meet him, relishing the tenderness and passion.

She knew then she'd always love him, heart and soul, or the part of her soul not destroyed with Alexi.

"Christos," she whispered urgently, drawing him deeper inside her, opening her mouth, giving him all of her body since he wouldn't take her heart.

The vivid swirling sensations built to a feverish pitch, his thrusts harder, faster, and for long mindless seconds she was at an insurmountable peak, nearing climax, her body warm, damp, straining against his, but not yet set free.

Christos plunged into her yet again, moving deeply, and suddenly she was his, all his, exploding in brilliant, breathtaking pleasure. Her pleasure sent him over the edge, and they came together, their bodies shuddering with rippling sensation, satiated and exhausted.

Still tangled together, her heart racing wildly, Christos kissed her again, long and hard. "Mine," he whispered against her mouth. "Remember that." And then his tongue rasped against hers in one final mind-spinning kiss that drew shivers down her spine, warmth from her belly, and flexed her toes.

He settled her to one side of him, pulling her hip in against his, one palm cupping her breast. For a long moment neither moved, nor spoke, their warm, weary bodies relaxed.

Alysia felt herself spiral down, down, down, but she never crashed, just floated in lovely suspended sensation, aware of Christos's fingers trailing in the curve of her lower back, and gently caressing the swell of her hip.

"You are worth all the ships in the world," he murmured, his voice husky, and she turned her head to look up at him, surprised by his words, but before she could ask him what he meant, he was breathing deeply, black lashes fanning his cheekbones. He was asleep.

They made love again later, toward the end of the night. Neither spoke, their bodies communicating in wordless expression. But later, after they'd recovered from the intensity of the physical pleasure, Christos pressed a kiss to the top of her head and eased out of bed.

"Where are you going?" she asked, sleepily sitting forward, sheet drawn to her breasts.

"Work."

"Now? It's so early!"

"It's five. I've a lot to do. Better to get started."

She sat up higher, pushed a fistful of hair out of her eyes. "Can I come?"

"No. Go back to sleep. You need the rest."

She pushed back the bedcovers, pressed her hands to her knees. "I could help you. You could put me to work."

"You know nothing about the industry."

"So teach me." She was warming to the idea, realizing she could try to win him over. Christos was like her father. He equated business with success, and he respected successful people. If she could find a way to be useful, contribute to his business, he might see her as more than Darius Lemos's spoiled daughter.

He might realize she had a brain. He might respect her.

He might even fall in love with her.

"Please, Christos, give me a chance."

"This is not a good day for show and tell. Today I have important conferences scheduled. Union bosses waiting to rip my head off. It's a day of hard bargaining, a little bloodletting—hopefully not my own. You'd be in the way. You'd be a distraction."

His good mood quickly evaporated as his wife flung herself from bed, her slim figure lunging at the floor, grabbing for her clothes. "I wouldn't be a distraction. I wouldn't get in your way. Christos, please."

"Alysia, be serious."

Her hands shook as she picked up her panties and stepped into the tiny scraps of satin. "I am. Completely serious."

"Alysia, you're a woman."

Daggers flashed in her dark blue eyes and with a furious glance in his direction, she yanked her white silk blouse over her shoulders, forgetting her strappy lace bra, the fabric hugging her breasts, outlining the full, round shape. "I can't believe you just said that!"

"I watched my mother slave on her knees

in other people's bathrooms. She worked her fingers to the bone and I vowed that when I married, my wife would never work, never be humiliated like that."

"I want to go into the office, not clean bathrooms." Her full, swollen nipples pressed tautly against the thin silk fabric and he felt his body harden, responding to her beauty and passion, unfazed by her anger.

"No. I will provide for us because I *can* provide for us. That is how it should be, and that is how it will be. Understood?"

With a strangled oath she flung her navy skirt at him. He caught it easily.

"Then go!" she spat, tossing her head, long silky hair swinging over her shoulders. "Do whatever it is you must do, but don't expect to come home and find me waiting!"

He stopped where he was, two steps from the foot of the bed, desire dying. He hadn't heard right. She was threatening him again. Unbelievable.

One of his hands circled her slim upper arm and he dragged her toward him. Her bare legs kicked, her hands pounded on his chest. "What did you say?"

"You heard me."

Anger swept through him, anger and impatience. He tilted her head back, holding her face captive beneath his. His kiss was an assault as much as it was an insult. He kissed her hard, a savagery in the rake of his tongue and grind of his lips. He wanted her to feel his wrath, wanted to remind her that in this house, he was the man, and she, the woman.

But even as he probed her mouth, his hard embrace gentled, his fingers releasing her chin to cup her cheek. She felt unbelievable in his arms, tasted like honey and crushed almonds. She was sweet and damn it, she was his.

She'd been his ever since she'd interrupted her father's meeting all those years ago. He knew then he wanted her, wanted her to be his. He'd protect her. He'd cherish her. He'd keep Darius Lemos from hurting her again.

Alysia's swollen mouth trembled beneath his, her slim body quivering against his bare chest. His kiss softened and he caressed the length of her neck, stroking her satiny skin, her body shuddering at each slow, lingering touch, playing her tenderly the way one would play the violin. She was melting in his arms, melting into him, and gently he released her.

He exhaled slowly, his breathing ragged, his heart pounding with the same fierceness that it surged through his limbs, gathering in his groin. God, he wanted her, wanted to take her and taste her, make love to her until she surrendered completely, admitting that she wanted no one but him, no life but theirs.

But she wouldn't meet him, not even halfway, and as much as he wanted to kiss her senseless, there wasn't time.

His brows flattened as he pressed the tip of his finger to her quivering mouth. "Do not, my rebellious wife, threaten to leave me again."

She heard the hardness in his tone and realized she'd pushed him too far. Shivering, she drew her blouse even tighter across her chest, wanting him yet again, craving him still. She should have more pride, want more from him than just sex, but desperate woman that she was, she took whatever he gave her, even the crumbs from his table.

Disgusted with herself, she lashed out. "I gave you what you wanted. You wanted me to perform my wifely duties, well, I did. I serviced you. Now give me what I want."

Christos stared at her, stunned, his expression revealing hurt, and betrayal. Then his dark eyes shuttered, leaving his chiseled features starkly remote. But she'd seen enough in his eyes to know her barb hit home. She'd wounded him.

Instead of joy, she felt remorse, and fresh shame. Before she could apologize, he was walking away, putting distance between them.

He headed for his bathroom, flicked on the lights and heat lamp before turning on the shower. She followed him into the bathroom, unsettled by what had just taken place between them.

The cold tile floor curled her toes. "Christos—"

Steam rose from the open shower door, fogging the white tiled bath. Christos turned to look at her. He was naked but completely uninhibited. "We have an expression in America. It's called 'low blow.' It means, you've hit below the belt. Do you understand what I'm saying?"

She swallowed hard, wondering how something so lovely, what took place in his bed, could now turn into something so ugly. "Yes, but—"

"Hitting below the belt is not acceptable. Not in this marriage. Not ever."

"I'm sorry, but you—"

"Like a child. So defiant. So unwilling to bend."

"Is that how you accept an apology?"

"Is that how you give an apology?"

She couldn't stand it, couldn't stand the way he made her feel so inadequate. "I hate you," she whispered, tears starting to her eyes. "I hate you and everything you stand for."

"Trust me. At the moment, the feeling's mutual." His dark lashes lowered, concealing his expression. "It didn't have to be like this, Alysia."

Tears shimmered in her eyes as she flung her head back. "Is that an apology?"

"No. A statement of fact."

"Why didn't you marry your good American-Greek girl and leave me in the convent?"

His mouth flattened, his dark eyes narrowing as his gaze raked her half-naked body. "I couldn't."

"You and my father are exactly alike. You love money before all else!"

"I tried to love you. But you won't let anybody near you. You won't allow someone to be kind—"

"Is that what you were showing me in bed?

Kindness?" She laughed, her voice high and strained, a hint of hysteria in the thin pitch. "Well, from now on, I can do without your acts of kindness." She balled her hands into fists. "Call a spade, a spade. Our marriage is nothing but a business deal. Dollars. Numbers. A bank account. What happened in there, in that bed, was nothing more than a business transaction."

His cheekbones jutted against the pallor of his skin. His nostrils flared with each short, ragged breath. "Fine, it's business. But it's an ongoing business. I'll take you when I want, and how I want, and to hell with the kindness you despise."

He pulled her into the shower with him, holding her beneath the blast of jets, water soaking them both, drenching her blouse, outlining her breasts.

Turning, he shifted her body behind his to take the brunt of the water. Clasping her face in his hands, he covered her mouth with his, lips parting her, tongue stabbing at her mouth's softness, taking her without pretense of tenderness.

The water beat down around them, splashing their bodies, dripping down their legs.

When Christos finally lifted his head, he slowly pressed a kiss to the corner of her throbbing mouth. His black eyelashes were spiky wet, his jaw glistening with water. "From now on I'll expect you to be ready for me, just like my banker's always on call, ready for my business."

"You're an ass," she whispered, hurt, and yet hungry for more skin, more pressure, more of him.

"And you're my wife." He unbuttoned her soggy blouse, dropping it in a puddle at their feet.

She tried to climb out of the shower. He pulled her back in, blocking the door with his body. He picked up a bar of soap and began lathering it between his large hands. He worked the soap into thick white suds, and then held the bar above her body. The foaming suds spilled from his hands to her shoulders and dripped down her breasts.

His gaze lowered, his burning gaze following the path of the bubbles as they slid down the sweep of breasts, her taut aching nipples peeking through soapy foam.

Reaching out to her, Christos traced the bubble path, his firm sudsy palm against her breast and distended nipple. He drew his hands across her, spreading the soapy lather down her flat abdomen, into the soft mound at the apex of her thighs. He washed her clean, rinsed the soap off, and lifted her chin. "I've washed you, I've made you mine. Your life, Alysia, is with me."

Shivering, she left the shower and wrapped a towel around herself and squeezed the extra water from her hair. Christos stepped past her, his hips bumping her bottom and she quickly moved out of the way. Reaching across her, he pulled a towel off the bar. "You have a half hour," he said flatly, no expression in his voice.

"A half hour?"

He looked at her with anger, and scorn. "Until we go. I won't leave you here and give you a second chance to run away. So you win, Alysia. You're going to work with me even though I don't like it one little bit."

CHAPTER TEN

During the helicopter ride into the city, Christos avoided looking at her, and she kept her chin firmly lifted, refusing to let him see that her hard-earned victory tasted terribly bitter.

She'd wanted to be a part of his world, but not at this price. Never at this price.

The moment they arrived at his office, walking through the frosted glass doors into a modern office furnished in navy, burgundy and cream, they joined a meeting already in progress and remained in the conference room all day.

Christos didn't glance her way during the three-hour-long discussion with the shipworker's union boss. And the discussion, so heated that at times she feared the union boss would come to blows, made her incredibly uneasy. But Christos remained utterly calm. He addressed the others without rancor, and yet he didn't bend, nor did he compromise.

The meeting adjourned for ten minutes so all could move around the room, use the bathroom, stretch their legs. Christos stood up, walked to the phone on the corner table, a table just inches from her chair, and made a series of brief phone calls without once looking at her.

Concluding his calls, he returned to his chair, again without a glance in her direction.

It was as if he was telling her, without so many words, that she could push him all she wanted, but that would never change the way he felt about her. He despised her. Clearly she meant nothing to him.

A bitter pill for a bitter victory.

They were silent on the ride home in the helicopter, landing on the cement pad in Christos's estate only twenty minutes after having taken off from the Manhattan skyscraper.

A car waited for them at the landing pad, driving them the short distance to the house. Mrs. Avery opened the door, welcomed them cheerfully, offering an appetizer tray and cold drinks.

Christos took his glass, and Alysia's, thanking Mrs. Avery with a warmth that Alysia couldn't miss.

"Mr. Pateras, your mother called late this afternoon to let you know your father had to work late tonight. She didn't think they'd be here much before eight."

"Thank you, Mrs. Avery. I know you've had a long day. Please don't feel you need to stay."

"But I can, and then you and Mrs. Pateras could relax a little. Unwind before your parents arrive."

Christos shot Alysia a speculative look. "We'll relax, don't you worry about us."

The moment Mrs. Avery was gone Christos ordered Alysia upstairs.

Her eyebrows shot up. Her stomach a bundle of nerves. "Pardon me?"

"Can you walk, or shall I carry you again?"

"You want me to go upstairs now, just before your parents come?"

He smiled coldly, no warmth in his dark eyes. "We've a good solid hour."

"You've got to be joking."

"Sweetheart, I never joke about sex."

I never joke about sex. How much cruder could one be? Her eyes smarted. Her throat closed, bottling the air in her lungs. "I'm sorry, but I'm not exactly in the mood."

He tossed back his drink, and shrugged. "Then get in the mood, because we made a deal. Business, right, sweetheart? You wanted to be a part of my world, well, I'm going to be a part of yours. I want you. Now."

"Don't do this."

"Why not? You treat me with as much contempt." He made a rough sound in his throat, reaching forward to run his finger across her cheek. "Ah, there it is, the anger. The hatred. It's all there, just for me." Christos turned, began climbing the stairs. "Now come. Business is business."

She wanted to hate him, wanted to shout something at him, but her voice failed her and her heart ached, craving something else from him than this.

As he took the stairs, she watched the length of his back, the powerful legs, and despite the anger and anguish burning within her, she felt another emotion, one awakened by the caress on her cheek.

She wanted him. She wanted to feel him over her, against her, the warm, hard planes of his body, her own warm acceptance. And slowly she followed him up the stairs.

They made love the first time with savage intent, nails raking, teeth nipping, kisses fierce and bruising. But after the first shattering orgasm, after the anger abated, Christos turned to her again, his touch softer, his expression almost gentle. He made love to her once more, this time giving rather than taking, kissing her through her second climax, holding her while she shuddered against him, murmuring assurances in her ear.

She nearly fell asleep in his arms but Christos stirred, and drawing back the covers reminded her that his parents would arrive in the next half hour.

He'd left the room and she bathed, but instead of dressing, she'd returned to the bed, curled on the foot in her towel.

She wanted more from Christos than skin. More than his mouth and fingers, his incredible satin and steel body. She wanted his heart, too.

But this marriage, their marriage, was paper and money, ships and inheritance. It wasn't love, would never be love. It was just business. Business and vengeance.

Her eyes burned, her throat sealed closed, and digging her nails into her palms she felt like the poor little rich girl again, the young Greek heiress whose fortune couldn't even protect her infant son.

God, how she hated her inheritance, hated the pampered world of nothingness.

The door to her room opened. Christos stood in the doorway, buttoning the sleeves of his crisp white shirt, the tail of it already tucked into dark wool trousers. "Alysia, you can't afford to dawdle. My parents will be here very soon. And trust me, you won't endear yourself to my mother if she finds you undressed."

She couldn't move, couldn't tear her gaze from him. He looked so cool and calm, so perfectly controlled, while she felt like a ball of warm wax, soft and changing, helpless in his hands.

She still felt him everywhere in her, on her, near her. She felt his mouth and hands, felt her body respond, and the dull pain in her heart.

Covering her heartache, she gave him a defiant glare. "Why not? You undressed me."

"Fine. I'll dress you. So much for independence, Mrs. Pateras." He stalked to her closet, plucking a silk skirt and cropped jacket from hangers.

"Wear these," he said, tossing them at her before digging through her drawers for appropriate lingerie. "My father loves lavender and my mother dislikes trousers. Wear your hair down but not too much makeup. I expect to see you downstairs in fifteen minutes tops. Am I clear?"

"Christos—"

"Am I clear?"

"Yes." She swallowed, gathering courage. "Your father, he must hate me very much."

He stopped at the door, but didn't turn around. "My father has no vendetta against you. My father is a compassionate man. A man far more tolerant than I."

He glanced back at her, his hard, handsome features without expression, his dark eyes intent, focused on her, observing the sudden tension at her mouth. "My father will be kind to you. Do not worry about him."

"And your mother?"

"She answers to my father."

Like a good woman should.

He didn't say the last part, but it hung there, unspoken between them. She smiled painfully. "I'll try not to embarrass you tonight."

"Just don't run away."

Downstairs she found Christos uncorking a bottle of red wine. Headlights gleamed in the driveway, reflecting through the dining-room window.

"They're here," he announced unnecessarily.

She stiffened, frightened at coming face-to-face with people her father had hurt so deeply. "Tell me what to say to your mother. Tell me how to act."

"Just be yourself," he said quietly. Her head jerked up. Her eyes met his. "My mother will be happy when I'm happy," he added more gently.

But I won't ever make you happy, she silently answered him, her heart aching, emotions so raw and new that she struggled to keep them in check. "Christos, it's not all business, is it?"

"You mean between us?"

Silence stretched, a humiliation of its own. Car doors slammed outside. Footsteps on the brick steps.

Bands of color burned her cheekbones. "Yes. Between us."

More silence. The shockingly loud ring of the doorbell. The knowledge that his parents were there, waiting, just on the other side of the door.

He didn't even glance at the door. "No. It's not just business."

She felt a bubble of emotion rise, higher, fuller, hope and pain, tenderness, too.

He crossed to the door but didn't open it, his gaze still on her, as if able to read her chaotic emotions. "I didn't marry Maria just because your father offered me money, and I didn't marry you to punish your family. I married you because I wanted you." And then, just like that, he swung the front door open, inviting his parents in.

Dinner with his parents was less of a disaster than she'd expected. With his father present, Christos's mother was subdued, silently following the conversation while Christos's father discussed business and matters of the church with Christos.

The elder Mr. Pateras made efforts to include Alysia, listening thoughtfully to her point of view, and treating her with what seemed to be genuine warmth and respect.

Following dinner they shared a sweet liqueur, a drink Christos said was made locally by a Greek family. Then his parents left after Christos and Alysia saw them to the door.

They stood together in the entry, neither moving from the door. After a long moment Christos leaned forward to tuck a tendril of golden hair behind her ear. "That wasn't so bad," he said

"No. Your father is lovely."

"I don't know if lovely is the right word, but it's obvious he likes you. I'm glad. I'd hoped he would."

"But your mother…"

"My mother is notoriously hard to please. With babies, grandchildren, I promise you, she'll have a change of heart."

Her own heart twisted, feeling like a traitor. She should talk to Christos, really talk to him, but how? What would she say? How could she tell him the truth? In some ways he was modern, open-minded, strong. But in other ways, when it came to women and family, he was impossibly protective. Almost chauvinistic. If she confessed to him, she knew she'd lose him.

Christos lifted her face in his hands, his expression somber. Then his head dipped and he kissed her with heart-shattering tenderness, savoring her lips, promising a warmth and a tangible hunger.

She clung to him, needing him, and as she kissed him, tears slid from beneath her closed lashes, spilling onto her cheeks.

Christos drew back, forehead furrowing. "What's wrong?"

She couldn't tell him. Words would only destroy the tentative bonds between them. Instead she drew his head down to hers again, covering his mouth with her own.

His lips felt damp and tasted salty from her tears, and a primitive emotion compelled her to kiss him deeply, sampling the trace of her tears on his skin. She tasted herself, and him, and it stirred dormant emotions, deep-rooted emotions of love and longing. She wanted him, to belong to him, not just now, but always.

The intensity of their lovemaking that night affected them both, but for Alysia, it was life-changing. She knew she'd never want any man, or love any man, the way she loved Christos. He was a perfect combination of strength and passion, pride and tenderness.

They made love again and his hands, body and mouth drove her to a shattering climax.

Afterward, he kissed her on the damp brow before returning to her lips.

"You might not know it, but you need me, Alysia, just as much as I need you."

She lay on the crook of her arm, gazing at him in the dark. She could see his eyes and the flash of white teeth, and she leaned forward to kiss his mouth, closing the distance between them. "I know, at least the part about me needing you."

She felt him tense, his breath catching, holding. At last he exhaled, his hand rising to her face, stroking her cheek, her skin still glowing with the heat of passion.

"I want to have a baby with you. I want to make a family with you."

Fear gripped her heart and she pressed her fingertips to his mouth to keep him from saying more.

"But you know that," he said. "You know it's what I want more than anything."

"I'm not mother-material," she answered hoarsely.

"That's not true. You're just afraid you can't conceive, but I'm sure with the right doctors, with new treatments—"

"Christos, you don't know!"

"What don't I know?"

The truth… You don't know anything.

"Alysia, you're my wife. I want you. I want a family with you."

Her eyes scalded, hot and gritty, and she tipped her forehead against his, hiding her face from him, hiding her past. If he knew the truth, he'd hate her, despise her.

"Talk to me," he whispered, drawing away and rolling her over onto her back. Lifting a strand of hair from the hollow of her neck, he pressed it to his mouth and then kissed her collarbone before kissing her mouth. "Trust me."

"I do." And she did, as much as she could trust anyone. *But what about the birth control pills?* A little voice whispered inside her head, stirring fresh panic. *He should know you're taking contraception.*

But another voice inside her protested. *He doesn't need to know now. You'll tell him someday, someday when he'll understand…*

"I'd do anything for you."

"Shh, you can't say such things."

"I can, because I love you."

She lay still, frozen, not daring to breathe. He couldn't have just said what she thought he said. It was her imagination, her need for acceptance, and forgiveness. Because he couldn't love her, not the real Alysia. The real Alysia destroyed those she loved.

"Look at me," Christos urged, his voice husky, firm fingers on her chin, turning her face to his, not understanding the tears in her eyes or the pain snaking through her heart. "We'll make a baby, and we'll be happy. I promise."

The weeks passed quickly; Christos was attentive, his desire something tangible and real. They slept together, woke together, took their meals together, and still neither could get enough of the other, seeking each other's company, wanting more touch, more passion, more pleasure.

After that stormy first week they'd managed to become friends, developing a relationship out of the artifice.

Christos invited Alysia to join him once or twice a week at his office, making a point of including her in big meetings, and other times, bringing home business reports and financial statements to discuss with her.

She found Christos's perspective on business fascinating, yet was bored by the myriad of details. While she liked understanding why he made certain decisions, she didn't want to pore over numbers or challenge his economic predictions. The fact was, his business bored her. What's worse, the endless columns of numbers looked meaningless after a while, just number after number, like little ants marching across the page.

"I hate this," she muttered, slamming the proposal closed and tossing it at the foot of the couch. "I can't stand it. There's nothing about this business that I enjoy."

Christos turned from the window where he'd been admiring the sunset, his mouth twisting. "I wondered how long it'd take for you to confess." He plucked the spiral-bound booklet from the couch and flipped through it, briefly scanning the charts and graphs. "Why don't you paint again?"

His tone was deceptively mild. She glanced at him, frowned. "You know I don't paint anymore."

"We could build a studio for you here—"

"I don't want a studio," she interrupted, jumping from the couch to confront him. "I don't paint. I'll never paint again."

"I thought you trusted me."

"I do."

"Then perhaps you can explain these," he said flatly. Something had changed in his voice, his quiet tone taking an edge. "I found these in your bathroom drawer." He drew a small plastic case from his pocket, lifted them high and tapped the plastic case with a finger. "These pills aren't iron tablets, are they?"

She went hot, then cold. "No." They were her pills. Her birth control pills. He knew, too, what her bottle of iron tablets looked like.

"Where did you get them? When did you get them?"

"In Athens." She swallowed hard. "From the doctor that visited me at your house, after I fainted."

"You've been on birth control pills for the last month?" His voice echoed hard, brittle, just like his features.

"Yes." She lifted her head, flinched when she met his gaze, fury blazing in his dark eyes.

"You lied to me."

"I didn't lie."

"You weren't honest."

No, she hadn't been honest, and it was all going to come out. She saw that now. The skeletons, the nightmare, the terror. The bones were stacked too high against the closet door and the door had been opened, just a crack, but a crack was more than enough to destroy her fragile control.

She turned, opened the door to his study and began walking away, quickly, heading for the stairs and the sanctuary of her room.

Christos followed her to the stairs, and she ran up the steps, flying as fast as she could.

He covered the stairs in half the time, able to climb three steps to her one. Grasping her by her shoulders, he spun her to face him. "What the hell is going on?"

"You don't know, and you don't want to know."

"Damn it, Alysia, I've had it with your secrets and your cryptic answers." His fingers held her fast, no escaping him now. "No more riddles. I want answers. Truthful answers. Why didn't you tell me you were on the pill?"

"Because you'd have taken them away, or tried to talk me out of them—"

"Yes!"

"That's why."

"But you knew I wanted children."

"And you knew I couldn't give them to you!"

She yanked away, stepping blindly backward.

She teetered on the top step, losing her balance. Christos caught her, pulling her roughly after him to the relative safety of her bedroom.

"No more pills, no more protection," he said, shutting the door behind them. "Do you understand?"

"I understand what you're saying, but I can't do what you're asking me to do."

"You mean you won't?"

She saw the hurt flicker in his dark eyes before being replaced by anger. "Please, Christos, trust me—"

"Like you've trusted me?" He turned away, covered his face with one hand. "God, I am a fool." He shook his head, dropping his hand. "Your father warned me you'd run away. He warned me you weren't very stable. But I didn't believe him. If only I had!"

"It would have saved us both a lot of trouble," she answered quietly, finding her pride, and her backbone.

She'd known from the beginning their marriage wouldn't last. She knew he'd discover the truth sooner or later and the relationship would end, as swiftly, as painfully, as it had begun. Only she hadn't expected to lose her heart to him. She'd never meant to fall so madly in love.

He stared at her as if he'd never seen her before, his dark eyes stripping her to the bone. "You were never going to have my child, were you?"

"No."

"How long would you have let me wait?"

Forever, she heard the answer whisper inside herself, forever, if it meant I could be with you. Instead she shook her head. "I don't know. Until you pushed for the truth."

"So you would have continued taking the pills, getting your period, letting me believe we couldn't conceive."

"Yes."

"God, I hate you."

She shriveled on the inside, dying. "I know."

"You can't. You have no idea how much you disgust me."

"I have a faint idea," she whispered, knowing he couldn't break what was already broken, and her heart had been shattered years ago. But still he was digging a fresh hole, dirt for her grave.

He closed the distance between them, lifted his hand as if to strike her and instead caught her face in his hands, kissing her hard on the mouth. "Why?" he demanded against her trembling lips. "Just tell me why. Let me understand."

His mouth felt so warm against hers, his skin smelling of cologne and musk and she reached up to cling to his chest, needing him more than she'd ever needed anyone.

But he didn't want her touching him, and he caught her wrists, pulling her hands off him. "I'm waiting."

"You don't want to know, oh, Christos, it's bad—"

"I don't care. I just want the truth."

She gazed at him helplessly, knowing she'd lose him—no, she'd already lost him—but fear held her back. She'd kept her secret so long, told no one, not even her father, what had happened in that Paris studio that unbelievable afternoon.

"Tell me."

Her heart lurched, her mouth so dry, it tasted of cotton. Where to begin? What to say first? "I...I had a baby."

"You what?"

The adrenaline surging through her veins threatened to make her ill. She couldn't look at Christos, didn't dare take a glimpse into his face. "Had a baby. A little boy."

"When?"

"With Jeremy. We were married, had been married for a little over a year when Alexi was born."

"And?"

"I lost him."

"Stillbirth?"

"No." She shivered, chilled, wondering how she'd ever get the words out, not wanting to see Alexi, not wanting the horrible pictures to fill her head again. "I delivered him, loved him, raised him. I took him on my jobs. He had his first birthday. And then…"

"And then what, Alysia?" Christos ground out, shaking her, almost violent in his impatience to hear the rest.

"I killed him."

CHAPTER ELEVEN

CHRISTOS couldn't believe it. He demanded the story again and again, ignoring her sobs, oblivious to her anguish, insisting she explain it all once more, from the beginning.

He struggled to piece her past together. She ran away with Jeremy after meeting him in Paris. They married thinking they could make a living by painting. That part made sense. That much was clear. But the rest of it...

"Christos, please, no more—"

He saw her cowering on the bed, but felt nothing for her. "How did the baby drown?" he demanded again.

"In water, in the bath—"

"You said the sink."

"Yes, in the sink. He'd been taking a bath."

"No, he wasn't taking a bath, you were giving him a bath."

"Yes."

"And what happened?"

"He drowned."

"How?"

"You know how! His little chair broke, I think. Or he wasn't in his chair—I forget, Christos, it's been so long."

"Not that long. Five years."

She closed her eyes, hugging herself. "Let me go," she whispered. "Let me go, let me go."

"I want to hear this. I want to know how you let your baby drown."

"I can't tell you."

"You can. You will." He stalked toward her, his face dark with anger. "Did the phone ring? Someone came to the door? How did you forget him?"

"Stop it!"

"How could you do it? How could you let your baby drown?"

"I was painting!" she screamed, her voice shrieking so high that it sounded like breaking glass. "I was painting."

"You were painting?" Christos stared at her aghast.

"I killed Alexi because I had to paint."

★ ★ ★

A doctor came, and Christos's parents. Alysia lay huddled in her darkened bedroom, unwilling to eat, or turn on a light. She wanted only to be left alone.

But the voices could be heard through her closed door, murmurs and exclamations, urgency in Christos, disgust in his mother's.

Sometime later the doctor entered her room, and despite her protests, turned on the light and checked her vitals. His examination was brief but thorough, shining a miniature flashlight into her eyes, listening to her chest, and taking her pulse yet again. Finally he asked her if she'd been taking any other medications lately, other than her birth control pills.

"No," she answered dully, just wanting him to go, wanting to be alone again.

But the doctor didn't move. "I understand you were in a hospital in Switzerland. Were you on something then?"

"Only when they first checked me into the hospital. It was a sedative...I fell apart at the funeral." Her shoulders lifted, a listless shrug.

The doctor didn't speak and lifting her head, her gaze met his. She expected revulsion in his expression. Instead she found only pity. Suddenly her eyes welled with tears and she begged him to go.

"I think you should rest," he said.

"I don't want to sleep."

The doctor sat down next to her on the bed. "Everyone makes mistakes."

"A mistake is burning toast."

"Good people can make tragic mistakes."

"Not like this." The tears filling her eyes clung to her lashes, blurring her vision. Every breath she drew felt like an agony. Every beat of her heart reminded her of what she'd taken from her own child. "I loved him," she sobbed. "I loved him more than I loved myself and yet look what I did—"

In her grief she hadn't heard the door open, or notice Christos standing silently in the doorway. She didn't hear when he stepped out again, soundlessly shutting the door behind him.

"I think," the doctor said quietly, gently pushing her back, settling her against the pillows. "You must rest now. Tomorrow talk about the future."

Alysia woke to a sunlit room, the curtains drawn back to welcome the warm light. Her head felt heavy, her brain groggy, and slowly she slid from the bed to stagger to the bathroom.

She caught a glimpse of herself in the mirror. Pale face, dark, sunken eyes, white pinched lips. She looked like a corpse. Then suddenly she saw Alexi, floating face up beneath the water, eyes open, mouth open, tiny hands outstretched and her knees buckled as she screamed, shrieking at the flood of memory.

A woman in black appeared—Mrs. Pateras, Alysia dimly registered—to take her by the arm, and firmly lead her from the bathroom back to bed.

Muttering in Greek, she pushed Alysia down and handed her a cup of tea. "Drink."

Alysia's hand trembled as she clutched the hot cup. "Christos?" she whispered, disoriented by the intensity of her emotions and the realization that she'd probably lost Christos forever.

"Gone," Mrs. Pateras answered coldly.

"Where?"

The older woman pushed Alysia's legs under the covers and drew the sheet up, and then the feather duvet. "Business."

Business. "Where?"

"Greece. Something to do with ships."

Ships, there'd always be ships. Ships, contracts, profit and loss. Tears filled Alysia's eyes. How could life be so black-and-white when she lived in shades of gray?

She missed Christos, needed to see him, talk to him. He was the one person she trusted. The one she loved most. "When is he coming back?"

"I don't know."

"I'd like the phone number of his Manhattan office."

"He's not there," Mrs. Pateras answered sharply. "I told you that already, now rest, or I shall tell Christos how difficult you've been."

The bedroom felt cold after Mrs. Pateras left, the corners swathed in shadows. How difficult she's been. Same words her father used to say. Alysia the difficult. But was she really that difficult? Was wanting love such a bad thing?

Alysia closed her eyes but she couldn't sleep, consumed by memory, confused by time. How could she have turned her back on Alexi? How could she have forgotten him?

It didn't make sense. She'd been a good mother, or at least, she'd tried to be a good mother. She never let him sit in wet diapers. She never skipped on his naps. Never left him out too long in the sun. She'd been young, but she'd really tried her best.

Until that day. That one day...

All this time later and she could still feel the weight of him, feel his limp body as she pulled him from the sink. She'd run with him into the streets screaming, *God, someone, anyone, help me. Help my baby. Help my baby.*

The day of the funeral, she destroyed her easel and canvases, shredding the paintings with a pair of sharp scissors, slicing them like a madwoman into long, tangled shreds.

As she destroyed her work, she howled, her agonized cries drawing the neighbors, and then the police. It was then they gave her the shot to calm her, and bundled her off to the hospital in Bern. They said she'd been talking gibberish, but it wasn't gibberish. She'd been weeping for Alexi, promising him she'd never forget him, and never ever paint again.

And she'd kept that vow.

Alysia woke to bathe and eat. Mrs. Pateras was there, presiding over the house, overseeing Alysia's meals, her iron tablets. She determined the routine, making it clear she was the mistress of the house, not Alysia.

Alysia didn't have the strength to argue. She

was still struggling to put together pieces of the past, wondering at the gaps in her memory, even as she dreaded reliving the pain. But there were too many holes in her memory, places where nothing fit and nothing made sense.

But now that the guilt had been fully awakened, she couldn't rest. Nor find peace. It felt as though she were on fire on the inside, her own form of hell.

Lying in bed was only making it worse. She had to get busy again, needed exercise, sunlight, work to do.

On the third day after the horrible confession Alysia appeared downstairs for breakfast. Mrs. Avery beamed with pleasure but Mrs. Pateras blocked the doorway to the dining room. "The doctor said you were to rest," she said stiffly.

Alysia felt a ball of tension form in her belly. She didn't want to fight with her mother-in-law, but she wasn't going to sit around any longer feeling sorry for herself. What had happened, had happened, and awful as it was, it wouldn't bring back Alexi.

"Mrs. Pateras, I appreciate all you're doing for me, but I think it's time I began to act like a normal human being again. Hiding in my room will not bring Alexi back, and it will not help me forget."

"Some things you'll never forget."

She met Mrs. Pateras' unforgiving gaze and flinched inwardly but held her ground. "It was a mistake, a dreadful mistake, but I'm not going to give up on life. I love Christos—"

"He doesn't love you. How could he?"

It was exactly her own fear, shouted at her in contempt. Alysia wavered, glanced at the stairs, and the front door behind her, then turned her back on the escape routes. There was no escape. She had to face herself, and the future. "It's none of your business," she answered quietly, far more calmly than she felt. "This is between your son and me."

The housekeeper disappeared into the kitchen and Mrs. Pateras took a step toward her, her finger pointed in accusation. "My son deserves better than you. He deserves a real woman."

"I am a real woman. I just happened to make a terrible mistake."

"You murdered your child. That's not a mistake, that's a crime!"

"I can't change the past. But I can promise Christos loyalty, and love—"

"Do you honestly believe my son will ever

be happy with you? Do you think he'll ever trust you?"

Mrs. Pateras was right, Alysia realized with a shudder, she wasn't thinking about Christos's needs, just her own. Christos deserved happiness. He was a good man, a loving man, he deserved a wife he could trust.

Sick to her stomach, Alysia turned away, headed for the stairs, hurrying back to her bedroom. At her closet she yanked clothes from hangers, a long gray skirt and a loose-fitting cashmere sweater in a paler shade.

Mrs. Pateras followed her into the bedroom. "If you were smart, you'd go now, before he returns. He could get an annulment, have a proper marriage."

"Leave," Alysia choked, facing her closet, her voice failing her. "I do not want you in here, nor do I need you here. Please leave now."

"Yes, Mother, please leave now." Christos appeared in the doorway, a dark coat over his arm, a briefcase in one hand. He looked exhausted, and pained. "I heard you, Mother, all the way into the kitchen. You have no right to speak to my wife like that—"

"Your wife? She's no wife—"

He cut his mother short, his voice rarely

raised now blistering with fury. "She is my wife, and I love her very much. If you have a problem with her, then you have a problem with me because Alysia is my heart. You speak to her like that again and I shall cut you off forever. Do you understand?"

Mrs. Pateras stared at her only child in shock, her mouth opening, eyes wide. And then she shook her head once, a slow, angry shake, before walking out of the bedroom and closing the door behind her.

Christos rolled up his shirtsleeves. "I'm sorry. I'm sorry she talked to you like that. I'm sorry I couldn't get back sooner."

Alysia stood rooted to the spot. She clutched the clothes tightly, too astonished, too overwhelmed to speak. The cashmere sweater tickled her neck, the long skirt rough against her bare arms. She could smell a whiff of her perfume on the sweater, a sweet light floral, a hint of Spring.

"You should have called me," he said, his features tight. "I left my numbers with my mother."

No point in telling him that his mother didn't share them. She swallowed, pressed the wadded clothes to her stomach. "Where were you?"

His dark gaze followed each jerky gesture, before lifting to her face, eyes searching hers. "I went to Paris."

She took an unsteady step to the chaise in the corner of the room and sank down. "Paris?"

"Then to London. I spoke with many people. People you worked for in Paris, the police there, and then on to Jeremy. He lives in London now. In a small dirty flat overlooking the Thames."

Jeremy alive, and well, Jeremy in a dirty flat near a river. But she didn't want to think of him, didn't want to be reminded of the grief they'd shared. Jeremy ruined her life once. She wouldn't let him ruin it again. "I don't want to talk about him."

"We have to."

"I can't, Christos, I can't. Please, not again. I told you everything—"

"No, not quite everything. You've forgotten the facts, Alysia, you've changed them."

She felt a tiny prick, almost like a beesting. "What do you mean?"

He moved across the room and sat down next to her on the chaise, drawing the bundled clothes from her arms. "It's time we talked about what really happened that afternoon in the apartment."

"I told you what happened."

"But that's not what happened. Look at me, Alysia. Look into my face." He waited until she dragged her gaze up, eyes meeting his. "The baby drowned," he said quietly, "but it's not your fault. You weren't even there. Somehow you've mixed the facts up, guilt and grief. You have to remember how it really happened, not the story you told me."

She couldn't speak, panic wrestling with hope and yet even as she dared to hope she remembered the truth. Alexi died, Alexi was dead, her baby, he was *her baby,* and it was *her fault*.

"Jeremy was the one watching him. You weren't home when Alexi drowned. You were painting—"

She struggled to rise but Christos caught her around the waist, drawing her back down, onto his lap.

His arms circled her, holding her fast to his chest. "You loved your baby, my sweet Alysia. You loved that baby more than anyone could love a child and you didn't fail him."

"I should have been there. If I were there

he wouldn't have drowned. I wouldn't have blinked, or moved a muscle. I wouldn't have turned my back, not for an instant, not for anything in this world!"

"I know. I know what a good mother you were. Your friends told me. Your neighbors told me. The police told me. That's what makes this such a tragedy. You did what you could—"

"It wasn't enough."

He stroked the back of her head, fingers detangling the long silky strands of hair. "Jeremy had been drinking. He claims he lost track of time."

"He drank too much," she whispered, awash in pain. It was awful, too awful to relive again and again and again. "He wasn't happy," she added dully, remembering his bitterness when he discovered that her father had cut her off, that there'd be no generous allowance, no financial support. He'd married her for her fortune and there'd been none.

"But were you?"

Her heart constricted. "I had my baby." She felt her throat close. "You see why I can't have children. And your mother is right. This marriage won't work. You must give the money back to my father. Find yourself a real bride."

"You are a real bride. You're my bride."

"But the dowry—"

"There was no dowry. Your father is bankrupt."

"Bankrupt?"

"I paid his debts, got rid of his creditors and set up a small nest egg in Switzerland for him. He needs something to live on."

Her mouth dropped open. "You mean, I have no inheritance? I've nothing?"

His lips twisted. "Nothing but me. I'm sorry, Alysia. I've been trying to figure out a way to break the news, but I didn't know how to tell you."

She felt a bubble of joy. This was actually wonderful news. She hated her father's money, had never wanted his money. Just his love. All she'd ever wanted from him was his love. "I don't suppose my father will give the money back to you," she said doubtfully.

"No, and I don't want it back, because I'm not about to give you up. I've waited for you for ten years. I first saw you over ten years ago in Athens, at a ship owners meeting. We were gathered in the living room and you interrupted the meeting to ask your father a question—"

"You were there?" she breathed.

His jaw thickened. "I hated what he did to you, I hated how he treated you. I vowed then and there to find you, to make you mine. I made a deal with your father, but it was for you, and me. I knew I could make you happy, and I will."

"How can you trust me after Alexi? Your mother, she hates me."

"I don't need her approval. I don't care what people think. I love you, and I want to be with you and that's all that matters."

"And there's really no inheritance."

"None. Zilch. You're as poor as a church mouse."

"That's too wonderful!" Tears filled her eyes, tears and a hint of laughter. For the first time in years she felt as though she could finally breathe. No inheritance, no pretense, no duty. Just love. And hope. "You really do love me?"

He stared deep into her eyes, his own dark depths full of emotion. "With all my heart and all my soul."

"Say it again."

"With all my heart, all my mind, all my body and all my soul. I was made for you, to love you, and only you." He kissed her then, stemming additional protests, silencing the intellect, letting emotion and sensation rule.

She woke the next morning nestled against him. It was early yet, not even six, and immediately her first thought was of Alexi, but instead of denying the flicker of pain, she drew a deep breath and said a prayer for him.

She did love him, she would always love him. As she finished her prayer Alysia felt a great wave of peace. The peace filled her, warm and light and bright, bringing tears to her eyes, but this time tears of happiness, and relief.

"Alysia?" Christos stirred, wrapped an arm around her waist, drew her closer to him. "What's wrong?"

"I said a prayer for Alexi." Her voice broke. "But it's okay, I understand he's in God's hands, and I owe it to him to make my life matter, to make it better. I owe it to him to be strong."

"As long as you live, Alexi will live on, in your heart, and in your thoughts."

"Then I must live a good long life and never forget the blessings we've been given." She couldn't swallow around the lump in her throat, and burying her face in Christos's shoulder, her mouth pressed to his bare skin, she let go of the anger and the guilt and the shame.

She cried for those she'd loved and cried for those she'd lost. She even cried for the relationship she'd never had with her father.

Christos held her throughout. But at last, there were no more tears, and exhausted, she lifted her wet face. "I'm sorry," she sniffed, reaching for tissues. "That was rather appalling."

He kissed her brow, the tip of her nose, her tear-streaked mouth. "It's what you needed to do. Grieve. Love. Feel. Especially feel. You can't live all shut down. You're not a robot, you're a beautiful, smart, sensitive woman." He kissed her again, her lower lip quivering. "You can talk to me about Alexi as much as you want. And if you ever want to talk to someone else, you could do that, too. Whatever you want. Whatever you need."

She pressed her cheek to Christos's chest savoring the even beat of his heart. "You give me hope."

"Then believe, Alysia, believe we will have a wonderful life together, a new life that will be better than anything either of us have yet lived."

"Is it possible?"

"I know it is."

"How can you be so certain?"

"I just know, the same way I knew that day in Athens that I would find you again and make you mine. I was made to love you. And I shall. Always."

EPILOGUE

"Careful! Watch out," Alysia called, jumping from the polished marble bench, shielding her eyes as she anxiously followed the toddler's progress down the flagstone path toward the fishpond.

"Gotcha." Christos laughed, swinging the wriggling little boy in the sailor jumper onto his shoulders. "I know where you were going."

"Fishies!" Two-year-old Nikos shouted, jabbing his father in the ear with a wet finger. "I wuv fishies."

Christos walked up the path, returning with the energetic toddler to the bench in the shade.

Alysia stood, arms outstretched to take the bouncing boy. Happily Nikos lunged into her arms, patting her face, kissing her cheek and then her mouth. "Mama."

Her heart turned over. "Yes, Mama loves you."

"Nikos wuvs fishies," he shouted, enthusiastically patting her face again.

"Careful with Mama," Christos said, reaching out to touch Nikos's small hand, gentling the tiny fingers.

"Mama," Nikos said again, kissing her cheek.

Alysia lifted her head, met Christos's dark gaze. "I'm fine," she whispered, even as the baby inside her moved. In just weeks there'd be another little Pateras running wild in the lovely rambling Colonial house.

Christos leaned down, placing a possessive kiss on her upturned lips. "You're so beautiful, especially now."

"You're blind."

"Not blind, just deeply in love." He kissed her again, over the top of Nikos's dark head. "How did we get so lucky?"

Her eyes burned and yet she smiled as tears welled up in her eyes, her heart brimming with happiness and love for Christos. It still staggered her, the joy she'd found with him. "I don't know. It's a miracle."

★ ★ ★ ★ ★

Don't miss the stories in this mini series!

PASSION

The Sicilian's Passion
SHARON KENDRICK
August 2012

Christos's Promise
JANE PORTER
October 2012

Available Next Month

Banished To The Harem Carol Marinelli

Not Just The Greek's Wife Lucy Monroe

A Delicious Deception Elizabeth Power

A Game Of Vows Maisey Yates

A Devil In Disguise Caitlin Crews

Revelations Of The Night Before Lynn Raye Harris

Defying Her Desert Duty Annie West

Painted The Other Woman Julia James

The Wedding Must Go On Robyn Grady
The Devil And The Deep Amy Andrews

Available from Big W, Kmart, Target,
selected supermarkets, bookstores & newsagencies.
OR call 1300 659 500 (AU), 09 837 1553 (NZ)
to order for the cost of a local call.
Visit **www.millsandboon.com.au**

Erotic fiction JUST GOT HOTTER

TWO WICKED READS EACH MONTH!

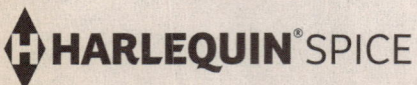

harlequinbooks.com.au

In-store October 2012

Wish Upon A Star
Sarah Morgan
Two beautiful stories of finding love in the festive season.

Regency Mistletoe
Louise Allen
Two sparkling Regency Christmas reads of romance and grandeur

---

Christmas Nights
Penny Jordan
Celebrate the holiday season with these three romantic treats of sizzling passion.

A Puppy For Christmas
Various Authors
Three tales where an unexpected companion leads lovers to find each other.

Order now at millsandboon.com.au

Mills & Boon™  HARLEQUIN

Australia's No.1 Bestselling Horoscope!

Australia's favourite astrologer Dadhichi brings you your complete horoscope guide to 2013.

OUT OCTOBER 2012

Get ready for the festive season

Last Christmas
Nora Roberts

Two heart-warming Christmas tales by *New York Times* bestselling author.

All I Want For Christmas
Home For Christmas

Glad Tidings
Debbie Macomber

Two delightful Christmas stories reflecting on family, forgiveness and good memories.

There's Something About Christmas
Here Comes Trouble

Order now at harlequinbooks.com.au

Mills & Boon™

Need something new to read?

All your favourite Mills & Boon™ stories are now available in eBook!

Order now at millsandboon.com.au

Mills & Boon™

Mills & Boon™

Find out more about our latest releases, authors and competitions.

 Like us on facebook.com/millsandboonaustralia

 Follow us on twitter.com/millsandboonaus

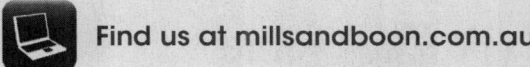 Find us at millsandboon.com.au